BLIND DATE'S BITTER END

BLIND DATE'S BITTER END

THE COOK AND INSPECTOR MYSTERIES

JOANNE PENCE

QUAIL HILL PUBLISHING

Quail Hill Publishing

Eagle, ID 83616

Visit our website at www.quailhillpublishing.net

First Quail Hill Publishing E-book: December 2024

First Quail Hill Print Book: December 2024

BLIND DATE'S BITTER END

1

Connie Rogers glanced down at herself to make sure her brand new, black lace underwire push-up bra was still doing its job and her boobs hadn't sagged as low as her spirits. She'd fixed herself up pretty hot for tonight's date in a leopard-print Lycra top with a plunging V-neckline, a short black polyester skirt, and sky-high black leather heels, size 7 narrow. She normally wore a medium, but the narrow looked a lot better, and they fit. Almost. Not to mention that she'd risked razor burn by shaving her legs and underarms even though she'd last done them just three days earlier. Okay, so maybe that was overkill, but a girl could hope, couldn't she?

She sat alone at a window table in the Wings of an Angel restaurant. Her feet ached and her skirt's seams screamed. She wriggled in the chair, trying to stop the waistband from digging in quite so tight. She'd dressed in hopes her date would like what he saw. If he ever showed...

If willpower alone could have caused him to enter the restaurant, he'd have bounded in doing handsprings. She'd already smoothed the white linen tablecloth, straightened the silverware, and twirled the single rose in the milk glass vase so many times half the petals fell off. The oversized gold-plated Anne Klein watch she'd splurged on at Costco showed 7:20 p.m. Not only was her date twenty minutes late, but since she'd arrived ten minutes early, if she were a thumb-twiddler, she'd have nothing left but stumps.

It wasn't as if she'd twisted his arm to go out with her. In fact, she'd never even talked directly to him. She was a victim here! A victim of a blind date who'd stiffed her. What was with that?

Earl White, one of the three owners of the Wings of an Angel and the one who acted as both maître d' and all-around waiter of the small restaurant, caught her eye. He was short and barrel-shaped, with hair resembling a shellacked brown helmet atop a face crisscrossed with wrinkles. He, too, glanced at his watch, then back at her with a shrug.

Being stood up was bad enough. The last thing she needed was an audience. She bet Earl had never been stood up. He was in his sixties, and not only single, but still bringing in a paycheck instead of living off Social Security, which made him one of the most sought-after cisgender heterosexual males at the North Beach Senior Center. It was rumored two women of a certain age even had a knock-down, drag-out over him.

Connie's best friend, Angie Amalfi, had helped Earl and his partners, Butch Pagozzi and Vinnie Freiman, build Wings of an Angel into a pleasant, albeit small, restaurant, and they'd grown close in the process. As a result, whenever Connie showed up, she, too, was treated like family. Maybe that was why Earl had taken such an interest in her plight a couple of days ago.

She'd been talking with him about getting herself a dog. A little dog, nothing big or troublesome, but just something warm and alive to greet her when she went home after work. Something that needed her, that would love her unfailingly, through good times and bad.

Okay, so she had a goldfish. It was alive; it needed her, but it wasn't anything she could give a big hug to. Talking to it, watching its flat eyes and lack of reaction as it went around in circles, no matter how heartfelt her story was, was an exercise in futility.

Earl had suddenly—rather rudely, truth be told—asked how her love life was going. She asked if zip, zero, nada was a clear enough answer. Before she knew it, he'd talked to his business partner, Butch, who was also restaurant's cook. Butch called a nephew—apparently the only one in the Pagozzi family who'd made a name for himself—and arranged tonight's turkey of a blind date.

In truth, Earl, Butch, and Vinnie had all made names for themselves as well, only they called them "reps," a prison term for "reputations." Bad reps, unfortunately. The three had met doing time in San Quentin, and when they got out, they decided to go straight, so to speak. Vinnie was the brains behind the operation. He kept the books and kept Earl and Butch in line. Sort of.

Connie put an elbow on the table, chin in hand, and stared at the entrance to the restaurant.

She'd been so excited and nervous she'd skipped lunch today, and was living off a snack of large fries and a diet Coke from McDonalds. Okay, so maybe fries were a little fattening, but they were a vegetable. She'd been starving, and they had fewer calories than a Quarter Pounder... she hoped. Now, her empty stomach growled, adding noisy injury to insult.

The nephew had sounded too good to be true, and so far, it seemed he was neither. His name was Dennis Pagozzi, and he played defensive end for the San Francisco 49ers. Connie might not be a sports fan, but she was quite willing to become one if it meant capturing the interest of a national conference player like Pagozzi, even if he was second string.

The way she understood it, he played only when someone else was hurt and pulled from the game. That meant his body shouldn't be as banged up as that of most football players. Generally, Connie preferred her men in one piece, although the way her love life was going lately, she'd settle for no-longer-on-life-support.

She drummed her fingernails on the table, then, horrified, stopped and made sure she hadn't chipped them. She'd spent a small fortune on fake nails that were painted at a diagonal—one half gold and the other red—49er colors.

A manicurist had worked on the design while a beautician cut, styled, and lightened her hair. This was a special date, so she splurged on a light ash blond color and a short cut with a shaggy fringe that framed her face. Dramatic and sexy. Sure to make Dennis Pagozzi's toes curl, and another part of his anatomy straighten. He'd be impressed... if he ever got here.

She tugged at her skirt again. The seams were beyond screaming. They were howling now.

A couple came in to the packed restaurant and picked up a takeout order. Connie took a sip of diet Coke and made sure none of it dripped from the glass onto her top. Many women having trouble with men could at least consider breast implants as a possible solution to their problems, but she was already a full D cup. If her experience was anything to go on, the size of one's bra wasn't the solution to anything beyond ogling.

Her best friend, Angie Amalfi, who was admittedly slim and petite, scarcely filled an A, and she had a boyfriend. San Francisco Homicide Inspector Paavo Smith was crazy about her and had proposed marriage. Actually, Angie's engagement to said cop had been the impetus that caused Connie this predicament. It had made her realize that time was slipping by and she needed to work harder at finding the man of her dreams.

She thought she'd found him once, but ex-husband Keith Trammel had turned out to be a nightmare. Some days it seemed the last time she had a good man to go out with, Calvin Coolidge was president. And she hadn't even been born yet.

All that was why she'd agreed to this blind date. If she were smart, she'd be home in her pjs, wrapped in a warm, comfortable robe and fuzzy slippers, while curled up on the sofa with a bowl of popcorn and streaming a romantic movie on the TV. Instead, she sat here uncomfortable, nervous, and hungry. What unlucky star hung over her?

"Here's some salad and bread, Miss Connie," Earl said. "I don't t'ink you need to starve just 'cause some jerk-off is late showin' up for your date."

"Thanks, Earl," she murmured. "But right now, I'm not even hungry." Okay, it was a lie, but she was too humiliated to eat.

"It's on da house." He left a green salad with Roquefort dressing, Connie's favorite, and walked away. The aroma of the French bread wafted up to her. She touched it. Warm. Firm crust. Soft center. Perfect for spreading butter, which unfortunately was loaded with straight-to-the-hips calories...

She checked her watch again. 7:30. Why bother with a guy who couldn't tell time? She decided to give him a few minutes more. It's not like she needed to hurry home. She kicked off her shoes and took a big bite of buttered, crusty bread. Heaven!

Just then, like magic, the restaurant's front door opened and a man alone entered. Connie's breath caught, causing her to nearly choke on the bread. She swallowed it in a scarcely chewed lump.

It quickly became obvious that the man who walked in was no football player. The only thing he resembled on a football field was a goal post—tall and slim. He held an arm across his ribs as if in some pain and stooped slightly because of it. His hair was badly in need of a cut and his ill-fitting gray overcoat and jeans looked as if he'd found them in a Goodwill bag. Not that Connie was a clotheshorse like her friend Angie, but she knew worn-out clothes when she saw them.

Earl sped toward the bedraggled fellow and, unless he was another takeout order customer, she expected Earl to throw him out. Earl confronted him just inside the door, near Connie's table.

"Excuse me," the newcomer said in a crisp voice. "I was told Dennis Pagozzi would be here tonight."

"You got a reservation?" Earl asked.

"No. No, I'm not eating. I just need to see Mr. Pagozzi."

"Dat makes two a you," Earl murmured, "An' he ain't here."

"Someone else is waiting for him?" The stranger's eyes traveled over the dining room as he drew his fingers through dark blond, wavy hair, pushing it back off his forehead. His face was narrow, and he looked as if he'd lived a hard thirty-five or so years.

"Yeah, but we ain't got no room for squatters," Earl said haughtily, or as haughtily as he could manage with his diction and grammar. "Maybe you better get outta here, and when Dennis shows up, I'll tell him somebody's been lookin' for him. What's your name?"

"Who else wants to see him?" the man asked.

"Uh, nobody." Earl's eyes darted toward Connie for just a second, but it was enough that the stranger glanced her way and visibly started. Only after a moment of staring did his expression ease.

To Connie's astonishment, he headed toward her, his mouth a hard slash and his jaw firm. "You're Dennis Pagozzi's friend?" he asked. His eyes were dark, his gaze cold.

"Not exactly," she answered. Who was this filthy creep?

"But he's expected?"

"Yes—"

"Good." He grabbed the back of an empty chair at the table and pulled it out as if to sit.

"Hey!" Earl, his chest puffed out, also grabbed the chair and jerked it away. "I didn't hear da lady invite you, fella."

The stranger looked down at Earl as if he were a human mold spore, then yanked the chair his way again. "I'll leave as soon as I talk to Pagozzi."

Earl tugged it back. "Why don't you phone him?"

The stranger's hand stilled on the chair. "His number is kept private to protect him from football fans."

Connie could feel the other customers laughing at the antics going on. It was bad enough being alone at a table without having some bum play tug-of-war with a chair and announce to one and all he didn't want to be there. How mortifying was that?

"How do I know you ain't some poivoit fan yourself?" Earl demanded. "It's time for you to go, mister!"

"Poivoit?" the man asked.

"Pervert!" Connie said sharply, implying more than an explanation with the word.

He faced her. "It's cold outside. The fog is in." Now, this jerk had the nerve to plead his case to her directly. "I've been trying to catch up to Pagozzi all evening."

She shook her head. "I don't—"

"A couple of minutes is all I need!" His voice was loud.

Connie's cheeks burned. He was a monomaniacal madman, but she didn't want more of a scene, and Pagozzi should show up any second—she hoped. "All right, already. Take a load off your feet. As if I should care."

"Miss Connie, you don't hafta do dis." Earl scowled pugnaciously.

"It's all right, Earl." Connie's teeth gritted. "I'm sure Dennis will be here soon."

A look of relief flashed across the man's slender face as he settled into the chair. He didn't say a word, but she noticed the ravenous glance he gave the bread. She realized he not only appeared broke, but hungry as well.

With a shake of the head, Earl turned to leave.

"Wait," she said, then to the stranger. "Since you're here, you may as well eat." Okay, she was being soft, and she knew it. What could she do? She was a nice person, even to a rude S.O.B.

His nostrils flared. "I'm fine."

Connie knew a hungry man when she saw one, pig-headed and vile or not. He looked exhausted, and judging from his stained and ragged clothes, probably hadn't eaten a decent meal for some time. Besides, much as she found him disagreeable, she could relate to anyone else stiffed by Dennis Pagozzi, the rat. "Why don't you bring him a salad, Earl? And more bread. What would you like to drink? Coffee, maybe? A coke?"

Her thanks was a fierce glare. "I said I'm fine."

Like hell you are, Connie thought. "It's no problem." She gave a firm nod to Earl. The waiter frowned, but went off to do as told.

"I'm Connie, by the way."

He glanced at her and swiveled toward the door.

He was even ruder than she first thought. "And you are?" Didn't she at least deserve to know the name of this seething mass of insensitivity sharing her table?

"Max Squire," he mumbled.

Connie wondered how much this fellow knew about her mystery date. "Did Dennis tell you he'd be here tonight for sure?" Could she help it if a part of her still hoped the evening wouldn't be a complete failure?

He nodded, giving a heavy sigh as he sank against the chair, eyes half shut. "A guy at the Niner's gym told me," he said finally.

She noticed a tightening of his mouth, fine lines forming at the corners as if he might be in pain. "Are you feeling all right?"

He smirked, his voice weary. "Sure. I'm just great." She'd rarely heard such heavy sarcasm.

Earl brought him a glass of Perrier with a twist of lime. Squire drained it.

When he put the glass down, his gaze caught Connie's as he picked up his napkin and brushed a thin sheen of perspiration from his brow. "It's warm in here," he muttered.

Her discomfort with the uncommunicative man increased with each passing second. He was looking somewhat ill. "You can take off your overcoat, if you'd like."

It was a gray, dusty, moth-eaten old thing. He removed it, trying to hold back a wince of pain, and let it drape over the back of his chair. Under the coat he wore jeans and a black turtleneck, faded and misshapen. His shoulders and chest were broader and more muscular than she'd expected. He simply needed some flesh on his bones. And a shower. He looked like he'd been sleeping in a dumpster.

Just then, Earl showed up with a salad, another basket of French bread, and more Perrier. The stranger practically salivated. "Eat. It's for you," she urged, wondering what had happened to the man, and why he wanted to meet her blind date.

The stranger swallowed hard and shook his head.

"I insist."

He placed his hands flat on the table. "I can't pay for it. It's the reason I'm here to meet Dennis. He owes me money."

Despite his harsh tone and blunt words, the blow to his pride was evident. "Uh oh. That means he won't be happy to see you," Connie said wryly, trying to lighten the mood. "So much for my great blind date."

He looked askance. "You have a blind date with Dennis? A woman like you?"

She couldn't tell if she'd been complimented or insulted. Was it her new hairdo? Didn't the style look good on her? She surreptitiously patted it, then attempted to twist a fringe into a feminine curl near her ear. "What do you mean by that, Mr. Squire?"

Her question seemed to puzzle him. Instead of answering, he faced the door again and simply said, "Nothing."

His irritating responses aggravated her. "So, your words mean nothing, and you're flat broke. Big deal." She waited until she had his attention again. "Now that that's settled, will you please eat the damn salad?"

Surprise flashed across his solemn face. Then, glowering, he considered the food. "What the hell," he murmured, and soon began to wolf down everything on his plate, plus the new basket of bread. As he ate, she ordered spaghetti and meatballs for both of them, asking Earl to bring it as quickly as possible.

"Want some wine wit' dat?" Earl asked.

She knew nothing about wine. House red? Did she want to spend the money? "I don't know..."

"A cabernet sauvignon would go well with your meal." Max's comments were off-handed, as if he was scarcely listening, but concentrating on eating.

"I'll go with that," she said to Earl. "If it's not too expensive."

"It'll be okay, Miss Connie."

She glanced at Max. "Make that two."

He looked up, as if chagrined, and then huddled over the bread again.

As requested, Earl soon brought out the entrees and the wine. For a while, Connie ate in silence, studying Max's thin, aristocratic nose, and high forehead. His eyes were intelligent, his mouth sensitive. When he noticed her staring, he made no comment. She turned her head but continued to try to figure him out. So far, she'd taken him for a bum, a jerk, and a creep. Yet something about him didn't mesh at all with his threadbare clothes or his "unpolished" state. She found herself intrigued.

"Are you new to the city, Max?" she asked.

He shook his head. "I used to live here."

"But not now?"

Reaching for more bread, he paused long enough to reply curtly. "No."

"Why not?" she asked, undaunted.

Dark brown eyes met hers, his lips curving thinly. "I go wherever the weather and my inclination lead me."

"Running away from something?" Connie asked.

His hand tightened on his fork. "Or trying to find it." The words were hushed.

The fierceness that radiated from deep inside him at those words alarmed her even as her curiosity about him grew. She drew back, her mind searching for something more to say. "Are you hoping to live here again now?"

"You ask a lot of questions." Only one piece of bread remained in the breadbasket. Connie slid it toward him. He took a piece to sop up the last of the sauce on his plate.

Connie ate about half of her spaghetti. "How about some of this? I'm full, really." He needed it a lot more than she did. Especially in this skirt. Her stomach was going to have permanent grooves circling it from the waistband.

He glanced from her plate to his, seemingly bewildered by the now-empty plate in front of him. "Damn!"

"It's all right. I expect a man to have a good appetite."

He again made no reply, his jawbone working as if he was filled with anger, but at what?

Earl came over, still grimacing at the stranger.

"We'll have some coffee, Earl," Connie said. "And would you put the rest of my dinner in a doggie bag?"

"Anyt'ing you'd like, Miss Connie," Earl said, picking up her dish with a flourish, followed by a sneer as he took Max's empty plate.

"Where the hell is Pagozzi?" Max said, eying the clock on the back wall. "I didn't expect to be here this late."

"He seems to have stood me up, that's for sure." She was

surprised she could say it with an indifferent lilt to her voice, as opposed to the horrible way she'd felt a short while ago.

"He's usually not so unlucky," Max murmured, more to himself than to Connie. He stared at the clock once more, then shook his head and sighed. "That's my area of expertise."

Earl brought them both some coffee and the doggie bag. Max looked down at the coffee, and he gave Connie a slight nod in thanks, his cheeks flushed.

Connie watched as, without a word, he took a sip of coffee.

She spent most days in Everyone's Fancy, her modest gift shop in a lazy corner of San Francisco. She ran it alone, except for a college student who helped out a few hours each week. Her apartment building was just a couple of blocks away from the shop.

Sometimes, like tonight, she enjoyed getting away from her own neighborhood with the hope of adventure, or at least avoiding the same old familiar routines. Unfortunately, this evening hadn't worked out the way she'd planned, although it hadn't been boring.

Max folded his hands around the coffee cup as if enjoying its warmth, and she wondered at a man who appreciated something so ordinary.

"Have you known Mr. Pagozzi very long?" she asked.

"Yes."

"So, you must have known him when he was just starting out in football."

"Right." Max sipped the coffee and said no more.

"Did you work with the 49ers?" she asked, thinking that might have been the connection between the two men.

He seemed to find her question funny. "Not at all."

"I see." She racked her brain for something more to say. "What about family? Are you married? Any kids?"

"No wife, no kids, no family who'll admit to it." His mood

shifted, and he glared at her. "I suppose you come from a big, warm, loving brood?"

The derision in his voice surprised yet troubled her. Who was he to act as if he knew anything about her? "Actually, I don't. For years, it was just me and my sister, and we weren't close." Connie hesitated, but something about the way he'd dismissed her, as if he was the only person in the world who knew trouble, made her add, "A while back, she was murdered."

Shocked, his gaze met hers. Then the moment passed, and he drained his coffee cup. "Shit happens."

His words stung. "That's one way to put it." The pain of Tiffany's murder had been overwhelming. The only good that had come of it—other than Homicide Inspector Paavo Smith finding the killer—was that she met Angie Amalfi. Oddly, she and Angie were much closer than she'd ever been with her sister.

"I'm sorry," he said, clearly shaken and regretful, giving a shake of his head. "I didn't mean to—"

Earl cleared his throat as he stood stiffly beside the table. "Butch an' Vinnie say da dinner's on da house seein' as how youse guys was here to see Butch's nephew an' he didn't show."

"You don't have to do that," Connie said. "No one's to blame."

"Please accept it wit' our apologies. An' Butch'll box Dennis's ears next time he sees him."

"He doesn't have to do that either," Connie said with a smile. Many years ago, Butch had been a prizefighter—bantamweight. He usually lost, and he was still a little scrambled-brained from a few too many head blows. "Thank you for the dinner, and be sure to tell Butch and Vinnie for me, too. I really appreciate it."

"Me, too," Max murmured uncomfortably.

"Yeah, well, I guess you're bot' welcome. Have a good night, Miss Connie." Earl scowled yet again at Max, and left.

She glanced at Max. "I suppose it's time for me to get a move on."

"Pagozzi's not coming here tonight." He sounded disgusted.

She tried not to grimace as she wriggled her feet back into their stiletto torture racks, then took out her wallet, trying to figure out a tip.

"I looked at the menu in the window," Max said. "For this city, food's not expensive here. But with the wine and coffee for two, it was probably at least eighty-dollars. Fifteen percent would be twelve dollars. If you want to go twenty, that'd be sixteen bucks."

"What are you, some kind of accountant?" Connie said with a laugh. She put a twenty-dollar bill on the table.

He looked stricken by her words, then stood and put on his overcoat. The color that had returned to his complexion while he sat and ate now vanished once more.

"Max?" she said, worried at his sudden pallor.

"I'll be all right." He slowly straightened, an arm pressed again to his ribs. He helped her with her heavy wool coat, a navy blue shapeless one that reached to mid-calf, the kind her mother had taught her was "practical."

On Columbus Avenue, a foggy breeze blew off the bay, slashing brutally through the North Beach area. Connie's stylish hairdo was whipped back and swirled from side to side as if caught in an eggbeater. So much for trying to look gorgeous, not to mention all the gel and hairspray she'd used so that this wouldn't happen. She burrowed into her coat, and Max raised the collar of his overcoat. Between the cold and the pain he was obviously in, he looked ready to pass out. "I can drop you off somewhere," she said.

"No, thanks," he replied, through unsteady breaths. "My hotel isn't far."

"It's no big deal. You look like you're hurting."

"Not... not really." He gasped heavily. "Is your car near? I'll walk to you it."

She was relieved to hear that. She didn't relish walking the city streets alone. "It's on the next corner. A little gray Toyota Corolla—over ten years old already."

He nodded, saying nothing.

As they walked, he seemed to become a bit shaky, even wobblier than she was in her heels. Had she known him better, she would have taken his arm to steady him. "The car's small enough that I squeezed it between a Caddy and a fire hydrant," she added. "Parking lots cost a fortune in this area."

"Yes." He paused. "So I've heard."

He worried her. "Are you sure you won't need a ride?"

"No. Let's get you to your car."

As they hurried on without speaking, Connie felt as if she should do something, but he was a stranger to her.

"Here it is." The back seat of the Corolla was filled with boxes of supplies for her store that she hadn't carried inside yet, while the front passenger seat had remnants of her last couple of MacDonald's drive-throughs. She usually kept her car neater than this—a little—but she'd been busy.

The car was too old and cheap for alarms and remote-control buttons and had to be unlocked the "old-fashioned" way, with a key. "Thanks for walking with me, Max."

"Dennis was very much a loser tonight for not showing up for your blind date. He's not really a bad guy. Don't hold this against him." He stepped back, studying her. A lamppost was beside the car, and he reached for it, gripping it as if the post alone was responsible for keeping him upright. Then, his voice soft and low, he added, "Take care of yourself, Connie."

His regard was unnerving, as if he found her somehow special. It'd been a long time since a man looked at her in quite that way. "You, too," she murmured.

She didn't know what more to add, but leaving like this seemed somehow incomplete. He was a strange man, but an interesting one. She waited a moment for him to say something more, but he didn't. Standing there gawking at him was childish, so she smiled and said. "See you." When he still made no response, she realized how foolish she must look rooted there, and hurried around the car to the driver's side.

He stood and watched, pale and wan under the streetlight, as she drove off.

What an odd man, she thought. She should just forget about him, reminding herself of how lucky she was to be going home to her cozy little apartment. But scarcely a half block later, she began to berate herself for having left him in such a sorry condition. He was hurting. What if he needed a doctor? She'd dumped him like a rotten Limburger. How cold was that?

On the other hand, he was penniless and dressed like a bum. Was she crazy? What did she want with him? Nothing! By two blocks, though, guilt had overcome her. She pulled over to the curb to build up the courage to face Max again and insist he let her drive him to his hotel or a doctor—his choice.

She angled the rearview mirror to check her make-up and make sure she didn't have a parsley flake stuck between her teeth.

Holy cripes! Her hair had frizzed from the heavy mist and stuck straight out from her head in weird, crinkly clumps. Any man who hadn't been appalled by such a sight was worth saving. Now, for sure, she had to make sure he was okay.

If he was walking along and looking fit, she'd just drive by and hope he wouldn't notice it was her. On the other hand, what did it matter if he did notice? She'd never see him again, anyway. Why should she care?

She made a U-turn in the middle of the block and headed back to the corner she'd left him on.

It was empty. She stopped the car and got out. He wasn't

walking down the block they'd come up, and she didn't see him on any of the adjacent streets, either. Apparently, he'd been able to move a lot faster than she thought he could.

You're such a jerk, Rogers! she thought. He'd probably been faking it all along. How much of what he'd said that evening was a lie? What was it about her that made men turn into a song parody, as in "don't believe their lyin' eyes."

Feeling used and foolish—those words should be tattooed across her forehead—she flung herself back in the car and was speeding down the street when she passed a dark pile of rags against a building. She'd driven past them before her mind registered what the "rags" really were.

Stomping on the brakes, she backed up, threw on her hazard lights and got out of the car.

She ran to his side, scared at what she'd find. He was curled up in a fetal position on his side. "Max?" She knelt down and touched his shoulder, and he opened his eyes.

"Ronnie..." he mumbled.

What was he saying? "Yes, it's me. Connie. I'm here."

"I'm late... too late... Ron..." His eyes closed.

"Max!" she cried, shaking him.

He struggled to open his eyes once more. Finally, they focused on her, clearly seeing her. Their eyes locked and his whisper sounded like a prayer. "Help me."

2

The next afternoon, Angie Amalfi drove her immaculate new pearl white Lexus NX SUV down West Portal Avenue looking for a parking place, otherwise known as a fool's mission in San Francisco. She was a little woman, with big brown eyes, and short brown hair with eye-catching reddish-blond highlights, thanks to her favorite Fairmont Hotel beauty salon.

Angie had recently bought the new car after her beloved Ferrari's cream-colored leather passenger seat became stained when someone who hated her doused it with blood. Other people claimed they couldn't see the "pink" tinge she swore was there. But whenever she got into the car, she not only saw the tinge, but remembered the entire creepy experience she'd had at that time.

Finally, she decided the time had come to trade the Ferrari in for a new car, especially a more "family friendly" type car like a mid-size SUV rather than a sporty car since, after all, her life was about to change.

Up ahead, an unoccupied yellow loading zone beckoned, and she eased right into it, much to the irritation of the people behind her who were most likely also eying the illegal spot. She didn't care. Let them honk and glower and pound their steering wheels. Life was good; luck was with her; and the world was a panoply of baked Alaska straight from the oven, a pouffy dark chocolate soufflé, and flaming crepes Suzette.

She was engaged.

The soon-to-be-married kind of engaged.

And she still couldn't believe it.

After an eternity of wishing, hoping, praying, hinting, and wondering if she'd have to resort to conjurers and mojo practitioners, two weeks earlier San Francisco Homicide Inspector Paavo Smith proposed.

Before turning off the ignition, Angie glanced once more at her hand on the steering wheel and her heartbeat doubled. Her engagement ring, an emerald-cut diamond in a platinum solitaire setting, gave her goose bumps each time she looked at it, and then everything but Paavo and love flew right out of her head. Maybe she was being silly, but so what? This was a life-altering, karma-enhancing, family-churning event.

She kept pinching herself to make sure she wasn't dreaming. And looking at her ring. And hugging herself. And looking at her ring. She'd gotten two manicures in two days, trying to find the perfect accompaniment for the diamond. A natural French manicure was winning at the moment since it didn't distract from the ring in the slightest.

The ring was especially precious because she knew Paavo had bought it with money he'd been saving for a new car. His Mustang was beyond ancient. If it was in good shape, it might be a collector's item. But the bailing wire and glue that held it together had destroyed any value beyond scrap metal.

God, but she loved being in love. She picked up her cell phone to call Paavo—just to say 'hi' and to wish him a happy lunchtime. She called his desk phone since, if he was there, he could take her call. His cell phone, during the day, was for emergencies only since if he wasn't at his desk, he was out on a case.

Paavo wasn't at his desk, and Inspector Bo Benson answered the phone. Benson told her Paavo and his partner were called to a job in Japantown at Bush and Scott Streets, and, surprisingly, it wasn't a homicide.

Not a homicide, she thought after thanking Bo and hanging up. That meant Paavo might not be out on a horrible case...

That gave her an idea. A brilliant idea, in fact. Gleefully, she made another phone call, and then, after rubbing a smudge off the dashboard, got out of her new car.

Now, she hurried along a block lined with specialty shops and delis to Everyone's Fancy where she expected blow-by-blow details of Connie's blind date. As she went, she couldn't help but hold her hand out in front of her to catch the sparkles of sunlight, until a quick halt stopped her from barreling smack into the closed front door. She tried the latch handle, but the door was locked.

Connie's store was never shut down at this time of day.

Angie knocked and peered through the lace curtain behind the glass door. Nothing moved inside. She'd talked to Connie yesterday, and she'd sounded upbeat and healthy. Why wasn't she at work?

Angie backed up and examined the store. Under a brick red awning, the window display hadn't been changed for at least three months. Boredom was hardly the way to entice neighbors into a shop they passed by every day. Connie needed to use a display with pizzazz, one that shrieked, "Buy me!" to window-shoppers. The linens, lace, doilies and glass bottles gathering dust didn't even whimper.

Angie purposefully hadn't telephoned Connie that morning, even though she was dying to find out all about Connie's blind date, because they'd agreed to meet at one p.m. Had Connie forgotten and gone to lunch without her? Or had something happened to Connie on her date? Was she in an accident? Or what if her date was some sort of crazed sex maniac or trafficker?

Angie tried to calm herself. After all, Connie might have been so enthralled with that jock, that Dennis Pagozzi, or whatever his name was, that she went home with him and decided not to come to work today? A long night of wild, passionate, raw sex?

No. That wasn't Connie's style. Or, to be more precise, it wasn't her kind of luck.

"Angie!" Helen Melinger, a broad-shouldered, well-muscled woman who owned the shoe repair shop next door, lumbered onto the sidewalk. "I saw you standing out here. Where the hell's Connie?"

"I don't know," Angie said. "Hasn't she been here at all this morning?"

"No." Helen folded her thick, muscular arms and scrunched her bulldog face. "I'm ready to piss my pants I'm so goddamned curious about that date she went on last night. What the hell's wrong with her, doing this to me? Where could she be?"

"Good question," Angie said.

"Aagh, it's probably just that she's got a hangover. You know Connie around booze. She never could hold her liquor."

"True, but she doesn't drink much when she's nervous. She knows it goes straight to her head. I don't see that as being the problem." Angie was suddenly worried. "I think I'd better go over to her apartment."

"If you run into her, tell her I don't give a damn how sick she is, she'd better come to work tomorrow, or I'm coming to get her, understand?"

"I got it," Angie said, wanting to smile, but not quite sure if Helen was joking or not.

"And congratulations," Helen added gruffly. "Connie told me you're getting married."

"Yes. My cop boyfriend finally proposed." She held out her hand to show off the engagement ring. Everyone she came in contact with had it stuck under his or her nose at some point before the conversation ended.

Helen took hold of Angie's finger, twisting it this way and that in the sunlight. "Look at that ice! It's a beautiful diamond. Not too big, but it's got great fire and saturation. Elegant." She dropped Angie's hand. "So, when's the big day?"

Angie was speechless for a moment, not expecting the gruff shoe-repair woman to know anything about diamonds, and especially not about fire and saturation qualities. "Well, we haven't chosen a date yet," she murmured finally. "There's a lot of planning to do."

"Yeah. I guess so. Not that I've ever found out." She gave a raspy, whiskey-and-smoke-laced laugh.

"Oh? You're single?" Angie eyed the woman. Fortyish, self-employed, strong, motivated. In other words, exactly the kind of woman for her neighbor, Stanfield Bonnette. He could use some discipline, motivation and hard-work in his life. He kept a job with a bank only because of his father's influence, not his dedication to the world of high finance. *Helen and Stan.* She liked it! And she could be the little Cupid that brought them together. Just like some good fortune had brought her Paavo. She smiled at Helen, starry-eyed. Ah, *amore!*

"Never found a man I could abide long enough to marry," Helen confessed. "Probably better off for it, too."

"You never know who might turn up when you least expect it," Angie said, her mind working. She was sure she could get Stan out to Helen's shoe repair shop on some pretext or other.

"Got to get back to work. Remember to tell Connie she'd better be here tomorrow or I'll kick her ass."

"Don't worry," Angie said. "There's no way I'd forget."

"I'm getting too old for this stuff, Paavo," Homicide Inspector Toshiro Yoshiwara groaned and huffed as he climbed down from the rafters in an abandoned garage. At nearly six feet tall, with powerful shoulders and legs, a thick neck and stubbly hair, he looked like he could play the lead role in a samurai movie.

"Come on, Yosh. It wasn't that high." Homicide Inspector Paavo Smith offered a hand as his partner leaped off a rickety wooden ladder, bypassing the last few worn-thin steps.

"I'm not complaining about the climb," Yosh said. "I'm complaining about trying to speak Japanese after all these years! You'd think the police department would have someone else on the payroll to do it."

"They probably do, but you happened to be right around the corner when needed. You did a good job. The kid was scared, and now he's back with his mother." Paavo watched the young Japanese woman tearfully hugging her son. Earlier, the six-year-old had gotten angry with her and had run away from home. Around the corner from their apartment was a boarded-up building, but a window leading into the garage had a loose board. The child crawled through it and climbed up a ladder and onto a flat piece of wood that had been placed across some rafters. It could hold a six-year-old's weight, but not an adult's.

The boy and his mother only spoke Japanese, and the boy refused to obey his mom and climb down.

Paavo and Yosh were two blocks away investigating a suicide when the call went out for Japanese-speaking assistance. As Yosh climbed up the ladder in the garage, he'd tried to remember the words and expressions he'd learned as a child.

When he reached the top of the ladder, the boy gawked at him and shrieked, and before Yosh had finished saying, *"Kon-nichi-wa. O-mawari-san desu,"*—or "Hello. I'm a cop,"—the child began to scramble toward his mother.

Once the boy was safe, Paavo grew curious about the rundown building he found himself in. "Who owns this?" he asked one of the uniforms who had stood under the rafter, ready to catch the boy if he slipped or the board broke.

"The neighbors say it's been abandoned for property taxes —a victim of rent control. The city owns it now but hasn't decided what to do with it," the young cop replied. "The upstairs flats are infested with rats, and they never see anyone go in or out."

Eight shoeboxes, arranged in a stack, were the only things in the garage that weren't coated with inches of dust and cobwebs. Paavo glanced at Yosh. "I wonder what's in them."

Yosh took out his pocketknife. "Let's find out."

Inside were baseballs. Yosh lifted one out and gawked at a valuable Roger Clemens autograph. "What the hell?"

Lifting out other balls, they found classic signatures from Barry Bonds, Pedro Martinez, Mark McGwire, and a number of lesser-known players. Paavo and Yosh opened the other boxes and found the same thing. Several ballplayers had signed more than once.

"I wonder if this is someone's baseball collection," Yosh said. "Why here, though? Unless they're hot."

"Or more likely, fakes," Paavo said. "Let's get them out of here before they 'disappear.'"

A number of patrol officers had gathered to watch the child's rescue, and Paavo got one to send the boxes of baseballs to the local station. As Paavo took out his phone and called Robbery to report the strange find, a short, chubby man with a pencil-thin mustache and wearing a black suit with a red carnation in the lapel walked up to them. A fireplug with a flower.

"Inspector Paavo Smith?" he asked.

Still on the phone, Paavo glanced at him. Yosh gave the strange guy an incredulous once-over before nodding and pointing to his partner.

Immediately, the little round fellow burst into a very loud, operatic version of the traditional Italian song, "O Sole Mio."

Paavo froze. *What the hell?*

Then it struck him.

She wouldn't, he thought. As the octaves rose higher and the volume louder, he was forced to admit the awful truth: she would. He jabbed a finger in his ear, and spun one-hundred eighty degrees, trying to finish his phone conversation. The singer followed, bellowing the tune with grandiose gestures, sobs and catches in his throat at the heartfelt lyrics, whatever they were. The fireplug had morphed into a singing windmill. A loud singing windmill.

People stuck their heads out of windows, cars stopped on the street, panhandlers forgot to ask for spare change, and a bus missed a turn and ended up on the sidewalk.

Paavo quickly ended the call and fled toward the city-issued Chevy. The tenor chased him down the block, still singing and gesticulating. Yosh was already in the driver's seat, his vision blurred by tears of laughter, while the other cops added a chorus of guffaws to the serenade.

With a diving leap into the passenger seat, Paavo glared at his partner. "Are you going to drive?"

As Yosh sped off, Paavo turned to see the singer in the middle of the street, hands over his heart, mouth opened wide in song, eyes shut. And a large truck was quickly rolling down the street toward him.

But then, Yosh turned the corner...

3

Connie peeked into her living room around one o'clock that same afternoon to find Max still asleep on her sofa. So much for going to work that day.

She might trust the stranger to sleep in her apartment, but no way would she leave him alone with all her possessions. They might not be much to others, but they were all she had, and she loved them. Besides, she'd let her renter's insurance lapse.

Her ex-husband had been the last man to sleep on her sofa. Lots of big rumpled cushions made it comfortable, and the color was a practical brownish-gray. She'd first used it in the small house she'd rented with Keith, her ex, and then brought it with her to this little one-bedroom apartment in an older building.

Dark hardwood floors in need of refinishing ran through the hall, living room and bedroom, and the walls in those rooms had floral wallpaper that had faded and yellowed with age. She tried to brighten up the apartment with white lacy curtains over dark wood window frames, posters of plays and art exhibits, and of course, her one completely impractical pleasure—the one her mother had called 'junk'—her stuffed animal and old-fashioned doll collections, which she displayed on shelves, window sills, and the backs of bureaus and table-tops throughout the apartment.

And now, as her décor's finishing touch—a man in the living room.

She studied him. Max Squire wasn't especially handsome. He wasn't bad, though, and probably a cut above average. Still, his face was a little too narrow, and his dark sandy-colored hair too shaggy to look good. His nose was a tad long, and his brown eyes could have been larger. Even his lips were perhaps a shade too well-defined.

Not that she was carefully checking him out or anything like that.

Her thoughts turned to last night, when she had helped him into her car. He had looked so pale and weak she wanted to take him to a hospital, but he'd refused. Max explained he'd been mugged earlier that day. The kids who'd robbed him of what little money he had—little Dennis Pagozzi wannabes in 49ers jackets—had taken a perverse pleasure in kicking him after pushing him to the ground. He thought his ribs had been badly bruised, but nothing more. He said he'd be fine in the homeless shelter he'd been staying at.

She couldn't help but wonder if he was being too optimistic about his condition. Against her usually cautious nature, she'd decided to bring him to her home so she could at least watch him throughout the night.

He leaned heavily on her while they slowly climbed the stairs to her third-floor apartment, she had thanked God she'd cleaned, vacuumed, and dusted the place earlier that day. She'd even changed the sheets—whether simply because they needed it or wishful thinking about her blind date, she wasn't sure. Well, actually, she was sure.

The sheets hadn't been all that dirty.

Once they reached her apartment, Connie ran a warm bath for Max and ordered him to take it not only because he was grimy, but she felt the water might soothe whatever was going on with his ribs. She handed him a large terry-cloth robe and the razor she used for her legs, including a fresh blade for it. He meekly took up her offer.

As he bathed, she'd put his clothes—other than the overcoat—into her washing machine, one of the few amenities of her apartment. She also covered the sofa with sheets, a blanket and a pillow. Normally, she wouldn't have dreamed of allowing a strange man into her home, let alone to bathe there, sleep on her sofa, and do his laundry, but he seemed in too much pain to be dangerous or anything else "bad."

And oddly, something about him touched her. She had no idea why. How many women ended up dead because a pitiable stranger had appealed to their compassion? Was she crazy, or what?

Or was she lonelier than she had realized? That, too, was a reason many women ended up dead. She vowed to be careful.

Then, when Max had come out of the bath, with his absurdly white legs protruding from the bottom of the robe, and his feet bare, she also noticed that he had some color to his face and his hair was soft and shiny. He definitely cleaned up quite nicely. Of course, he also looked so exhausted she knew she would be safe that night. Her life as well as her honor.

The way he grimaced as he lowered himself onto the sofa caused her to ask if she could take a look at his ribs. A trip to Emergency might be needed whether he wanted to go or not.

He slumped wearily. "If they were broken, you couldn't do anything about it, so why bother?"

God, but he's negative. "I could wrap them for you," she'd pointed out. "At least you wouldn't feel as much pain with each breath."

He kept the bottom of the robe clutched close about his

waist as she slid the top off his shoulders. His arms and shoulders were milky white while his chest, back, and ribcage were livid red and purple.

"You poor man!" Just looking at his bruises had made her wince. But no skin was broken, and no bone seemed to be jutting out unnaturally. She found an old pillowcase and tore it up. As she gently wrapped it around his ribs, she said, "When you were passed out, you mentioned being late or too late. Is there anything I can do to help you with that? Anyone you need to call?"

"I don't know what you're talking about," he mumbled.

"You were muttering the words. You sounded agitated."

"You must be mistaken." His voice was firm, almost harsh, and his eyes bored into her.

When she finished with the padding, she'd lifted the robe back onto his shoulders and gave him three Aleve, doubting the usual two would work.

But then, to help ease him down onto the pillow, she had wrapped one of her arms around his shoulders for support. As she lowered him, bending with him, their eyes met. His were like pools of dark coffee, rich and penetrating. She quickly looked away, doing her best not to notice.

As soon as he reached the pillow, she'd pulled her arm free and stood, stepping back from him, her face nearly as red as his bruises at the reaction she'd had to his nearness and the way he was looking at her—as if she were a beautiful version of Mother Teresa.

She wasn't a horny teenager anymore, but a thirty-plus divorcee. Okay, so maybe it had been a long time since her last fling, but this guy was a stranger, a fairly handsome, brusque, mysterious stranger.

So maybe she was a horny divorcee. *Get over it, Rogers.*

She shut her eyes a moment and did her best to shake off

those memories. The man was a stranger; he meant nothing to her.

That morning, she gave him more pain pills along with a couple of scrambled eggs, toast, and coffee, shocked at herself for cooking an almost traditional breakfast. Angie would be proud.

It'd also been years since either bacon or sausage had found their way to her refrigerator, not because she was a vegetarian or anything, but because they were too fattening. Also because toast or chocolate-flavored granola bars made for a quicker and easier breakfast. The fanciest she ever got was Egg-O waffles with diet margarine and lite syrup. She debated leaving Max alone while she ran over to Safeway to buy sausage, but since he fell back asleep before finishing his toast, she guessed he needed sleep more than sausage anyway.

Now, hours later, he finally began stirring and muttering.

The doorbell rang. She jumped at the unexpected sound.

The clock read 1:20 p.m., and she suddenly remembered... Angie! She slapped her forehead. They were supposed to meet at one for lunch.

She had to decide, quick. Did she dare tell Angie that not only had her blind date stood her up, but then she'd taken a complete stranger—a *homeless* stranger at that—into her home? Even to herself, that sounded really pathetic.

Angie placed her hand on the door handle, ready to push as soon as Connie buzzed it open.

Instead, after a long wait, Connie appeared in the doorway. "Hi, Angie," she said brightly as she stepped out onto the sidewalk.

Angie eyed her outfit—a stretchy pink top with a low-cut vee-neckline that showed off Connie's cleavage, tight black stretch slacks, and pink sandals with high, chunky heels. Plus she had put on makeup. Lots of makeup. This was not the appearance of a woman at death's door. Or of one who'd just crawled out of a bed of passion. More like looking to crawl into one.

"Were you just leaving?" Angie asked. "Heading for your store? Or, maybe, somewhere else?"

"No, not at all," Connie replied cheerfully.

"Oh?" Angie was confused. "Why didn't you buzz me in?"

"I figured it was you," Connie answered.

That was a non-answer. Connie always buzzed Angie in. What was going on here? "I went to the shop to meet you for lunch."

"Oh, shoot! That's right." Connie looked contrite. "With all the excitement of my date, I forgot to tell you I had a dentist appointment this morning, and my part-time clerk was busy, so I just left the shop closed."

"I'm sorry." Angie hated going to the dentist. "Was it so painful you decided to stay home all day?"

"He had to use a lot of novocaine... and it's taking forever to wear off. My face puffed up like a chipmunk's. I couldn't go to work like that. Slurred speech, face swollen. What would people have thought?"

"Well, you look fine now," Angie said with a compassionate smile. "Shall we go to lunch? I can't wait to hear every little detail of your date last night."

"There's nothing to tell." Connie folded her arms. "Not enough for a five-minute break, let alone an entire lunch. He stood me up."

Angie didn't think she'd heard right. "Dennis Pagozzi stood you up?"

"Neither hide nor hair. Look, I've got to go."

"Go where?" Angie stared at her. "But wait! I can't believe Dennis Pagozzi didn't show up. He's Butch's nephew."

"Believe it, Angie." Connie's mood deteriorated with each word. "The guy must be flaky. It was embarrassing. On the other hand, what else is new? It isn't the first time a blind date's ended up that way for me, and I'm sure it won't be the last. But I'm a big girl. I can handle it."

Angie's indignation over her best friend's treatment soared. "What a slime bucket!" She cried, hands on hips. "I never thought Butch's nephew would be such a...a..."

"Dickhead?"

"Exactly!"

"Who cares?" Connie said.

"That's the attitude!" Angie's jaw was firm, her whole being determined to make things right. "I'll find the perfect man for you. The world needs more love it in."

"Sure it does," Connie said without conviction. "And while I'm holding my breath, I'm going back inside to nurse my sore mouth."

"Connie, wait!" Angie cried as Connie turned away. None of this made any sense. "What's going on? What aren't you telling me?"

Connie stepped inside the foyer to the apartment building and left the door open just a crack as she faced Angie again. "Nothing. I told you. I want a break today, that's all. Don't worry about me. I'll be back at work tomorrow."

"But—"

Connie sighed. "You're so pushy, Angie."

"I'm pushy?" That took her aback. "Well, yes. Maybe sometimes. With good reason—"

"Goodbye!"

Hands on hips, Angie stood facing the closed door. That dentist story didn't hold an iota of truth. Connie never dressed up for her dentist. She was clearly hiding something.

If Connie didn't live on the third floor, Angie would have tried to see just what was going on inside her apartment. Never before had they held a conversation out on the street or, come to think it, had she been given such a brush-off.

She didn't even get to tell Connie about her brainstorm regarding her neighbor Stan and Helen the shoe repairer.

As she walked back to her car, the sense that whatever was causing Connie to act so unusual had something to do with last night struck her. She checked her wristwatch—just for fun waggling her ring finger to watch the diamond sparkle as she did so. There wasn't time now, but tonight would be here soon enough and, if no one had been murdered today, Paavo could join her in sleuthing it out.

Fortunately, he loved the food at the Wings of an Angel.

4

Chuck Lexington no sooner hit "send" on one e-mail, when another appeared. It seemed answering emails and reading bulletins from the home office was all he did these days. The job was a complete bore compared to the old days when he was in the Fresno police force and drove around in the streets in his patrol car, eyes on everything around him. He'd enjoyed that time, even though he'd put in so many hours his kids grew up without him ever getting to know them. Eventually, he'd felt to guilty about them he changed jobs.

He was still technically in law enforcement, he guessed, but being a fifty-year-old parole officer babysitting released convicts was nothing like being a young stud working the streets. Now, he felt more like a clerk between talking on the phone and staring at a computer screen for hours at a time. The phone rang while he was reading yet another e-mail.

He sighed and glanced at the clock above his desk—1:32 p.m. Still three hours before he could leave his boring parole officer job. He answered the phone.

"This is Joe Neeley at McDonald's down on Main Street," a

male voice said. "I was told you're Veronica Maple's parole offi-cer. She applied for a job here and was supposed to show up this morning, but she hasn't arrived. Do you know if she's been released yet?"

Lexington wasn't sure what to make of the call. Maple wasn't one to consider serving Big Macs. "I don't know how you heard that. Her release isn't for a couple of days."

"I don't think so. She told me she'd be out today and needed the job," the fellow said.

The question made Lexington uneasy. Nothing about Veronica Maple was ordinary, and especially not the woman herself. "Impossible," he muttered as he pulled up her records on the computer.

What the...!

"I was wrong," the parole officer admitted through clenched teeth. The information on the screen shocked and infuriated him. "She was released this morning."

"Thanks." The phone went dead.

Lexington stared at Maple's records with growing anger. How the hell had her release date changed without him being notified?

He got to work tracing her movements from the time she left jail. She'd been given a debit card, which would help him see what she was up to until it ran out of money.

But as he thought about it, something about the phone call bothered him as well. It didn't sound like a boss checking a reference, especially the way the guy quickly hung up. Lexington hit star-six-nine on his phone. Some aspects of low tech he liked. "The number of your last incoming call was four-one-five-three-nine-two..."

He scribbled down the number. Four-one-five was San Francisco's area code. He used the reverse phone directory on his computer for the full number. It belonged to a woman named Constance Rogers.

He jumped to his feet, staring at the phone.

What in the world is going on here? Who's Constance Rogers? Who's the guy calling from her phone? And where the hell is his parolee, Veronica Maple?

Sometimes computers could be helpful, he thought, as he searched California state files for names, phone numbers and addresses.

After Connie had finally gotten rid of Angie, despite feeling sorry she'd had to be so rude to do it, she raced upstairs to her third-floor apartment. On the last half-flight, she slowed down to catch her breath, smooth her pink top, adjust her bra, and push at her rock-hard hair so that it'd poof up a bit. One bad thing about this short hairdo was that gel tended to make it flatten against her skull and look like a bathing cap.

Max just might be awake.

Why, she asked herself, did that matter? Although he did look at her as if she was somehow special. That was nice. Even —okay, it was colossal admission time here—she liked having someone who needed her in her house, in her life. The words and tune of a schmaltzy old Broadway musical song popped into her head, "*As long as he needs me...*"

She waltzed up the rest of the stairs lightly singing to herself, then quietly unlocked and opened her apartment door. She actually was a very good singer. In high school, she'd had important roles in any musicals her class put on. Never the lead, but important enough.

No sound came from the living room. Tiptoeing to the doorway so as not to disturb Max, she peeked at the sofa.

It was empty.

He must be in the bathroom. The door was open. Cautiously, she approached. It, too, was empty.

Was he in the kitchen? Hungry, perhaps? Some runny eggs and a piece of toast weren't enough for such a tall man's appetite. What had she been thinking? She should have gone to the store and bought *both* sausage and bacon—and maybe splurged on a quart of chocolate Häagen Dazs or maybe Ben and Jerry's.

At the far end of the kitchen the back door was ajar. The apartment building had back steps for tenants to take down to a small yard where trashcans were kept. Connie always kept that door locked.

Max's clothes, which had been folded and draped neatly over a kitchen chair, were gone, and in their place was the terry-cloth robe she'd lent him.

He wouldn't have snuck out on her like that, would he? She wanted to believe he'd merely stepped outside for a moment, maybe to have a cigarette, and would be back soon. She wanted to believe anything except that she'd done it again—that she'd opened her home and heart to a man whose own troubles left no room for her or her feelings. The last thing she wanted was to get involved with that type again—her ex had been a complete course in needy personalities.

Good thing she found all this out about him before she got any more involved! And this made it even better that she hadn't mentioned him to Angie. This way, she could forget that she'd ever met Max Squire, or that he even existed.

Too bad she kind of liked him.

As she stepped into her cozy living room, she gasped. Her big, brown shoulder bag lay open on the oak coffee table. When she picked up her wallet, her heart sank.

All her cash—about a hundred eighty dollars' worth—was gone.

5

"Isn't that sweet?" Angie thought. She'd returned home after her unhappy encounter with Connie and was on the sofa going through her mail when she came across a letter from *Bon Appétit* magazine. It was an offer for her to become their Bay Area correspondent, since the current one resigned to become a full-time cookbook writer, and they were aware of her through the occasional but always wonderful restaurant reviews she wrote for the regional magazine, *Haute Cuisine.*

They enjoyed the whimsical style of her writing and thought she would add sparkle to the stories she wrote for them.

"Sparkle?" she murmured with a smile. She did have plenty to sparkle over these days, that was for sure. Diamonds, champagne, Paavo, love.

The offer from *Bon Appétit* dropped from her hand as she stared dreamily out the window. The magazine recently had a particularly nice spread on savory tea sandwiches, the sort that would be lovely to serve at an engagement party...

Sidney Fernandez, known as El Toro by friends and enemies alike, stretched out on the back seat of his black limousine and watched the bright neon glow of the city at night. He loved his limousine. He loved the plush red leather seats, the fully stocked bar with all his favorite liquor, the television, the satellite phone that worked no matter where he was. He loved the way he never had to worry about parking. He just had Raymondo drive him around and around, picking up friends and acquaintances, and once in a while pulling up to a gas station so he could use the crapper. That was the only thing still needed so he'd never have to leave his limo at all—a toilet.

He didn't even care if he never took a bath or a shower again. He washed up for other people, not himself. He was getting so rich, so powerful, no one would have the *cojones* to object to his stench anyway. Come to think of it, they already didn't.

"What you laughing about, Toro?" a nasal voice asked, snapping him out of his reverie.

"None of your business, Ju-li-us," Fernandez replied, harshly eying the nervous, sharp-nosed, goateed man. "So keep your trap shut."

Julius Rodriguez sulked, as usual. Fernandez didn't give a damn. He owned the guy. Rodriguez had been one of Fernandez's guys since they started out in one of many street gangs in Los Angeles. Lots of guys from the barrio wanted to call him "Hu-li-o" but since Julius—like Sidney Fernandez himself—was third generation and his knowledge of Spanish was limited to swear words and common phrases, he preferred the Anglo pronunciation. Anyway, Fernandez also found "Julius" more in keeping with being a big shot's main man.

"I was just wondering," Julius said. "Where we going?"

"No place. I'm thinking." Fernandez's three-hundred

pounds lumbered over onto his back, so his head lay on a stack of pillows covering the armrest, his feet braced against the one opposite.

Julius perched on the seat facing him. "No place. Great."

Fernandez glared at him. "Is she out yet?"

"She's trouble." Julius stared out the window. "You can't trust her."

"Who says I trust her? I want this job. That bitch owes me."

"And then?" Julius asked.

Fernandez smirked. "That's for me to know. So, she out?"

Julius sighed. "She got out this morning. I took care of everything for her. She's ours now."

Fernandez sat back and shut his eyes. *"Bueno."*

After a few more blocks and silence, Julius said, "Why don't we go find ourselves some chicks? I'm tired of just sitting."

Without moving, Fernandez ordered, "Get out."

Julius stared at his boss. "You joking?"

"You're tired of sitting, and I'm tired of listening to you complain." Fernandez struggled to sit up. "Raymondo! Stop here!" The car stopped in the center of Nineteenth Avenue, one of the major thoroughfares through the western side of San Francisco. Brakes shrieked and horns blared.

"Come on, boss. I didn't mean nothing," Julius said.

"Me neither. No hard feelings."

"But—"

Fernandez pulled out a .357 Ruger. Julius leaped out the door and dashed down the sidewalk. Laughing, Fernandez gave Raymondo the signal to take off.

As the limo rolled through Golden Gate Park, Fernandez once again stretched his flabby bulk across the back seat. "Drive along the ocean. I got to relax. The sound of waves, they relax me."

"You got it, boss."

"This is gonna be big, Raymondo."

"I know, boss."

Fernandez rested his bulbous head and shut his eyes, remembering Veronica, and what it had been like between them. He wanted to think of her without Julius's constant nagging and worry. He wanted to think of the way it used to be, and could be again. He was the one who had come through for her, to help when she needed it most, and she owed him. Also, she knew what he'd do if she tried to get away without paying. She'd help; no doubt about it.

"It's gonna be the biggest job of my life," Fernandez said to his driver. "After this, I may even think about retiring. What'll you do, then, without El Toro to drive around?"

"I'll be very sad, boss."

"I'm sure you will, Raymondo. I'm very sure you will be."

"Who cares that it's a corny old song?" Angie sat across the table from Paavo at Wings of an Angel and listened to him describe how cringe-worthy it had been when the tenor started to sing in the midst of a bunch of cops. "The sentiment is beautiful—that there's the sun in the sky, but my own sun, *sole mio*, is you before me, *sta 'nfronte a te*. It moves me to tears just to think about it!" She sighed dreamily, her gaze slowly moving over Paavo's face. It was handsome, and to her eyes, the stuff of songs. Some people might think that it was too angular and hard, with his high cheekbones and intense blue-eyes. Not her.

His hair was dark brown and wavy, and he wore it short and brushed conservatively back from his face. He was trim and fit, and about a foot taller than Angie's five-foot-two, which meant she usually wore fun shoes with wondrously high heels around him.

"Well, maybe it's not such a bad song," he murmured, then cleared his throat, as if to hide the way her words had touched him. "Anyway, the cops with me sure enjoyed laughing about it."

She grinned at his discomfort. He hated showing any iota of sentimentality, yet hidden under a brusque exterior, he was one of the most loving and tender-hearted men she'd ever met. "I'm sure they thought the singer was wonderful. They just didn't know how to tell you."

"Angie." He reached across the table and covered her hand with his. "It was thoughtful, unexpected, loving—but no more singers. Please."

She smiled ruefully. "All I wanted was for you to know how happy I am."

"I know, believe me. And now, the entire police force of the City and County knows as well."

"Good." She laughed. Even Paavo chuckled, proving he wasn't nearly as upset as he pretended to be.

Earl White scurried from one table to the next, serving desserts and coffee, collecting checks, and clearing dirty dishes, while continuing to provide for a steady stream of takeout customers. Angie hadn't realized Wings of an Angel had started such a service. It appeared to be successful, amazingly so. Who would have thought so many people would have a yen for cash-and-carry spaghetti and meatballs?

Angie leaned toward Paavo, and in a lowered voice said, "As soon as Earl is free, I'll ask him what happened here last night between Connie and her date."

"So eating here wasn't due to a sudden desire for Butch's cooking," he said, one eyebrow knowingly lifted.

"If I was taking care of my desires," she said saucily, "we wouldn't be here now, believe me."

He grinned, obviously liking her response.

She and Paavo had finished their green salad and small bowls of minestrone, and were working on the entrees— polenta and Italian sausage for Paavo, and Butch's spaghetti and meatball special for Angie—when she saw that Earl was free, and used her engagement-ring-laden hand to wave him over.

"How're you guys doin' now?" Earl asked as he bustled closer. "Wait! I almost forgot." He filled his lungs, spread his arms wide, and in an ear-splitting voice that grated like a flat bugle, erupted into, 'O so-o-o-le mi-i-o!'"

The other customers gawked in stunned silence, then burst into applause and laughter.

Paavo cringed as Angie beamed. "How did you know?" she asked.

"Da last takeout guy was a cop. Tol' us all about it. What a hoot! Miss Angie, you're too much."

Since Paavo looked ready to chew the table, Angie quickly changed the conversation to Connie's date. Earl told them all about the stranger Connie had dined with after Dennis stood her up.

"Did they leave together?" she asked.

Paavo studied Angie's expression. "You don't think she'd take some stranger home with her, do you? She's smarter than that."

"Why, then, didn't she tell me about him?" Angie wondered.

Earl had an answer. "Maybe 'cause dis stranger looked like a bum."

"Well, something kept her home from work, and me out of..."

The door opened and two men walked into the restaurant. The one in the lead dripped magnetism, money, and sexy good looks. Angie stopped talking and eyeballed him. Rarely did she see a man she'd call a hunk—other than Paavo—but this guy definitely fit that category.

He was at least six-three or four, with shoulders that stretched from one wall to the other, and thick, jet-black hair with an evocative lock carefully draped to lightly touch his forehead. His eyes were hazel, framed by long, black lashes, and his face chiseled. His clothes reminded Angie of a recent Calvin Klein ad, from his chestnut brown leather sports coat, to the gold chains against a cream pullover, black slacks, and Italian brown leather loafers. On his pinky rested an eye-popping diamond in a chunky twenty-four carat gold setting.

She scarcely noticed the older, thinner, and smaller man in a dated, off-the-rack pinstripe suit with wide lapels. He seemed to fade into the woodwork, while the first one lit up the room.

"Oh, my! Who's that?" Angie whispered to Earl.

"Not'in' like a day late an' a dollar short," he murmured. "It's Dennis Pagozzi."

It took all Angie's willpower not to swivel around and stare at the man and his cohort as Earl led them to a back table. Dennis Pagozzi looked like part of the high-rolling world of celebrity sports stars, the kind of man who'd have starlets and showgirls throwing themselves at him, while Connie—despite her love of loud, too-tight clothing—was really a down-home kind of girl.

On the other hand, Angie thought with a thrill, it might be time for Dennis to settle down with a real woman. Why should he bother with young, sexy playgirls when he could have Connie? A question better left unanswered.

Even his Uncle Butch seemed to think Connie was exactly what Dennis needed, and Butch obviously had Dennis's best interests at heart. Connie's, too.

"Very interesting," Angie murmured, mental wheels churning and spinning.

Paavo cocked an eyebrow and glanced at the man who'd caused such a reaction in Angie. "He looks like a lot of jocks who've hit the big time," was his only comment, until, "Uh, oh."

Angie didn't like the way Paavo was frowning. "Why did you say—"

The question lodged in her throat as Dennis Pagozzi cast a

huge shadow across their table. She looked up and realized she had to lean way back to meet his eyes. "Hello."

He held out a large, strong hand. "I'm Dennis Pagozzi." His deep voice rumbled. "I just learned you're Angie Amalfi, and you've been a big help to my Uncle Butch and his friends getting this restaurant off the ground."

"Thank you," she said, her hand still swallowed up in his. "This is my fiancé, Paavo Smith. We've just become engaged." She freed her right hand and lifted her left toward him, ring finger extended.

"Very nice," Dennis said, then offered congratulations to Paavo as they shook hands. "Care if I join you?" he asked as he pulled a free chair from another table. "I feel terrible I missed meeting your friend last night. Man, my Uncle Butch is really piss—, I mean, angry at me about it. See, what happened was, I got knocked out during a pickup game with some friends, which means I'm on a disabled list for a couple weeks— concussion protocol. Anyway, I spent my dinner in the infirmary. Do you think she hates me so much if I call her she'd hang up? I hear she's a great gal."

He looked so hangdog as he relayed his tale of woe that Angie couldn't help but laugh. "If you tell her what happened, I'm sure she'll listen."

"Cool!" His face lit up with a big smile. "This restaurant's great, isn't it?" He looked around, eyeing everything much like a little boy in an ice cream parlor. "I've been suggesting to Butch that they expand it so they can fit in lots more customers. I could help out, take part in it myself."

"Expand it?" Angie was shocked. "Don't you think that'd ruin the place? It's a small, romantic, eight-table restaurant."

"Isn't that the problem?" He shrugged, then rose. "Well, I don't want to interrupt. Just wanted to say hello. What if some-time we get together and, you know, toss around ideas about how to make this place bigger and better? I've been told you're real creative."

"That would be most interesting," Angie said, pleased that someone, somewhere, appreciated her creativity. She tried to be innovative, not that she'd often succeeded, but she always tried.

"Before I forget," Dennis said, "one more question. What was your friend's name again?"

A short while later, Angie was getting into the passenger seat of her car—Paavo preferred to drive—when she realized she'd never gotten an answer to her question. Had Connie left with the stranger last night or not?

6

Dennis Pagozzi was asleep when he heard the doorbell ring. He lived in a mansion in Sea Cliff, one of San Francisco's most exclusive neighborhoods. Most of his friends and teammates lived with family and kids south of the city in big suburban sprawlers with land and swimming pools. Dennis enjoyed city life, so the thirty-five hundred square feet of high-tech luxury he called home suited him just fine.

Few people knew this was his home, however. And those who did had better sense than to come to call at two a.m.

He went to the security video in one corner of his bedroom and looked to see who stood at the door.

He couldn't say his visitor was unexpected. He walked back to the bed, took out the Beretta he kept in his nightstand, and put on a black silk robe.

Holding the gun, he padded downstairs. The bell rang once more as he reached the door.

"Who is it?" he called. No sense letting on that he knew.

"Veronica."

Hearing her voice was like a knife through the belly. "Are you alone?"

"Of course!"

He opened the door a crack, giving her a quick once-over, then pulled it wider. Her gaze fell to the gun.

"Are you serious?" she said. "Is that how you greet me?"

"Since when weren't you dangerous?" He slid the gun into the robe's pocket and held open the door as she entered. She looked good, damned good for a woman who'd done time, in a tight, silver dress and gray stiletto heels. Her blond hair appeared freshly trimmed and feathered long and sexy. He remembered how silky it used to feel—how silky she used to feel.

She perused the living room, slowly walking around over the white carpet, eying the two black sofas with a couple of black and gray checked throw pillows on one of them, the gray loveseat. She lightly fingered the big screen TV, the audio and video entertainment systems, and the entire wall filled with a variety of video game systems and monitors. "Still into toys, I see," she said, her voice curling around him, as husky as he remembered it.

His chin tilted upward, glad she could see how far he'd come, yet smarting at her criticism. "So? No harm done."

"You've done well," she said abruptly. "Extremely well. Almost suspiciously well, I might add."

"Don't worry. It's all legit. From football. Not everyone is like you, Veronica."

"You had me worried there for a minute, but I should have known better." She laughed aloud as she sat down on the sofa and opened up the onyx cigarette box on the chrome and glass coffee table. "Cigarettes? That's all?" The mocking tone in her voice grated. Lifting out a Benson and Hedges, she held it between long, red nails. "You aren't the man I used to know."

She put the cigarette in her mouth and waited for him to pick up the lighter.

"I don't even use nicotine now. That's all I keep in the house, and they're for company." He held the flame steady as she drew on the cigarette, then sat down across from her. "I'm a respectable member of the community, in case you didn't know."

Her deep, throaty laughter rumbled inside him and made him want her in his bed. In the past, she had nearly cost him his career.

"Of course you are, lover." Her head dropped back, and she slowly blew smoke high into the air. He eyed her long, smooth neck, the lightly throbbing pulse at the base of her throat.

"How did you find out where I live?" His words turned clipped and dry. "I figured you'd phone when you got out."

"We have a few mutual friends," she said coyly, "whether you want to remember that little fact or not."

"I remember," he said with a frown. "So, when did you get out?"

"This morning. Or, considering it's now past midnight, I should have said yesterday morning." She took a deep drag and let the smoke billow around her.

He inhaled it, remembering. "You didn't waste any time getting here."

"Why should I? I've waited for this a long time."

He smirked. "For me? I should have known."

Her red lips slanted in a half-grin, half-derision. "You're such a sick bastard. You know what I'm here for. It's time to hand it over."

He raked his fingers through his hair and wished he was dreaming. She was more than he could bear. "It's not that easy, Veronica."

"What the hell are you talking about?"

"I got bills. Lots of them. My career... things... aren't quite as good as they were earlier."

Her jaw tightened. "I sat in jail three years—"

"I know, but it's been tough," he shouted, then softer added, "the economy is going south. My contract... I don't think it's getting renewed."

Her face hardened. "What are you saying?"

"I need the money a lot more than you do."

She jumped to her feet. "Max Squire put you up to this, didn't he? You two bastards think you're going to screw me again!"

"No! I haven't even seen him. Not... not for years."

She pulled a gun from her handbag and pointed it at him. "Where's Max?"

He took hold of her wrist and turned the gun away. At the same time, his free hand captured her waist, holding her in place as moved close. First their bodies touched, then as his gaze locked with hers, their lips met.

<hr>

Connie woke up to a raging headache and black circles under her eyes.

Most of the night she'd lain awake berating herself for having been such a sucker. When she saw Squire lying on the street two nights ago, she should have called the cops! How far would he have gotten trying to steal out of *their* wallets, hmm?

When she finally fell asleep, she dreamed she had tracked him down. After devastating him with her charms into a mass of quivering unfulfilled desire, on his knees, all but chewing the carpet with frustration, she picked his wallet from his back hip pocket, took out all his money, rolled it up, and slid it into her ample cleavage.

"Connie, forgive me!" he'd begged.

"Die, worm."

She sashayed away in a blaze of bright yellow and matching four-inch spike heels. Comfortable ones, which told her she was definitely dreaming.

She got up, showered, and used half a tube of concealer to hide the bags under her eyes before putting on the rest of her makeup.

Yesterday, she'd searched her apartment for anything Squire might have left behind to give her some clue as to where he was living, but she'd found nothing. Big surprise. He didn't *own* anything to leave behind.

He'd told her he was staying at a shelter near Wings of an Angel. She wondered if that was true. Maybe he didn't even know Dennis Pagozzi, and the whole thing was a scam to get a free dinner, a free night's lodging, and some ready cash.

What a stupid, schmaltzy, ignoramus sap she was! She was going to swear off men forever. She'd had it. End of story. Finito.

She was almost out the door to head for work when Angie phoned, singing the praises of Dennis Pagozzi.

"I'd like to know why you met him when he was supposed to have been my date," Connie snapped.

Angie's reply was measured. "He was sorry he missed you, and he's going to call."

Like this girl was born yesterday. "Well, let's forget about my job," Connie mewled. "I'll just sit here holding my phone all day."

"He's handsome, and a sharp dresser. You'll be gaga over him, trust me in this," Angie urged.

"If gaga is close to nuts, I don't have far to go," Connie muttered.

"Anyway, what's this I hear about you having dinner with some stranger?" Angie asked. "Earl told me about it. Some bum who was looking for Dennis as well? What was that about?"

"Damned if I know," Connie said brusquely. "Earl was right. He was a bum. I don't know and don't care anything about him. Now, I'm going to work."

Connie hung up the phone, in no mood to hear any more about how great her missed blind date was, or how much Angie was in love, and definitely not how Angie thought everyone else in the world should be in love as well. Sometimes she could be really hard to take.

Before stepping out of her apartment, Connie looked at herself in a mirror to make sure no one had taped a sign to her back that said "SUCKER." How did guys like Squire even find her?

Right then and there, she was determined to find *him*, and when she did, he'd be one sorry bastard. His ribs might not be broken now, but just wait.

Helen Melinger, the shoe repair shop owner, was sweeping the sidewalk when Connie approached. "Hey, there! Glad you're back!" Helen barked in her usual gruff way. "So, how was your blind date?"

"Buzz off!" Connie unlocked the door and slammed it behind her.

Helen leaned on the broom, gawking in complete surprise at her usually friendly and cheerful neighbor.

7

Early morning was hot in Chowchilla, California, a dusty town in California's central valley. It was located about forty miles from the "big city" in the area, Fresno, which the inmates referred to as an armpit of the world.

San Francisco was a hundred-fifty miles away. It seemed more like a hundred-fifty light years.

Max stared at the sprawling, unadorned, concrete gray buildings. The Central California Women's Facility, six-hundred forty acres that made up the largest women's prison in the U.S., and probably the world, had beds for two-thousand inmates, and housed a lot more.

Max almost felt a pang of pity for Veronica Maple having spent three years there. Almost. A sour-faced female guard led him through security to the visitor's area of the cellblock Veronica had called home.

He sat on a stool facing a thick glass wall with phones on both sides. After some ten minutes, a jailer led a young woman to a chair opposite his. Her name was Harmony Givens and Max had learned she had been Veronica Maple's cellmate for at least the past year, if not longer.

"Who're you?" Harmony asked. Her acne-scarred face was hard and the scowl she wore made it even fiercer.

"I'm a friend of Veronica's," he said quietly. "I was supposed to meet her, but she isn't at the hotel. I'm hoping you might have some idea why or where she might have gone."

The woman eyed him suspiciously. "You Dennis?" she asked. Her voice and mannerisms were as rough and tough as her appearance.

Dennis? The past came at him in a rush. He wobbled dangerously on the stool, his head light and dizzy. After Veronica had been sent to prison, he'd gotten the impression that she'd had an affair with Dennis, among others. He had no idea, though, that their relationship was at all serious, or that it had continued.

Dennis had been one of his few clients who'd been kind to him after his "troubles" and had offered help. He'd thought it was because Dennis had considered him a friend. Now, he wondered if it wasn't guilt.

"I'm surprised," he said finally. "I didn't think she'd tell anyone my name. She must trust you a lot."

The woman shrugged. "Guess so."

He tried to look worried. "I waited all day yesterday for her. She was released yesterday, wasn't she?"

"Yeah. Lucky bastard. Me, I got four more years here. She told me you're rich. Can you do something for me? Help me get out?"

"I'll see what I can do. But first, I've got to find Veronica."

"Why don't you ask her PO?" she said.

"I did. But the parole officer didn't even know she'd been released."

"She said she was going to San Francisco, man. You should try her there. Isn't that where you live? Maybe she's at your place, waiting for you."

Not very likely, Max thought bitterly. But then his imagination turned to Veronica with Dennis Pagozzi; the two of them together and laughing over what a lovesick fool Max had been.

It shouldn't be too hard for him to find Pagozzi's home, and then to visit her there with the Saturday night special he'd picked up with Connie's money.

Damn them both!

For now, he smiled warmly at the woman. "To think, I came all the way down here to meet her. Did she say she was going to San Francisco right away?"

"That's what I thought. Why the hell would she want to stay in this crappy town one minute longer than she had to?"

———

Connie's mood wasn't any better when she returned to her apartment that evening, especially when Mrs. Rosinsky, her landlady, confronted her on the stairs and demanded to know if she had a man living in her apartment. She should be so lucky. But then the landlady asked if another woman lived there.

"What are you talking about?" Connie asked. "You know I live alone!"

"A police officer of some kind came by here," Mrs. Rosinsky explained. "He first asked about you and then said he was looking for a man or woman who might be staying in your apartment. I told him you lived alone, and had been a good and quiet tenant for a couple of years. But now, I want to make sure I hadn't lied to the police."

"The police were asking about me?" Connie murmured, confused and chilled by the thought.

"He wasn't a regular SFPD cop—that's all I can tell you. I wasn't about to question him. Anyway, he left, so don't worry about it," Mrs. Rosinsky said as she headed back down the stairs to her apartment.

It was all too weird, Connie thought. Now, on top of everything else, she wondered if she had given sanctuary to a man wanted by the police. But even if he was, how would they know he'd spent one night in her apartment? It made no sense, did it?

She kicked off her Hush Puppies as she flipped through the mail. Two bills, four advertisements. At least the numbers weren't reversed.

Tossing her jacket onto a chair, she went to the refrigerator for a bottle of diet citrus tea and to ponder the food situation for dinner. It wasn't pretty.

The few customers who'd come into the shop that day were picky and hadn't bought anything. Many more days like that and she'd end up back at the Bank of America as a teller. Standing on her feet for eight hours giving money to other people was not her idea of a good time.

The hundred-eighty dollars Max stole from her was impor-tant. Most of it was grocery money. As she sprinkled some food into Goldie Hawn's bowl, she wondered if she might be reduced to eating fish food before her business turned around.

Goldie Hawn was lucky she was so small. Any larger, and she might end up battered and fried.

Connie cooked some instant rice, then sautéed onion and garlic in a frying pan, added about a quarter pound of hamburger, crumbled, a half can of peas and a little powdered ginger. When it was cooked, she mixed it together with the cooked rice, sprinkled soy sauce over the concoction and, voilà, "Connie's Fried Rice." Okay, so it wasn't anything she'd serve company—and she wouldn't dare mention it to gourmet-cook Angie—but it was easy, filling, and most importantly, cheap.

With each bite, irritation at Max Squire grew. How many times is one burnt so badly? She should track him down like a crazed bloodhound, then glom onto his arm like a rabid pit bull until he coughed up her money.

Dennis Pagozzi supposedly knew Max. Old friends—wasn't that what Max said they were? Maybe Dennis could tell her how to reach him. If she called Butch Pagozzi, he could give her Dennis's phone number.

God, but she hated the thought of phoning a man who'd stood her up! On the other hand, she was desperate, financially speaking.

She was steeling her nerve to call the Wings of an Angel when her phone rang. As she crossed the room, she was sure the caller was Angie wanting to get together "to talk." Why did people who had everything going well for them think that other people's problems could be solved by talking? God knows, if it was that easy, she'd talk so much she'd rival Oprah.

But when she picked up the phone, the caller was unknown. "Hello?"

"Is this, uh, Connie?" A man's deep voice asked.

"Yes," she said hesitantly.

"I'm Dennis Pagozzi. I called to apologize for missing you the other night. I was knocked out cold in a pickup game. Spent the night in the infirmary."

Dennis Pagozzi! He'd actually called her. Was on her telephone. Right now.

She swallowed hard as her head began swimming with all the movies and books she'd enjoyed recently in which women had sexy Italian boyfriends. Could it finally be her turn?

It took a moment to find her voice. "How awful!" she croaked, then nervously cleared her throat.

"It's no big deal. I'm okay. I was wondering if we could try again."

To hear him say those words was even more of a shock than the call, no matter how nice Angie had claimed he was. Cautiously, she said, "What did you have in mind?"

"How about dinner tomorrow night? I'll come by to pick you up. My uncle didn't like the way you ended up sitting there all alone with no one but a guy who knew me years ago to keep you company. It was pretty cold. I never treat my women that way—not any woman. I feel bad about it."

Something about his pat little speech grated. On the other hand, the way he said "my women" with that growling, masculine voice, caused her heart to beat a little faster. God, what was with her? "Tell you what," she said, taking a couple of deep breaths. "I'll meet you there, but I'll get there on my own."

"Don't trust me?" he asked, sounding hurt.

"Why should I?" was her quick retort. Despite his sexy voice, he was a long way from being anyone she wanted to depend on for anything. Of course, she did want information on Max Squire's whereabouts, and perhaps he could give it to her.

"Hey, you're one tough woman." He chuckled. "I like that."

She smiled. "Maybe, if you're lucky, I'll feel the same about you someday."

"You will, Connie. You can bet on it."

After arranging a time, they said goodbye. Connie ended the call, but instead of feeling elated by it, despite Angie's assurances, something made her uneasy.

Maybe she was gun shy because of her rotten experience with Max. Or, maybe she just wasn't blind date material.

8

As Paavo returned to Homicide the next morning after a grueling time in court, he was tired and cross. The defendant's attorney was good, but with his client obviously guilty, his only chance was to make the police look like the bad guys in the case. It didn't help Paavo's mood any to know it was more a show for the jury than anything else.

The first thing he saw as he stepped into the bureau's main room, was an ornate silver coffee urn on a table near the entrance, and around it, yellow, green and gold floral demitasse cups more than half filled with cold coffee. On platters were fancy little sandwiches, no crusts, cut into heart and flower shapes. A number of them, with one bite taken out, lay abandoned on plates besides the cold coffee.

He looked out over the large rectangular space that held the Homicide detail of the San Francisco Police Department. Homicide was a specialized department, part of the Bureau of Inspections, and housed centrally in the Hall of Justice rather than scattered over the neighborhood stations. Although homicide was the top level for an officer not interested in supervision or administration to aspire to, right now, those few tough cops on the premises had their heads buried in their paper-work, refusing to meet his eye.

Elizabeth Havlin, Lieutenant Hollin's secretary, and de facto all-around helpmate for the homicide inspectors, a usually pleasant and chatty woman with dyed hair, currently red, and glasses, stepped into the room, saw him, and froze.

"What's this?" he asked as she scurried by, almost as if she didn't want to be anywhere around him.

"Don't ask me." She picked up the out-going mail, then all but ran from the room.

Heads bent lower as he headed toward his desk.

On the desk was an envelope with his name, written in Angie's neatly rounded script. Eyes peered at him as he opened it.

I hope you and your staff enjoy this treat—and it makes up for the singer. Love, Angie.

His own partner was one of the cowards. Paavo stared at him until he looked up. "What's wrong with it, Yosh?"

"Try it."

Paavo slowly walked to the coffee urn and poured himself a cup. From the smell alone, his stomach began to sink. He took a sip and nearly gagged. Rebecca Mayfield, the city's only woman homicide inspector, stood beside him. She was an attractive blonde, intelligent, tall, and with a figure sculpted to near perfection by workouts at a gym. Everyone in Homicide knew, including Paavo, about her "secret" crush on him. And they all thought she was a lot better suited to him than Angie.

"Strawberry?" he asked.

"Strawberry and vanilla cream flavored coffee, as far as we can tell," she said, her lips pursed.

"It's awful." Paavo's cup joined everyone else's on the table.

"Wait until you taste the sandwiches," Rebecca warned, unable to suppress a smile.

"What are they?"

"The watercress isn't bad, if you like veggie sandwiches, which these guys don't. But it was the pâté that really got to them."

"Christ," he muttered.

"You call it pâté. To me, it's chopped liver." Calderon's voice boomed across the room. Luis Calderon was homicide's resident grouch. He could have easily played the guy in a Stephen King movie who scared little boys and girls. "I tried to wash it down with that strawberry crap. Thought my damned tongue would shrivel up and die."

Rebecca patted Paavo's arm. "I'm sure she meant well. It probably sounded very, uh, romantic to her. It's excellent pâté, if you can stand that kind of thing."

"I can't even think of where to send it," Yosh finally got the nerve to speak up from behind his desk. "If we offered it to the guys in city jail, it'd probably cause a prison riot."

The entire detail laughed.

———

Angie walked two steps from her car and stopped, staring down at one of her black Ferragamo pumps with high platform soles. Stan Bonnette, a slim, preppy looking man in tan Ralph Lauren slacks and a suede Brooks Brothers jacket, stood beside her. She'd convinced him to go to Connie's shop to buy his mother a birthday gift. "Before we go into Connie's, Stan, I've got to get the heel of this shoe fixed. It feels loose."

"How can you tell with those things? I think you need a blacksmith more than a shoe repair." He laughed at his joke. She didn't.

"A shoe repair is right next door to Connie's. Isn't that handy? Let's go inside."

Helen Melinger was concentrating on the sole of a man's

shoe when the two entered. "Hi, Helen," Angie said. "How are you today?"

"Well, look who's here. What's up, Angie? I saw your pal drag herself next door this morning. I guess she's settling down a little, finally." Helen's greeting was good-natured as she swung the hammer down with a resounding clang.

"I hope. I'd like you to meet a dear friend of mine, Stan Bonnette. Stan, this is Helen Melinger."

The two shook hands. Angie waited for "Love In Bloom" to sound. "Stan is my neighbor," she chirped. "He's also a good friend of Paavo's." Heaven forbid Helen get the wrong impression about her and Stan.

"Oh, nice." Helen scarcely looked up. Her muscled arm swung again. *Clang!*

"He works in a bank." Angie pretended not to see Stan scrunch his face up and cringe with each blow.

"Is that so?" Helen glanced up at the clock. Two p.m. "Banker's hours are getting shorter every day, aren't they?"

"It's my day off," Stan said petulantly. He was sensitive about his work habits, or lack thereof. "Why don't you show her your shoe, Angie?"

She turned to Helen. "Oh, yes. My shoe. The leather piece on the end of this heel feels loose. I think it needs another nail or glue to hold it in place." She put the shoe on the counter then faced Stan. "Helen is a wonder at fixing things, Stan. Shoes, purses, belts, um..."

"Motorcycles," Helen added with a wink and a smile, giving the shoe she'd been working on a couple more whacks, then smiled in a job-well-done way. "I have a big Harley that sings like a bird." She picked up Angie's shoe.

"Isn't that exciting, Stan?" Angie asked.

"Sure. Except that they're dangerous," Stan added.

Helen finally looked up at him. She put Angie's shoe on the

work table, the hammer still in hand. Her eyes narrowed slightly. "Not if you know how to drive them properly."

"It's not *how* to drive them, it's the way they're driven," Stan proclaimed. "I hate how bikers drive along the line that divides lanes, zipping between cars stuck in traffic. They should stay in one lane or the other the way cars do. But instead, if you change lanes and you bag some guy on a motorcycle while he's where he shouldn't be, usually in your blind spot, it's the car driver's fault."

Helen put the hammer down and folded her arms. "You need to understand that motorcycles aren't like cars. They have only two wheels, in case you hadn't noticed. You've want to keep them moving if possible, so they don't fall over or stall."

Angie pointed at her shoe. "There's—"

"If they can't handle traffic like everyone else," Stan pontificated loudly, "they shouldn't be on city streets. A no motorcycle zone, that's what this world needs."

"My shoe?" Angie hopped a little closer to Helen. Both Helen and Stan ignored her.

"What kind of a pig-headed attitude is that?" Helen growled. "If everyone drove motorcycles instead of big gas guzzlers, this country would be a lot better place. We could save the environment."

Stan threw back his head and brayed a phony laugh. "A Sierra club Harley rider? Now I've heard everything. A two-wheeling tree hugger."

Helen came around the counter toward him with deadly deliberation.

"My heel... over there!" Angie pointed vigorously at her shoe, trying to get Helen's attention.

"You haven't heard nothin' if you bad mouth Harleys *or* the Sierra club, buster."

Helen looked ready to deck him, and Angie had no doubt

about the agonized outcome for Stan if it came to that. So much for matchmaking. "Uh, Stan, I think it's time for us to go."

He waved her off. "I can say whatever I want, *lady*—and I use that term only because I don't think it's polite to say what I'm thinking."

Angie couldn't believe her ears. Stan was squeamish, nervous, and your basic wuss. He never stood his ground. Was he drunk?

Helen put her hands on her wide hips. "You can say what you want, you pencil-necked weeny, as long as you have the balls to back it up."

Angie wobbled dangerously on one shoed foot, tugging at Stan's arm, trying to get him out the door.

He brushed her off. "Well, maybe mine aren't quite as big as you wish yours were—"

"Why you little!"

"Stan!" Angie grabbed him around the waist and pulled. "Let's get out of here!"

"Hi!" Connie said. She'd been standing in the doorway watching the bizarre scene. She waved to Helen as Angie dragged Stan out of the shop onto the sidewalk. Connie followed them, a huge smile on her face. "I thought I heard familiar voices. I was just heading home to get ready for my date with Dennis Pagozzi, thanks to you, Angie."

Angie gave a whoop of joy at Connie's news. She was thrilled, even though she'd left her shoe in Helen's shop. She'd retrieve it later. For now, she wanted to bask in Connie's happiness. Her matchmaking failure with Stan and Helen was, clearly, nothing but a onetime-only aberration.

9

Connie gelled her hair into spiky strands that stood up on top and sprayed it into place. With this new hairstyle she should buy stock in all kinds of hair products. She then added globs of black mascara to her lashes, gray eye shadow, and pink blush. After sheer black tights and black strappy sandals, she squeezed herself into a slinky black dress with a skirt so short and a neckline so plunging that if either was much shorter or lower, they'd have met.

Eat your heart out, Pagozzi.

She hadn't particularly believed his concussion story, but it didn't matter. Having him call made her feel a lot better about him. Angie's predictions about how much she'd like him, though, carried no weight after watching Angie try to matchmake Stan and Helen. She'd viewed enough while standing in Helen's doorway to recognize exactly what Angie was up to.

Covering up with her sensible, long and bulky navy-blue overcoat, Connie headed for Wings of an Angel. When she walked in, she spotted Pagozzi immediately and, as she approached his table, all thoughts about him feeling remorse for missing their date vanished. Who was she kidding? The guy was drop-dead, mouth-wateringly gorgeous. He stood up as she walked in, all six-feet four-inches of him in a deep red cashmere sweater and well-fitted black slacks. She all but stopped breathing. "Connie?" He smiled pleasantly as he stepped forward to greet her. A dimple. He even had one dimple when he smiled.

"Hi, Dennis." She fought for composure. She was supposed to be cool here, not gape and drool like some brain-dead groupie. "How nice to finally meet you." They shook hands. He held hers a little longer than necessary.

"Same here," he answered. "I'd like you to meet a good friend of mine, Wallace Jones. Everyone calls him Jonesy. Jonesy, meet Connie. She's the chi—, er, gal, I was telling you about."

When she could finally tear her eyes from Dennis, she saw an older man also sat at the table. Skinny, wearing a pinstriped suit with wide lapels, his left eye twitched as he looked at her.

He stood up and shook her hand, giving her a quick nod. His hand felt dry and scaly, and his teeth looked the same.

Dennis held out a chair for her as she removed her coat. His pleasant expression expanded into a wide, happy grin, and he murmured, "Wow."

Ecstatic, she sat and then, to hide her nerves, turned her attention on his friend. "What do you do, Mr. Jones?"

"It's Jonesy, ma'am. I'm a collector."

She raised her eyebrows in surprise. "How fascinating. What do you collect?"

"Sports stuff, I mean, mem-or-a-bi-li-a," he said slowly, as if he'd just learned the word and was testing it out.

"That's right," Dennis said enthusiastically. "And if we make this place into a sports bar, like I'm thinking would be a real good idea, Jonesy will supply the stuff to sell, and we'd all get a cut."

Facing him, she was struck anew at what a stunning man he

was. "Why would you care about a sports bar when you play football?"

"A guy has to think about the future. Someday, when I retire, I'll need a backup plan," he said. But then quickly added, "Of course, my contract will be renewed for next season. It's not like there's any problem."

"I see," she murmured, although she didn't. Still, a man who thought about the future was excellent in her book.

Dennis placed his hand on Jonesy's back. "No sense talking business tonight, friend. I'll call you." Jonesy took the hint and left.

The evening went by in a haze of glory. Dennis Pagozzi treated Connie like a princess, and he was large enough she felt almost petite around him. His hazel eyes had a way of gazing at her as if she were both interesting and intelligent.

She kept pinching herself to make sure this evening was real. That she was here, and so very happy.

Much too early, Dennis escorted her to her Toyota. She'd hoped he'd ask her to go out to a nightclub or to go dancing. How many times could a girl say she loved to dance without appearing too obvious? But, no luck.

It was just a first date, she reminded herself. He should call back. And maybe he really did have a concussion. At this point, she'd have believed him if he said he'd missed their blind date because he'd turned into Superman and saved Metropolis.

"I almost forgot," he said as they neared the car. "You talked with Max Squire the other night."

Max, who? was her first reaction, but she smiled and said she had.

"Did he say anything about how I could get hold of him?" Dennis asked. "I heard he was looking for me, but he didn't leave a phone number or anything."

That was the question she'd planned to ask Dennis, back when she was able to hold a thought in her head. "He didn't say specifically. Only that he lived near here—in easy walking distance. Perhaps in a, um, a homeless shelter. But I may be wrong about that. I don't really know him at all."

"I see..." Dennis nodded, looking around. "Anyway, I got to go. See you around, Connie." With that, he hurried down the block to his Jaguar.

Connie hadn't even put the key in the ignition when she saw him drive off. Why was he in such a hurry?

Veronica Maple sat in a coffee shop across the street from Wings of an Angel. When she first arrived in the city, she'd taken buses everywhere. But now, staying with Dennis, he'd let her borrow his Prius. It was too small for him. That night, she'd used it to follow Dennis, hoping he was going to meet Max Squire. She didn't trust either of those guys.

All she wanted was her money, and then she'd split.

Instead of going to meet Max, Dennis went first to a run-down apartment building in the rough China Basin area, where he picked up a sleazy looking little guy with a pinstripe suit and an eye tic, and then to the restaurant.

From the outside, the restaurant looked like little more than a dump, although it did a decent business, especially in take-out. She'd peeked in the window and saw that it was clean and kind of cute, if you liked the cozy and intimate look. Definitely not what she'd consider a Dennis Pagozzi go-to place.

Before long, the skinny guy left the restaurant, but not Dennis. When he finally did leave, he walked out with some stacked blond. They took separate cars, and judging from the different directions the cars went off in, they weren't reconvening at some love nest.

She had to find out what Dennis was up to. He wasn't nearly as malleable as when he was younger, and she didn't like his new assertiveness. He even had the nerve to say "no" to her about her money. She harrumphed—as if he thought he could stop her that easily. Nobody said no to Veronica Maple. She thought he'd learned that years ago.

The three years she'd been in jail must have been long enough for him to forget. Or, perhaps, he thought her time there had softened her. If anything, it had made her harder and tougher than the girl she once was.

She never did completely trust him, not even back then. That was why when she'd come up with a clever plan. She'd figured out a way neither one of them could simply take what they wanted and double-cross the other. It was her way to keep things straight between them.

Now, though, he was balking at turning over the money—including her share. She had to find a way to get him to go along, or find a way around him. Somehow, she would. Years ago, Dennis Pagozzi would do anything she wanted. Given enough time, she would once again have the guy wrapped around her little finger. No matter what it took.

Max Squire was the opposite. He knew too much, and after what she'd done to him, she was sure he'd do anything he could to screw her over. With him, she needed to make sure she controlled the situation.

The more she looked at the restaurant, the more she decided to check it out. What if Max was in there meeting Dennis? What if the blond was just a ruse?

She entered and stood at the door, looking around cautiously, peering at every corner, her right hand inside her large shoulder bag, her fingers wrapped around the handle of her Smith and Wesson—one she'd picked up cheap at a pawn-shop before she ever reached San Francisco. Inside, the restaurant was filled with the smells of Italy, cloth-covered tables with candles and single roses, wooden chairs, bottles of wine, and frilly, white lace curtains adorning the tops and sides of the large window facing the street.

"You wanna table?" the waiter asked from his stand a little past the front door. Behind him were a couple of tables and swinging double doors to the kitchen. Most of the tables were to the right, as was the window.

She didn't see Max, or anyone else she knew. "I'm looking for Dennis Pagozzi. Do you know him?" she asked, stepping back from the disgusting little man.

"Sure. He's da cook's nephew. He just left. I don't t'ink he'll be back—"

"Butch is the cook here?"

"Yeah. You know him? He's—. Hey!"

She slipped past the waiter and headed for the kitchen. He tried to step in front of her, but she ground the heel of her boot on his instep. As he hopped around in agony, she shoved both swinging double doors open and marched in.

She'd know Butch anywhere. Short, with wiry salt-and-pepper hair, a pugnacious grimace and upturned nose, the only difference between the fleabag before her now, and the one she'd met years ago when she first started hanging out with Dennis, was that Butch's hair was no longer black.

Butch glanced up at her and stuck one hand behind his back. He grimaced. "What the hell are you doin' in town?"

"Isn't this interesting," she murmured, looking around the all-stainless steel kitchen with its commercial size ovens, sinks and refrigerator, until her perusal hit the takeout boxes. She flipped open a Styrofoam lid and smirked.

"Hey!" the waiter yelled, and pulled the box away from her, too late.

"What're you doin' lettin' her in here, Earl?" Butch demanded.

Just then, another man bounded up the stairs from the basement at the noise.

"I didn' do not'in', Vinnie!" Earl cried, turning from Butch to the equally elderly fellow who had just joined them. "She ran past me. I tried to stop her!"

Vinnie, wheezing from his dash up the stairs, was short like Earl and Butch, but where Earl was stocky and Butch was wiry, Vinnie sagged all over—cheeks, jowls, chest, stomach, even his feet seemed to splay all over the floor. If a pear could melt, it would end up shaped like Vinnie.

Vinnie eyed the situation. The tension in the kitchen couldn't be missed. "Who's she?" Vinnie asked the other two.

"If you're lookin' for my nephew," Butch growled at Veronica, ignoring Vinnie, "he ain't here. He ain't in town, even. An' he don't wanna see you. You keep away from him!"

She laughed. "Do you really think your Dennis is so clean?"

"What's goin' on?" Vinnie shouted as if trying to get someone to pay attention to him.

Again, Butch ignored him. "His only mistake was gettin' involved with you!"

Veronica smirked. "Funny man." She took a Benson and Hedges out of her purse and grabbed a book of matches. "You always hated me, didn't you? Maybe that's because you were jealous. You wanted me for yourself, didn't you, Butch? But I belonged to Dennis."

Butch's upper lip curled in disgust. "You're sicker than I thought!"

She looked around the kitchen. "You've got a nice place here, Butch. With a couple of your friends, I see. Friends from San Quentin, right?"

Vinnie and Earl's heads swiveled back and forth from Butch to Veronica.

"What you gettin' at?" Butch asked.

"I think you know. Dennis told me all about you, Uncle Butch. You got caught twice, didn't you? First time was just a little thing—auto theft, right? Still, it's a felony. And then the second time. Burglary, wasn't it? Another felony. That makes two strikes, Butch. You get a third, and you know what that means in California. The jailer could throw away the key."

"Butch!" Vinnie yelled so loud his face turned beet red. "What the hell is this about?"

Butch glared at her. "She's an old girlfriend of Dennis's. She just got outta jail."

"An ex-con?" Earl muttered, his eyes wide and confused.

"I'd hate it if Dennis's uncle got into trouble." She smiled coyly at Earl and Vinnie while walking around the tabletop, her fingers lightly tapping the takeout boxes, one by one. "It's too bad all of you left so much evidence lying around. It's my civic duty to tell the police, don't you think?"

"Get out the hell out of my kitchen!" Butch rushed at her. Earl grabbed his arm, pulling him back. "The only thing I want to go to jail for is killin' you! It'll be worth every minute I'm there!"

"Easy, Butch," Vinnie said. "Nobody's gonna believe nothin' from her."

"You stay away from my nephew!" Butch bounded on his toes like in his old prize-fighting day, unsuccessfully trying to yank his arm from Earl's grip. "So help me..."

"It's too late for that, sweetheart." Veronica smirked.

"Damn you!" Butch lunged again, but before he could break free, Vinnie hustled Veronica out of the kitchen and out the front door of the restaurant.

Instead of being angry at him, though, she laughed.

The full moon cast a ribbon of white on the ocean just beyond the wide, gritty sand of Baker's Beach. Paavo and Angie took off their shoes and socks and walked barefoot. It was a rare night in San Francisco: no wind, no fog, only a peaceful stillness. To the north, the Golden Gate Bridge spanned the narrow entrance to the bay, and to the south, high, steep rocks supported the posh neighborhood known as Sea Cliff. Waves from the Pacific lapped at their feet.

Angie was restless. She knew Connie had a date with Dennis that night, and she was wildly curious about how it was working out. She hoped Connie was having a good time. She deserved it. Life hadn't been easy for her.

Between anxiety over her friend and planning for her upcoming wedding, not to mention dreams of matchmaking, Angie was afraid that if she and Paavo had gone out to dinner, she couldn't have resisted staying away from Wings. So, instead, she had suggested they eat at his place and then bundle up and go for a walk on the beach, even though it was late autumn, and the weather was chilly. On the other hand, in San Francisco, beaches were nearly always cold and windy, if not foggy. So it didn't make that much of a difference.

The cold water stung as it hit Angie's toes and she ran, lifting her feet high, to dry ground. Paavo chuckled at her. "Sissy," he said.

"You never told me if Homicide liked the coffee and sandwiches I had catered," she said suddenly, à propos of nothing.

"They thought it was... quite romantic of you."

She liked that answer. "Oh, good! I didn't want to send anything plain or boring."

"Not to worry," he said, then smiled at her.

She beamed at him. She couldn't help herself. Everywhere, all the time, with nearly every breath as she thought about him, ideas would pop into her head, ideas that she absolutely knew would please him and let him know how much she loved him. Also, after the gut-rot motor oil the guys at the Hall of Justice drank, and the greasy doughnuts they ate, gourmet coffee and tea sandwiches had to have been a wonderful change.

"I'm so glad," she said, relieved. "Isn't it great to share a bit of romance with your friends at work?"

Paavo looked a little stricken, which worried her. But then he calmed her fears. "It's different," he said.

He walked through the icy cold waves without flinching, while Angie darted back and forth out of their reach. But then, he might be part Finnish, which would explain the name "Paavo." He didn't know much at all about his parents, having been raised by an older Finnish man. In any case, after Angie learned that Finns enjoyed jumping out of a hot sauna to roll around in the snow, she knew she'd better be prepared for just about anything from Paavo. Her Italian blood couldn't begin to understand doing anything like that. Just looking at Paavo's blue toes made her shiver.

"This has been the happiest time of my life," she said, beaming at him.

He walked to her side on dry land. "For me, too," he admitted as he tucked her close by his side while they continued their walk. "You know, now that we've got this 'being engaged' thing down, and we both like it," Paavo said, "have you ever thought about eloping?"

"Eloping?" She stopped dead, her jaw dropping. She hoped he was joking. "I've dreamed all my life of a big, beautiful wedding. I just sent in subscriptions to *Bridal Guide, Vogue Weddings*, and untold online magazines. I've bought an armful of books, including *Priceless Weddings, Planning a Wedding To Remember,* and *How to Set Your Wedding to Music.* I've already checked out four wedding boutiques and have seven more to go, from Carmel to Tiburon. I even tape every *Married at First Sight* episode so I don't miss any of the wedding scenes."

After a long wait, he quietly said, "I always thought eloping would be romantic."

She couldn't miss the hopefulness in his voice. "It is. But

when I think of the two of us giving our vows, I can already see it in my head..."

"Oh?"

His voice sounded so bleak, she could help but smile. "Just think of it this way, you'll be standing at the altar looking so very handsome, and I'll be wearing the most beautiful gown in the world. At least a dozen bridesmaids will lead the way—"

"A dozen?"

"And my father will escort me to your side—"

"Scowling the whole way. The guy hates me, Angie."

"We'll have a mass as part of the ceremony—"

"Not just quick 'I do's'?"

"With a children's chorus singing traditional hymns, several of them—"

"Angie, are you sure you don't just want to go to Reno? Or, maybe Las Vegas?" Paavo asked with increasing desperation.

His question pulled her out of her reverie. He just didn't get it. She would have worried, except that she'd watched each of her four older sisters go through the same thing with their spouses before the wedding. She threw her arms around his neck and met his gaze with a big smile. "Positive," she replied.

His arms circled her as he gave a resigned sigh. "That's what I was afraid of."

"This is a picture of the woman I'm looking for," Chuck Lexington handed Veronica Maple's mug shot to Luis Calderon. Calderon and his partner Bo Benson were the on-call inspectors at Homicide that week, which was why Calderon was in the Homicide bureau at seven-thirty that morning, finishing up paperwork on a death he'd been called to at three a.m.

Benson was home catching up on sleep, while Calderon decided to go to his desk to get some paperwork done before the next call came in. And one would. In a city the size and with the crime stats of San Francisco, there was a homicide, on average once a week, and a suicide or otherwise mysterious death that Homicide needed to take a look at, two or three times as often.

But Calderon never expected to have a parole officer from the Central Valley show up.

Calderon took the photo, then glanced at the man standing over his desk. "Sit down. Begin at the beginning."

Lexington gave him a brief summary of Maple's background and prison term. She was an embezzler, and had been released after three years for "good behavior."

"How do you know she's in the city?" Calderon asked when Lexington's explanation ended.

"She bought a Greyhound ticket here. I thought I had a lead on her whereabouts, but so far, it hasn't panned out. That's all I can tell you. That, and the fact that she killed a pawnshop owner. She was caught on a video camera across the street going in and out of the shop, and a Smith and Wesson nine-millimeter automatic is missing from the gun case. I want her caught."

"So, she's a lot more than a skip," Calderon said. "She's a murderer, now armed and dangerous."

"You got it. That's why I'm here," Lexington said. "I'm responsible for her leaving the Chowchilla without a word. There was a mix-up with the paperwork, and she was gone from the prison and the area before I knew it. And an innocent man is dead as a result."

"If she's still in this city, we'll find her," Calderon said, steely-voiced. He didn't need any soft, overweight parole officer getting in his way. "You asking for an A.P.B. to go out on her? Where's your local PD? We usually work with them on cases like this."

"They're doing their own thing, apparently happy she's no longer in their jurisdiction. I'm the one who tracked her to San Francisco." He tightened his lips. "They aren't listening much to me. But she was my case—and it's my job on the line now that she's vanished! I'm not about to sit around while the bureaucrats play hot potato with this case."

Calderon grunted, his most common form of communication. None of what the parole officer was saying surprised him. "We'll do what we can."

"When, or if, you find her, I want to know about it."

Lexington leaned closer. "She's already killed once. I don't want to chance her doing it again!"

Calderon slid back in his chair, his mouth firm. "In this department, we know how to handle ourselves."

Angie was in Stella's Bakery in North Beach carefully going over a recipe for a "success cake," basically a meringue cake made using ground almonds instead of flour. She wanted to be sure all four cakes she'd ordered were perfect. And, heart-shaped.

The cake, one of Angie's favorites, literally melted in the mouth, but it required more time and concentration than she wanted to give. For each cake, three heart-shaped layers of meringue, mixed with ground almonds, were baked separately. After baking, the layers were stacked, with caramelized almond butter cream spread over the bottom and middle layers and along the sides, and chocolate-flavored butter cream on top. Slivered almonds were pressed against the sides of the cake and chocolate rosettes or other designs could be added on top for decoration. Angie was convinced the difficulty in making it was why French pâtissiers often wrote "Le Succès" on the cakes.

The baker was growing increasingly unhappy with each of Angie's comments. Meringues turned crisp and brittle after cooling, so the cake was definitely a tour de force to make. Nevertheless, she was convincing him to give it a try, sure the boys in Homicide would be ecstatic over it, when who should walk in but her old friend and sometimes foe, Nona Farraday, restaurant reviewer on the staff of *Haute Cuisine*, a regional magazine for gourmands. Once, Angie would have crawled through ground glass to get a full-time job on that magazine.

On top of that, Nona was everything Angie would have liked to be. Tall, thinner than a breadstick, with high cheekbones, big, round, green eyes, and silky blonde hair, she could wear clothes like a Vogue model. Her lips were a lot poutier than Angie remembered, and she wondered if a little collagen hadn't been added. Basically, she was someone Angie could easily hate, and often did.

"As I live and breathe," Nona cried. She threw her skinny arms around Angie, bending slightly, as they air kissed. "Whatever have you been doing with yourself? I heard your name come up in connection with something, but for the life of me, I can't remember what."

"My name?" Angie asked in surprise.

"Oh, I remember now! There's going to be an opening at *Haute Cuisine*." She smiled demurely. "I guess someone mentioned you. You might want to apply. You might have *some* chance. Perhaps."

"If I were interested, I'd take *Bon Appétit*'s offer."

Nona reached for the countertop to hold herself up, then laughed. "I couldn't have heard right. I thought you said—"

"I did," Angie stated. "But, more importantly—my big news hasn't been announced in the papers yet, and I'm still trying to figure out a date for my engagement party, but look." The last word came out as a squeal as she held out her hand.

Nona's mouth distinctly down-turned before she recovered with a big smile and a squeal that outdid Angie's. "Can it be? You're engaged! How wonderful. Is it the cop?" Nona asked.

"None other."

"He's so sexy, I'll have to grant you that, Angie."

"Isn't he? I'm here ordering some special cakes for Homicide. That way, Paavo's friends can enjoy our happiness."

Nona's teeth clenched as she focused on the cakes behind the glass display. "I've got to get some cake for an open house one of my friends is holding at her art gallery. It would be much more fun, I'm sure, to be buying sweets for my fiancé's friends."

"It is fun."

Nona rested one hand on the counter, the other on her nearly non-existent hip and angled toward Angie. "Maybe you've gone about this the right way," she said. "You've found a regular guy, maybe not real exciting, but *basic,* a guy who believes in things like marriage." Angie's eyes narrowed as Nona gave a toss of her head, making her hair whiplash away from her face. "Here, I've been going out with artists, chefs, restaurateurs, even a couple of film directors—poor ones, which is why they're here instead of Hollywood. What good has it done me?"

Angie stiffened. "Well, I don't know how 'basic' Paavo is—"

"I'm not getting anywhere!" Nona cried. "Those men are so busy trying to figure out themselves, they can't begin to take on the problems a woman might have, especially a strong, business woman like *moi.*" Nona ran a hand through her hair. She was a melodramatic nightmare.

Angie had had it. She turned back to the chef, whose eyes were starting to glaze over. If she wasn't putting out big bucks for the meringue, he'd have bounded back into his kitchen the minute Nona started talking. "It isn't," Angie said to the chef, "as if my fiancé jumped onto the marriage bandwagon first chance he got, believe me, and—"

"You know what I mean, Angie," Nona interrupted. "At least there was *hope* for the two of you." She folded her arms. "All right. I'll admit it. Much as my life, my dates, my sex life, have been wild and successful and exciting, I wish I knew someone like Paavo."

Angie did a double take as she heard past Nona's snarky words to what the woman was actually confessing to her. Angie tossed her recipe at the startled chef and gave him a quick thumbs up. He clutched the recipe to his chest and escaped.

She then faced Nona, her mind quickly racing through the unmarried homicide inspectors she knew—and just as quickly came up with the perfect match. "No problem."

Dennis sat at a table at La Rosa D'Italia, a popular North Beach restaurant. He was early for their lunch meeting, but he was anxious to see Max Squire. He'd left word at the 49er office that if anyone should try to reach him, to give out his cell phone number. Sure enough, Max had called, and they arranged to meet.

The waiter, a young man with green hair, one gold earring and a well-scrubbed demeanor, brought him a Johnny Walker Red and water and put it on the table. "Say, you aren't Dennis Pagozzi, are you?" the man asked hesitantly.

Dennis focused on the earring. "Yeah, I am."

"Wow! I watch the 49ers all the time on TV. Games all sold out, so can't buy a ticket"—he chuckled—"even if I could afford one! Man, seeing you here is great. Want to order? Wine? An appetizer? I'm Scott, by the way."

"Let's give my friend a few minutes to show up," Dennis said. "In fact, here he comes now."

Scott turned and tried not to look shocked as he glanced from Max back to Dennis, as if to be sure he had the right man. "I'll show him to your seat," he said, baffled.

Dennis could understand why. Max's gaunt and grubby appearance stunned him as well. He'd seen better dressed beggars.

He stood. "Good to see you, old buddy," he said, hand outstretched.

"Dennis." Max shook his hand, his lips smiling, but his eyes hard. "Thanks for seeing me. I wouldn't have contacted you if it weren't important."

The waiter hovered near. "Can I get you something to drink, sir?"

Max glanced at Dennis's scotch and began to shake his

head when Dennis said, "My friend will have the same drink as I've got here, but make it a double."

"Thanks," Max murmured as Scott rushed off.

"So how you been?" Dennis asked.

"Not so hot, as you can see," Max said gesturing at himself. "But that's not the reason I wanted to talk to you. You see—"

"Wait. After we order lunch. I didn't eat breakfast today." The waiter brought Max his drink, and Dennis ordered antipasto, soup, pasta, and prime rib for them both. "That okay with you, Max?" Dennis asked.

"Sounds great."

"And don't take too long," Dennis said to the waiter. "We're two hungry guys here." Scott dashed toward the kitchen, about ten feet off the ground.

"So, things haven't come together for you since that trouble a few years back?" Dennis asked.

As the table became loaded with bruschetta, capicola and cheeses, Max turned the conversation back to Dennis and his football career, as if he didn't want to talk about his own troubles. Not when he had a chance at a feast.

It wasn't until they were well into the prime rib that Max said, "Veronica Maple was released from prison three days ago."

Dennis tried to act surprised. "Really? Why do you care?"

Slowly, Max lay down his fork and knife. "Don't play dumb. I know you kept in touch with her."

"But I didn't!" Dennis protested.

"She told people you did. People in the prison."

"Why would I? She meant nothing to me. Think, man! She ripped me off, too."

Max looked, at first, as if he didn't believe him. But then his eyes softened. Dennis hoped Max remembered he had been the only one that helped Max three years ago.

"I'm on your side in this," Dennis said with intensity. "I always have been."

Max ran his fingers through his greasy hair. "She's still got the money. Most of my clients were paid off like you were. The insurance company did right by you, didn't it?"

"Hey, Max. Calm down. All your clients did okay, eventually."

"It's just me. I'm the one she ruined." Max's fists clenched. "I can't wait to get my hands on her!"

Dennis frowned at Max's anger. "You've got to forget about her. This isn't going to do you any good. Leave the city. Keep away from her."

"I won't do it. She's got what I want!"

"Max, let me give you some money." He pulled out a wad from his pocket. "How much do you need? Five hundred? A thousand?"

"It's not what I need now. It's the whole thing. She stole eight million dollars from my clients! Do you know what that did to me? To my reputation?"

"Here." He pushed a wad of bills toward Max. "Forget the eight million. It's water under a bridge now. If you need more, you let me know. You were the greatest, Max. You helped me invest my money and make nearly twenty percent return on it. You stopped me from doing a lot of stupid stuff I wanted to do. If it weren't for you, I'd have nothing."

Max stared at the money. "Tell me this. Did she contact you?"

Dennis waited a long time before he whispered, "No."

Max's eyes bored into him, colder than Dennis had ever seen them. "Tell me how to reach her."

Dennis slowly shook his head. "I don't know."

"Damn it, Dennis! If you're lying!"

Dennis noticed that the other customers looked up,

concerned. "Forget her! She'll only cause you to do something that'll get you into more trouble."

"Like what? Kill her? Believe me, I'd love to. Once I get my money back."

"Max, listen to me." Dennis picked up his money and held it toward Max. "Take this money and leave town. Do it."

Max stood and knocked the money away, sending the bills flying across the restaurant. "I don't want a goddamned hand-out! I want what's mine!"

Dennis stood as Max stormed from the restaurant.

"I'm so sorry," Scott said crawling around the floor picking up hundred-dollar bills. "Was he threatening you?"

"No. Not at all. He's just very upset." Dennis quickly counted out enough cash to pay for lunch and a substantial tip. "When the pre-season games start, call the Niner office. There'll be a couple of tickets waiting for you." Then he ran from the restaurant.

The waiter's mouth dropped open. "Oh, wow. Oh, man!"

11

C onnie's part-time helper was scheduled to work at Everyone's Fancy that afternoon, so Connie took the opportunity to go to Angie's apartment. She wanted to tell her about her date with Dennis.

Angie had never been so right about a guy. All morning Connie had been unable to keep still, leaping around the shop as if it were a step aerobics class, thinking about him. He was so cool.

Angie wasn't home. Didn't that just figure? The once she had something exciting to tell her best friend about, said friend skipped out on her. What nerve!

Connie got in the car to go back home. The weather was clear, crisp and warm, and going back to her solitary apartment wasn't her idea of a good time. She drove, enjoying the day, and soon found herself in North Beach, driving down the street where she'd found Max Squire passed out.

Whenever she thought about Max, she felt like a dork over the way he'd snookered her. Nothing like that had happened to her since high school, and then it had been over sex, not money.

Of course, her ex-husband had been the champion at really screwing her. Compared to him, Max was a piker.

Even in her family, it had been her beautiful younger sister, Tiffany, who got all the attention and the love from their parents. Tiffany had been no more than a secretary, but a secretary in San Francisco's City Hall where she hobnobbed with local politicians. That made all the difference.

It also, unfortunately, had led to Tiffany's death.

Still, Tiffany's job had been far classier than Connie's who, back then, had worked as a Bank of America teller and later as an insurance agent for All Farm. While Tiffany could talk to their folks about political intrigue, Connie could only talk about the need for liability insurance. Who was she kidding? She was dull, even to herself.

Connie's ex, Keith Trammel, had only added to her misery. Like her, he only had a high school education, but he belonged to a construction workers' union, made good money, and was handsome as sin. Even Tiffany could scarcely keep her eyes off him.

Connie knew he'd had problems with drugs before they'd met, but he told her he'd been clean for over six months. They dated another four months, then went to Reno and got married.

Soon after, winter came, and construction slowed. Keith spent more and more time at home, while Connie went off to work. Money was tight. Two couldn't live as cheaply as one, especially when Connie's job was low paying, and when he worked, Keith's was comparatively high. He was used to buying what he wanted, without a wife or anyone else to answer to.

Connie wasn't one to sit by with her mouth shut while he blew their money. The resulting fights were scary. Connie shuddered to remember how close to violence they had been. That should have been a sign of both their immaturity and inability to cope with crises. And more importantly, their incompatibility.

Before winter ended, Keith was back on drugs. He stopped in spring when work started up again, but then he pulled a back muscle and had to lie around the house while it mended. Drugs helped ease the pain, he'd said. Connie had lived in dread of going home each day after work, wondering if she'd find the loving man she'd married or his evil twin.

Ironically, she had wanted to stay married to him through this time. She remembered the man who had charmed her, and she wanted him back. She tried to do whatever she could think of to get him back, including going to meetings for families of drug addicts.

For two years she tried, but the stress, financial strain, and unhappiness became too much. She contacted a divorce lawyer.

Keith couldn't believe she would abandon him that way. He needed her, while she wanted a husband she could depend on. Luxuries meant nothing to her, and she would have been perfectly happy with a couple of kids and a comfortable home. The kind of warm family life she'd never really known. Was that too much to ask?

Was she bitter? Could she have gladly sent him through Angie's commercial strength meat grinder? Never doubt it for a minute.

When All Farm Insurance downsized, she took her severance pay and used it to set up Everyone's Fancy. By that time, her parents had passed away, and soon, her sister would be gone as well. Her little shop became everything to her—her haven from the world.

The whole mess had bummed her out until she met Angie and life began to pick up again. She had been living like a loser because she'd let herself feel like one. Around Angie, she was different. Angie even looked at her with respect—Connie ran a business, while Angie couldn't find the right job or business, no matter how hard she tried.

Respect didn't mean that Angie wasn't always after her to do something to add a little zing to the shop. Maybe she should think about ways to spruce it up, make it more inviting for return visits, and attract more drop-in traffic. Maybe Angie would be willing to help.

Some day, Connie might ask her.

Thoughts of past travails flew out of her mind as, with a jolt, the current one appeared before her eyes.

Max walked along the sidewalk, and running towards him was Dennis Pagozzi! The two were supposedly friends, so it shouldn't have been a shock to see them together, but it was.

Dennis caught up and put a hand on Max's shoulder. The way Max spun toward him, Connie thought they were about to fight. But after a few words, the two seemed to relax and continue to talk.

It was all Connie could do not to drive up onto the sidewalk and confront Max herself! Seeing Dennis with Max made her wonder about Dennis as well. If he got in the way of her fender, she couldn't say she'd be too broken up.

But instead of confronting either of them, she stepped on the gas, driving as fast as she could to the corner where she turned. Almost immediately, she realized she should have watched to see what the two men were up to. At a minimum, she ought to follow Max to demand her money back. Unfortunately, by the time she made her way around the traffic-congested block to where she'd spotted them, they were gone.

At the same time, Angie was entering the offices of KYME radio, otherwise known as "Why Me?" radio, and approached the large reception area with a high, circular desk. Beyond reception were the executive offices and radio recording studio where Angie had once worked on a call-in talk show, "Lunch with Henri," with chef Henri LaTour.

She was there now to pick up a list of top floral arrangers in the area. Last week, one of the station's talk show hosts discussed big events planning—weddings, bar mitzvahs, baby showers, graduations, and engagement parties. Angie telephoned and spoke with her on the air, and the host offered a list of decorators who specialized in live floral arrangements, but it hadn't arrived. Most likely, it was stuck in clerical hell, the place requests wait for clerks to find the time to fill them.

There were some things a girl shouldn't have to wait for, and choosing the right help for her engagement party was one of them.

She explained why she'd come to the receptionist, who went off to search for Adrianne Marceau's list. As she waited at the desk, one of the station managers, a young curly-haired fellow with horn-rimmed glasses and a bowtie, walked in.

"Angie!" he cried. "Joel Witcomb. Remember me?"

"How can I forget?" she asked. Back when she worked there, most of the time she wasn't allowed to say a word on the show, but had to listen to Chef Henri mangle recipes. "I'm here to pick up floral recommendations because I'm—"

"You were such an angel to help us in the past here," Joel said, cutting her off. "I can't believe we let you go!"

"Well, we all make mistakes." She laughed, and he actually joined her. "Not that such things matter in the least anymore because I'm—"

"I'd like to remedy that," he said with a toothy smile. "Pierre Takizawa, our current chef, will be leaving on Friday. His ratings just aren't what we'd hoped. We're going to be playing Country-Western music in that time slot until we get a replacement, which I pray will be soon, or we'll have no listeners left at all."

The other name for KYME popped into her head in neon colors: *cwime*. As in that station's broadcasts were a *cwime* to anyone with eardrums.

"As I said, I'm here for the floral arrangers because—"

"I think *you* could do it," Joel enthused. "Let's put the Angie Amalfi Hour on the radio! You could talk about Bay Area restaurants, and also perhaps present a favorite recipe each day. What do you think?"

"As I started to say—"

"At other times, you can talk about how to prepare something exotic. And we could round out the hour with people calling in asking you questions. How does that sound?"

Just then, the receptionist returned with Angie's list. "Thank you." She gave the helpful woman a smile then turned to Joel. "Goodbye."

"What's wrong?" He chased after her, flabbergasted as she reached the elevator. "Aren't you interested? Are you working on another radio show—"

"Goodness, no."

"TV?"

"Heavens!"

"Newspaper? Magazine?"

"No. Nothing like that."

"What then?"

"I guess I've simply got other things on my mind at the moment." The elevator doors opened and as she got on, she waggled her left hand in the air. "I'm engaged."

"It's too bad she won't elope," Yosh said to Paavo, then took a big bite from a slice of linguica and artichoke heart frittata.

"I'm glad she won't!" Benson said, taking another slice. Dapper, African-American, and streetwise, he dressed like Will

Smith, and went through women like a rock star. "This is even better than yesterday's mixed hors d'oeuvres platter. They tasted good, but a couple of bites and they were gone."

"Just hope she forgets about sending any more pâté," Calderon groused.

"Especially for breakfast," Bill Never-Take-A-Chance Sutter said between mouthfuls. In his late fifties, he kept threatening to retire from the force, get his pension, and then he'd probably find an easier, safer, and possibly higher paying job. Nothing like having someone around with his attitude to build up morale. "But now, if Paavo's engagement will be a long one, I might postpone my retirement."

"I thought you already had," Rebecca Mayfield said sullenly to her nearly worthless, mind-on-fishing-holes-and-future-bridge-games partner. She cut herself a little more frittata—luckily Angie had sent two of them—as if to drown her sorrows in food. "So, why not elope, Paavo?"

"She won't go for it. Plus, her mother's probably planning to rent out City Hall to fit all the people she wants to invite to the reception. Maybe Golden Gate Park. What else is big enough in this city?"

"The Cow Palace," Calderon called over. Not that he and everyone else in Homicide were eavesdropping. Not that they'd admit to it.

"That's scary," Yosh continued. "Can't you talk her out of doing something so huge?"

"Have you ever met Angie's mother?" Paavo asked.

"No."

"That's why you asked that question."

Yosh chuckled. "I now know who Angie takes after."

Paavo visibly shuddered. "Don't remind me."

"Here's something to take your mind off your wedding," Calderon said, handing them a mug shot. "The name's Veronica Maple. She was released from Chowchilla Wednesday and apparently killed a pawnshop owner, stole a Smith and Wesson, and took off for the city. She has ties with a small-time gang lord named Sid Fernandez, called El Toro. He used to make his money on drugs, but bigger fish are moving in. He's having some trouble keeping his territory, I hear. Vice doesn't know where he might pop up next. Anyway, her parole officer, a guy named Chuck Lexington, was here trying to get help to find her."

"Why a PO?" Paavo asked.

"Sounds like he screwed up the case and his job is on the line. He wants to bring her in himself. I told him we don't go for cowboys here. Not our own, and for sure not outsiders from the valley. I don't know why, but something about the woman, the whole case, smells like trouble."

Paavo nodded.

"Thanks for the info," Yosh said, studying the photo.

Just then a florist walked into Homicide wheeling a cart with filled with flowers—a huge bouquet of red roses, and ten smaller ones with amaryllis, daffodils and lilies. Out of Lt. Hollins' office came a loud *aaah-choo.*

"I had to see for myself if you were here, or if you were lyin' as usual," Butch said when Veronica opened the door to Dennis's home.

"Now, you see. I'm living with him. For now." She was dressed in a high-necked, long-sleeved black jumpsuit. "What do you want?"

He pushed past her and looked around for Dennis. "I want to see Dennis. Where is he?" Butch said. He walked to the bar and poured himself a stiff straight shot of Chivas Regal.

"You make yourself at home, don't you?" She gave the front door a shove and listened to the latch click.

"You have." Butch took a sip, and let the smooth warmth drift down to his stomach. "Why're you here? What the hell do you want from him?"

She stared at him, her gray eyes flat and soulless. "It's none of your business."

"I don't trust you, Veronica," Butch said. "And if Dennis does, he's a fool. Is he home?"

She smiled at him, a smile that never reached her eyes. "He's out buying some steaks for our dinner. Filet mignon. Just like an old married couple, wouldn't you say?"

Butch's body tensed. "Damn you, Veronica. You almost ruined his life once. Wasn't that enough?"

"Get out of here, old man."

He poured the rest of the Scotch down his throat and slammed the glass on the bar. "I'm going, and so will you."

"Don't count on it," she taunted.

He left the house before he did anything he'd regret, but when he reached the sidewalk, he turned and looked back at it. He frowned, scratching his head. He had to admit he hadn't used his brain much lately, maybe that was because he knew it didn't work so good anymore.

Nevertheless, as he pictured Veronica with his nephew, his sister's pride and joy, he knew what he had to do.

The question was, did he dare do it?

"So, tell me about your date with Dennis!" Angie and Connie finally caught up with each other and now were at the Cliff House, a restaurant overlooking the ocean. They were there for dinner.

Before Connie could answer, the waiter came by to take their orders. Connie chose the golden red snapper in a coconut lime sauce, and Angie, the fricassee of chicken with tomatoes, raisins and olives.

"Say, aren't you Angelina Amalfi?" the waiter asked.

"Why, yes, I am." Angie tried to remember if she'd met the young man before.

"I saw you on YouTube some time back, doing a review of a new French restaurant where a friend of mine is working. You spoke well of it. I'll have to get the owner. He'd love to meet you."

"Sure," she said, watching him dash off. She turned back to Connie. "Isn't that amazing? I thought no one watched my reviews, yet this fellow actually recognized me. But, I interrupted you. You were saying about Dennis..."

"I met him at Wings of an Angel, and—"

"Here she is!" The waiter beamed as he ushered in a distinguished gentleman with a fringe of gray hair, a large jaw, and a picket fence of false teeth. "Miss Amalfi, I'd like you to meet the owner, Donald Kaufman."

"Miss Amalfi! What a pleasure to have you here," Kaufman blurted, his teeth clattered as he spoke—loose dentures, Angie guessed.

"Thank you." She introduced Connie. "Your menu is a wonderful combination of Southwest plus San Francisco seafood."

"Do you think so? That's grand! Just learning you were here has given me an idea, if I might be so presumptuous." He pulled out a chair and sat. "I was wondering if you might be willing to work with me on this menu."

Angie stared. *What's with him?* "Work on it how?" she asked.

The waiter came by with a complimentary bottle of Charles Krug Cabernet Sauvignon Blanc as the owner explained that he'd like to hire her as a consultant.

Connie caught her eye and nodded enthusiastically. *What's she nodding about?* Angie wondered. "I'm sure you don't need a consultant," she said firmly. "Your restaurant is doing just fine. Now, my friend and I are here for some *girl* talk. We wouldn't want to bore you..." *Hint, hint!*

Kaufman's face fell. "Think about it, please. Give me a call when you're ready to talk." He handed her his card and left.

"Angie," Connie marveled. "What's wrong with you? He was offering the chance of a lifetime. The kind of job you've always wanted."

"No, no, no!" Angie rolled her eyes. "I want to hear about *amore*. That's what life is really about!"

"Well, if you're sure..." Connie glanced back at the hopeful owner, letting her gaze wander through the fine restaurant with the gorgeous Pacific view.

An appetizer of seviche—raw halibut marinated until "poached" in lime juice, chili, onion, tomato, oregano and olive oil—was placed on the table. "Compliments of Mr. Kaufman," the waiter said.

"Thank you," Angie said dismissively. Then, to Connie. "Tell me, did you like him?"

"Kaufman?" Connie's eyes widened.

"No! Dennis!"

"Of course. What's not to like?"

"Will you see him again soon?"

"I don't know. He didn't ask me. I went home right after dinner ended. And he didn't phone today. But it's still early, sort of. And I'm sure he's very busy."

Angie's face fell.

"So, what did you think?" Kaufman materialized at the table. "Too much lime juice, perhaps? Seviche is temperamental."

Not nearly as temperamental as I'm going to be, Angie thought. She wanted to get back to Dennis not calling Connie, but before she could say a word, a bevy of waiters paraded from the kitchen, each carrying a plate with a small portion of an entrée.

"I've died and gone to heaven!" Connie cried. Kaufman hovered over them, grilling Angie with questions while Connie oohed and aahed with each dish. One of the waiters took over as a sommelier, pouring wine to help Angie cleanse her pallet from one dish to the next, while another stood off to the side and wrote down almost every word she said.

Finally, she could stand no more. She grabbed Kaufman's arm, dragged him to a far wall and poked him in the chest. "Listen, I'm here to talk about love! I want to have a conversation with my girlfriend, but she's too busy stuffing her face to talk! Will you, please, leave us alone?"

He twisted his tie. "But you know food, Miss Amalfi! Just to watch your expression as you take each bite is a full course in gastronomy. You're a dream come true to me."

"I can become a nightmare very easily."

"All right, all right. Be that way." He stiffened his upper lip. "Go, now. I won't bother you."

"Thank you!"

She marched back into the dining room, to find Connie in full swoon over a strawberry Charlotte.

12

The next afternoon, Paavo and Yosh walked out of the Northern police station where they had gone to talk to a couple of uniformed cops about the stash of baseballs and autographed sports paraphernalia they'd found in the abandoned garage. The items were all counterfeit. No lead yet was available on who put them there.

As they hit the sidewalk, Yosh stopped, bent forward and slowly peered first to the left and then to the right.

"What is it?" Paavo asked.

He held his finger against his lips a moment, then lowered it and whispered. "Just making sure there aren't any bakers, florists, or Italian tenors waiting to waylay us."

Paavo growled.

Yosh chuckled as they walked toward the car. "The good news is that Angie's so busy buying and making you stuff, she isn't snooping into your cases."

The two froze.

A man was getting out of a van with a huge stuffed bear.

In stark horror, San Francisco's finest fled to their car and sped off.

Veronica walked two blocks from Dennis's house to the street corner where Sid Fernandez's limo had been double-parked and waiting. Fernandez, aka El Toro, knew where Dennis lived. He was the one who'd given her the address, but she wanted to make sure he and Dennis didn't see each other unless it became absolutely necessary. She could control them better if they remained separated.

She got into the limo and took a seat beside Fernandez. His main man, Julius, had a seat facing them.

"We'll work together like in the old days." Sid Fernandez said as he placed his hand on Veronica's thigh and lightly stroked it.

"I think it'll be great fun," she murmured, and with a toss of her head, looked over at Julius. "I love your plan." She flashed a smile meant for him alone.

"You make our little 'strategy' perfect, Vero," Julius said, using his pet name for her. *Vero*—a play on 'verdad,' the Spanish word for true. It made her want to puke, but that was all right. He was lots less revolting than the so-called El Toro, The Bull, who didn't even have the good fortune to be built like a bull where it mattered most.

"What's this Vero stuff?" Fernandez asked, squeezing Veronica's thigh hard. "We call her Ronnie, don't we?"

"Veronica is the name," she said forcefully.

He squeezed harder. "I thought you liked being called Ronnie?"

She faked a smile. "You can call me anything you like, Toro. You know that."

"*Bueno, puta.*" Calling her the Spanish word for "whore" caused him to laugh hard. Julius joined him, as did Veronica. Fernandez was everything she despised in a man, but she needed him, and he didn't like his jokes dissed. He'd been the only one to help her when she was in prison, and he counted on her loyalty as a result. And had it. Up to a point.

"Now, it's time to get serious," Fernandez said. "In three days, Julius will have your identification. Everything is set. It should be perfect."

"It will be, boss," Julius promised.

"That's it, then. It's up to you, Veronica, to get us in. Then the diamonds, all of them, will be ours."

"As long as I get my share," she said, "I can do it."

"You think I'd try to gyp my little *puta*?" Fernandez asked.

God, but she hated the fat bastard. "Only if you want to see your *puta* gut you," she replied.

He roared with laughter. "*Dios,* I love this woman!" He rose his bulk up, all but pounced on her, and nearly smothered her with a wet French kiss. She could feel Julius's eyes boring into them, into El Toro's broad back as he leaned over her. She reached a hand out toward Julius, and felt his fingers wrap around hers, their grasp hidden from El Toro's view.

Fernandez lifted his head a moment to look down at Veronica. Plus, he needed to catch his breath—she was driving him wild, and he could feel his heart pounding hard in his chest. It was time to order Julius out of the car. Things were moving fast and Fernandez didn't like an audience watching 'certain' activities. He knew he'd missed Veronica too damn much to be healthy, but she was the one soft spot remaining in his heart. Something about her had burrowed deep inside him years ago, when they were little more than kids, first starting out.

Also, Julius had made it clear he didn't approve of the way Fernandez felt about Veronica, as if Fernandez cared what Julius liked. His hand cupped her breast, feeling her softness, how perfectly she was shaped. His entire body trembled with desire. For years he had searched for a woman who thought like he did, and now that she was once again out of prison, she'd be with him, work with him. He lowered his head to kiss her again...

The glass-covered bar area in the limo was polished until it shone like a mirror and his gaze was distracted by a movement in it. He didn't quite understand, for a moment, what he was looking at, everything slightly distorted in the glass. But slowly, it made sense.

Julius was leaning forward, his outstretched hand clasped Veronica's and his thumb slowly, gently, rubbed against her fingers, as if they were lovers....

Paavo could smell pizza as he and Yosh walked down the hall on the fourth floor of the Hall of Justice. Normally, that would have made him feel good. A shared treat usually meant the successful conclusion of some particularly sticky or horrible case. He had his doubts, though, that homicide was the cause of the celebration that day.

As he neared, he felt a knot in his stomach grow. Then he saw that pizza tray was heart-shaped.

Not again.

Even as he thought that, he knew he was wrong.

Again.

No pizza remained on the tray, however.

"What's going on?" Yosh asked.

"Hey, Paav," Benson called. "That was great. Pepperoni, Italian sausage, three cheeses, loaded with mushroom and olives. Outstanding. The shape was a little weird, but no matter. We're getting used to heart-shaped food. In fact, heart-shaped steaks would be nice."

"Too bad pizza gives me heart-burn," Calderon grumped.

"Heart-shaped barbecued ribs!" Sutter added, ignoring Calderon's remark.

"Heart-shaped ravioli, with a rich beef sauce." Rebecca was practically salivating.

"Heart-shaped biscuits and gravy"—Sutter drooled—"with a slice of heart-shaped sweet potato pie on the side."

"Knock it off," Paavo said. "This isn't funny."

Yosh said nothing. He was too busy staring longingly at the empty pizza tray. A glob of cheese and a piece of pepperoni had been left on it, and he scooped it up and ate it. The way he licked his fingers attested to Benson's raving about the pizza.

"It's all gone already?" Angie's voice bubbled over with good cheer as she walked into Homicide, her sometime friend, Nona Farraday, behind her. "Did you like it?" she asked Paavo as she gave him a quick peck. The Hall of Justice was not a place for displays of affection. Even Angie was quelled by the somber surroundings.

"Paavo, dearest!" Nona squealed, not intimidated by the serious surroundings at all. "Congratulations!" She threw her arms around him in a bear hug that, if it had gone on much longer, would have resulted in Angie grasping a fistful of blond hair.

Paavo backed up and thanked her, while Bo Benson, Homicide's resident Romeo, moved in. "Hey, there." Benson acknowledged Nona, and without removing his eyes from her, said, "Angie, are you going to introduce me to your friend?"

"Sure. Nona, meet Inspector Bo Benson."

Benson was coolly extending his hand to grasp Nona's with some snappy comment, when Angie hooked her arm in Nona's, spun her away, and marched her up to Luis Calderon's desk. Paavo's eyebrows rose in wonder.

Calderon slowly lifted his head from his reports, his eyes narrow, and focused hard on the two women before him. "Yes?"

"Inspector Calderon," Angie said, "I'd like you to meet my dear friend, Nona Farraday."

Nona held out her hand. Calderon lifted himself to his feet, his knee cracking, and with a look of utter weariness shook hers.

Benson smoothed his jacket and took a step toward them, but Paavo put out his arm to stop him. Their gazes met, and Paavo shook his head. Benson's eyes widened, then his mouth spread into a grin, as the situation hit him.

"Who died?" Calderon asked gruffly.

"Died?" Angie asked. "You misunderstand. My friend is just here for a visit. She knew you were all having pizza for lunch, so she brought along a little dessert."

She glanced at Nona, who was gaping at Calderon as if her brainpower had bounded away like a slinky toy. Angie elbowed her. "The dessert," she whispered.

"Oh! Of course! Here you are." Nona lifted a cookie tin out of a shopping bag and put it on his desk, right on top of his papers. His scowl deepened. Then she opened the tin.

The smell of alcohol filled the room. Rum, to be precise.

"Holy Moses!" Bill Sutter cried, walking over to Calderon's desk. "Is it happy hour already?"

"What did you do?" Angie asked, puzzling over the soggy chocolate chip cookies in the tin. "The recipe called for only a tablespoon of rum."

Nona gave a come-hither look to Calderon. "I wanted them to be *adult* chocolate chip cookies, so I tripled it." She lifted one out with her fingertips and offered it to Calderon. "It's my recipe—Nona's Pecan Rum Chocolate Chip Cookies. Try it. You won't be disappointed."

Calderon noticed the other inspectors silently watching his every move. "Forget it. I don't eat pizza, and I don't eat sweets."

"You don't?" Nona dropped the cookie in the trash and

stepped a little closer. "I don't either. It helps me keep my weight down." She held her arms out to the sides.

Calderon coughed lightly. "I see." He picked the cookie tin off his desk and handed it back to her. Without even looking at what they were, he grabbed a handful of papers and his suit jacket. "Got to go investigate a murder."

As Angie and Nona stared, he hurried out of the bureau.

"I'm sorry," Angie said.

"Don't be." Rubber-kneed, Nona sat on the edge of Calderon's desk and sighed longingly at the door he'd just exited. "He's so... *masterful.*"

13

"Come join us, Connie," Angie cried as Connie entered Wings of an Angel to have dinner with her. Paavo had gotten called on a case that evening, so she invited Connie to join her.

"What a surprise to find you both here," Connie said, eying Angie and Dennis sitting together.

Angie smiled innocently. "Butch made some lasagna, Dennis's favorite. He called Dennis, who was all alone when I arrived, so I invited him to join us."

"I'm glad to see you again, Connie." One of Dennis's cheeks dimpled when he smiled.

Shades of Tom Selleck, Angie thought. He used to be her ideal man when she was a little girl and watched him on TV with her mother. She wondered whatever became of him. Old age, she guessed. None of us was getting any younger, and since she was soon to become a wife, she was feeling more mature and sophisticated by the minute. Although it was too bad Paavo didn't have dimples.

"Dennis has an idea to expand the restaurant," Angie said

as enthusiastically as she could. Frankly, she hated the idea. Still, as she looked at Connie and Dennis, she hoped love would blossom between them, and had decided this dinner would be the way to give them a little nudge.

"So I've heard," Connie said.

"Say, Angie," Dennis turned to her, "wouldn't you say Connie is the perfect person to run some ideas past? I've heard she's got a good head on her shoulders. Practical. Sensible. I like that in a woman."

"You do?" Angie asked, delighted. "I'm so glad! Those are wonderful qualities, and Connie is one of the most practical, steady people I know. That's her—Constant Connie, in the flesh."

Her smile slipped a notch as Connie's foot met her shin under the table.

"Constant?" Dennis asked, confused.

"Dennis is also constant," Angie said to Connie. "He's loyal. Generous. Handsome." She was running out of adjectives.

"Well, he's more constant than some friends," Connie sniped.

Dennis looked lost, as if he couldn't hear his quarterback's audibles. "About the restaurant," he said, "I'm hoping to make this place hit the big time. Give some competition to The Porcupine."

Angie frowned. What was Dennis thinking? She didn't want to call him on it in front of Connie, but the Porcupine was supposed to have outstanding, expensive food, despite its casual ambiance—sort of like jeans that cost hundreds of dollars. Angie just realized, for all she'd heard about the place, she'd never eaten there yet. She faced Connie. "Isn't it great how Dennis is full of ideas for business?" she mused brightly.

Just then, Butch bounded out of the kitchen holding a bottle of wine and candles. Earl followed with a violin.

Angie smiled and clapped to welcome them.

Connie glowered at her.

Dennis cleared the table of the menus so Butch could put the candlesticks down and open the burgundy. Last week's vintage. At least it didn't have a screw top.

Earl tucked the violin under his chin and began sawing away at something that vaguely resembled "You Are the Wind Beneath My Wings." Unfortunately, it sounded like a different kind of wind.

Other customers stopped eating, dumbfounded.

"If I'm part owner of a sports bar," Dennis shouted over the cacophony. "I could probably get some of the guys on the team to drop in."

"They'd love this, all right!" Connie yelled back, sarcasm dripping from every shouted syllable.

"Absolutely!" Dennis's voice strained.

Angie made expressions at Connie to smile and be nice. It didn't work.

Butch poured the wine.

Connie snatched a breadstick and broke it in half. Instead of eating it, she reached for another and broke it as well. Angie didn't like the way Connie was eying her as she did so.

Butch had to strike a half dozen matches to light the candles.

Earl switched to "Feelings," a nails-on-the-chalkboard rendition that must have had the entire neighborhood of dogs, cats, and mice running for their lives.

As Dennis announced "salute" and hoisted his wine glass toward the middle of the table to clink with others, Connie, who was scowling at Earl, reached for another breadstick. Their hands bumped. The jostling caused the wine in Dennis' glass to slosh high into the air and land with a splat on Angie's dress. As Dennis looked on with horror, jerking the wine glass back, his arm smacked against a just-lit candle that fell over kamikaze-style onto a paper napkin.

The napkin caught on fire.

As Angie's matchmaking plans went up in smoke, she doused the napkin flambé with water from her glass, while Butch smothered the tablecloth before it, too, caught fire.

The violin's tune changed as Earl began to saw away at Johnny Cash's "Ring of Fire."

They were all standing now. Angie was dabbing water on the wine staining her dress, Connie and Dennis were both apologizing, and Butch was trying to get the violin away from Earl, when into the restaurant walked a man Angie hadn't seen before. He stopped at the door and stared hard at the group around her.

Connie gawked at him, then sat once more, trying hard to appear nonchalant. The stranger gazed at her for what seemed like an eternity. What, Angie wondered, was going on?

As the stranger approached the table, his attention turned away from Connie. "Hello, Dennis."

Dennis's expression turned serious. "Hey, Max. Good you could make it."

They shook hands and Dennis introduced him. "Ladies, this is an old friend, Max Squire. Max, this is Angie Amalfi, and this... oh, wait a minute, you two already met, didn't you?"

"Is that so?" Angie's eyeballs had quite a workout as they bounced from Connie to this Max Squire.

Max shook Angie's hand first, then turned to Connie. "Miss Rogers and I met briefly the other night."

Connie slowly lifted her hand to his.

Angie gaped. Max Squire's clothes were crumpled and worn—jeans and a once-navy blue pullover that had been washed a few times too many. His shoes were scuffed on top. She hated to think of what the soles must look like. At the same time, she watched his gaze hold Connie's a long time. Connie's face began to redden until, finally, she pulled her hand free.

"Have a seat," Dennis said, seemingly oblivious to the interaction between his friend and Connie.

"Thanks, but," Max continued standing, "I didn't mean to interrupt anything. I can come back when you're free, Dennis."

"No, no," Dennis said. He grabbed a chair from a nearby table and slid it between his chair and Connie's. "Sit. I asked you here for a reason. We're discussing expanding the place, and that's where you come in."

"I do?" Max asked as he took the seat. Angie sat back and watched. Max seemed to look everywhere but at Connie, while Connie was clearly trying to concentrate on Dennis without a lot of success.

"Exactly," Dennis said. "When the restaurant expands, we'll need more help."

Max folded his hands on the table and looked around. "It's a nice place as is."

"We'll have some work for you here. We'd hate it if someone as reliable as you went off and found work someplace else. We could use you, especially when the business starts to take off." Dennis was all sincerity and trust. Angie guessed he was offering Max a job as... what?

"Not me." Max shook his head.

Beggars can't be choosers, Angie thought.

"Definitely you, pal. Let me go get Butch." Dennis jumped up and headed for the kitchen.

Angie immediately faced Max. "So, you and Connie met when she was waiting for Dennis the other night?"

He gazed at Connie and didn't answer until she dropped her eyes to her lap. "That's right."

"You didn't tell me," Angie said to her friend.

Connie forced a laugh. "I don't tell you about everyone I

meet in a day." She tried not to look back at Max, but failed miserably.

"Have you been in the city long, Max?" Angie asked.

"Not very," he said.

"Just passing through?"

"Not sure yet," he replied.

"I see. But you're here looking for work?" she prodded.

"Not really."

She sat back, arms folded in exasperation at how tight-lipped he was. Connie stifled a smile.

Just then, Dennis reappeared, a big hand on Butch's elbow as he guided his little uncle into the dining area. Butch's bibbed apron hung below his knees, and the sleeves of his blue shirt had been rolled up to reveal forearms with an anchor and the logo of the US Navy tattooed on one, flowers and ~~MOM~~ on the other. The MOM was a little jagged, as if it might have been adapted from some other name sometime in Butch's history. Angie had heard that back in the days when he was a prizefighter in the bantamweight division, before he lost many fights and began to grow jangle-headed, Butch used to have a lot of women after him. At least one probably caught him a few times. The MOM might have been the last in a whole string of names.

"Uncle Butch, you remember my old friend, Max Squire, don't you?" Dennis said.

Butch frowned. "Yeah, Squire." He stuck out his hand. "How's it goin'?"

Max stood, and they shook hands. "Not bad."

"Max needs a job," Dennis said. "He might not admit it, but he does."

Butch's gaze went from a grimacing Max to his nephew. "Yeah? I don't know nobody hirin' right now. Times is tough."

Vinnie and Earl came puffing up behind the others.

"What's goin' on?" Vinnie asked.

"Dennis's friend needs work," Butch said.

Vinnie rose up on, almost on tiptoe, and stood before Dennis's chair. "We don't need no more help."

"You guys are going to need someone to work here with you when the business takes off. Earl is slow now; he'll be completely over his head in the future."

"What d'ya mean, slow?" Earl put his hands in fists and approached Dennis.

"The restaurant needs improvement." Dennis glanced at Angie for confirmation. When she didn't move an eyelash, he turned back to Vinnie. "Me, Max and Angie are the ones to do it. Oh, and Bonnie, I mean, uh, Connie, too."

"Leave me out of this!" Angie muttered.

"Are you bailing on me?" Dennis was shocked.

"We don't want no more help," Vinnie said, his jaw stuck out. "We don't need it. Business is great as is." Just then two customers came in and Earl left to take care of them. They were there to pick up a takeout order. "See, what'd I tell ya?"

"It can't be great," Dennis countered. "The place is too small. I'm surprised you three have held on this long. Don't you understand—"

"I understand you're gonna get a flat nose if you don't stop badgerin' me." Vinnie waved a fist. "We like things the way they are. *Capisce?*"

"Forget it, Dennis," Max said. "I don't want the job anyway."

"Sure you do!" Dennis insisted, whirling toward Max now.

"I don't like it either," Butch said. "Too many from the past showin' up, first her, now him. What's going on, Dennis?"

Max paled, staring hard at Dennis, then, with a quick glance at Connie, he rose to his feet and stormed out the door.

Connie also stood now. "Max!" she called.

Dennis rushed out after him.

"What in the world is going on?" Angie also jumped to her

feet and gripped Connie's wrist, stopping her from going after them. "Do you understand any of it?"

"Not at all." They sat back down, but Connie's eyes never left the window as she watched Dennis and Max outside.

Soon, they parted, Max heading south, and Dennis north.

"Excuse me." Connie stood. "I'm not feeling well. I'd better go home right now."

"But—" was as much as Angie could utter before Connie also hurried from the restaurant.

<hr>

Connie spotted Max about a block ahead of her, walking south on Columbus Avenue. Staying within the shadows of the buildings, she followed him. He turned onto Mason, a street lined with three-story flats and a couple of small apartment buildings. As he walked up three steep blocks, she followed, gasping for breath by the time she reached the third. At a corner, he turned onto Vallejo and halfway down the block entered a yellow building with brown trim. She hurried after him, stopping when she read the sign beside the door, a homeless shelter, just as he'd told her.

She pushed open the door. Max stood at the registration desk.

"What are you doing here?" He sounded angry.

"I want my money." She lifted her chin.

The clerk handed him a ticket with a cot number and a folded gray cotton-flannel blanket. He tucked the blanket under his arm and faced her. "It's gone."

"Gone?" If he lived like this, how could he have spent a hundred-eighty dollars already? "You spent it all? On what?"

"It doesn't matter. It was wasted." With a sneer, he walked away. His dismissal of her stung worse than his words.

"You wasted my money! You rat! You thief!" She dogged his

heels. Visions filled her—of slapping him, kicking him, grabbing him by the throat and shaking sense into him, anything to get him to react to her and the awful way he made her feel. "How dare you do that to me when I was just trying to help you?"

He spun on her, his mouth twisted with bitterness. "You saw what just happened at that restaurant. Would I have put up with that... humiliation... if I had money?"

Shocked, she stared at him.

He walked into the men's room. So angry she didn't hesitate, she followed and slammed the bathroom door shut behind her. "I need it back! Why don't you get a loan from your rich friend Dennis? You two are so chummy! Why take from me? How am I supposed to live? I should move in to a place like this right beside you, maybe? That money was important to me!"

He leaned toward her. "Of course it was. You're a woman, aren't you? Love is never enough for you." His voice dropped, as if his words were reflecting something in his past rather than Connie.

"What are you talking about? I invited you to my house—"

His head snapped toward her. "That was as stupid a move as I've ever seen."

Beyond fury, she yelled at him. "You were sick, damn you! That's what I get for caring!"

He bent over the sink and ran water onto his cupped hands. "You want money so much"—he splashed the water onto his face, then patted it dry with a paper towel—"put your money on Geostar Biotechnologies. It sells over-the-counter as GSBT. It'll make you back what I took and lots more."

"What kind of smarmy line is that?" She yanked the paper towel from him, wadded it and hurled it at the back of his head. "I'm supposed to take stock tips from a guy who lives like this? You're even crazier than I thought!"

An elderly man wearing a knit cap and layers of dirty,

stained clothes, suddenly walked into the restroom, saw the two of them and backed out.

Alone again, Connie and Max stared at each other.

"The hell with you, Max Squire!" she yelled, then turned and ran out of the dreadful place and into the street. There, she stopped, half hoping he would follow her out, apologize, anything. The brown, paint-chipped door stayed shut.

"To hell with you!" She repeated even louder and stomped her way through the streets to her car.

14

Dennis and Veronica sat at a small table in The Porcupine, one of the best new restaurants in the city. She took a sip of Moet's champagne and smiled as the bubbles tickled her nose. As Dennis watched, his heart thrummed. Champagne and oysters Rockefeller had been her dream when she was young. Now, he'd gotten her both.

"I'll tell you where Max is, okay?" Every ounce of willpower Dennis possessed was needed to keep from shouting at her to pay attention to him. "I convinced my uncle and Vinnie—Earl's opinion doesn't matter—to let him set up books for their business and even prepare their income tax forms. He'll be in the restaurant trying to make sense out of the papers and receipts they've got stashed all over the place. I doubt they've ever filed before, and if the business is legit, they have to."

"So little Dennis wants to run a sports bar," Veronica sneered. "A legitimate, tax-paying sports bar. What a loser you are!"

Each word was like a stab to his chest. "You just don't know how to think big, do you?"

"Right. A sports bar in a dump is big thinking. I'm so

impressed." She leaned forward. "Listen, you pig, I'm sick of waiting for you. I don't give a goddamn about Max Squire as long as he stays the hell away from me. I want my cut now, and I want out. Do you understand?"

"The money I got isn't going to last forever, Veronica," Dennis said, his face burning with indignation. "I got to think of the future—our future—and a sweet little legitimate looking operation like that can do a lot for us."

"Don't give me that 'our future' crap. I gave up listening to you years ago."

"Hey, you and me. It's always been about us."

"No. It's always been about you and football. And now it's dumped you. Just like I'm going to do. You've got two days, then life won't be so easy for you, Dennis."

"You can't threaten me."

"I think I just did."

His teeth clenched. "Without me, you'd have nothing."

She smiled wickedly. "You forget about Max."

The words spat from his mouth. "You really think Max would do anything to you other than put a bullet through your cold little heart?"

"I know he would." She laughed in his face. "And now that I know how to locate him..."

"I could kill you myself. You bitch!" he shouted.

"That's what you've always loved about me, sugar, and don't forget it." With a dismissive sneer at his sputtering outrage, she smugly returned to her champagne and oysters.

Angie shivered as another blast of cold air hit her. The Porcupine was crowded, and she and Stan were stuck right near the front door, which meant every time someone came in or went out, she felt a chill. But at least she was here. She'd forgotten about the place until Dennis mentioned it last night.

Tonight, she didn't want to stay home. Paavo was still on call and a lot of weird cases had come in, and Connie was still fuming over their aborted dinner the night before. Stan was her last resort, and anyway, she owed him for dragging him across town to meet Helen. He'd barely escaped that encounter with his life; Angie had expected Helen might turn him into a human pretzel.

The seating arrangement didn't say much for a restaurant that had the best buzz in town. Just to by-pass the reservations, she'd had to use her father's name with the maître d', something she didn't like to do routinely. Salvatore Amalfi had started as a shoe salesman and grew to become the owner of a chain of shoe stores—which he'd since sold—and several buildings in San Francisco. He had more than a few friends in high places.

The restaurant wasn't at all what Angie had expected. One wall was brick, looking more like an outside wall than the inside of a top restaurant, and in keeping with the rustic "theme," black rafters showed on the ceiling. Brown paper was placed on the tabletops instead of fine linen, and when the bread was delivered, the waiter dropped a small, freshly made loaf directly on the tabletop.

She guessed it was a rich man's rustic chic décor—alley dining at its finest.

She carefully looked over the customers. The noise of conversation was surprisingly high, as was the clatter of the kitchen that stood open in one corner of the room, separated from the diners only by a high counter. At least the customers could be sure the cooks weren't spitting into the soup or anything else.

Her breath caught. Seated at a far table was Dennis Pagozzi, and with him, a woman. Angie's eyebrows rose at the sight. *What do we have here?*

She hadn't noticed him when she and Stan entered. She hadn't noticed much at all, since they'd been immediately seated by the door. Maybe her father's name didn't have quite the clout she thought it had.

Suddenly, Dennis and the woman stood to leave. She stared at him, gaping.

What about Connie? Should she tell Connie she saw Dennis out with another woman? He wasn't exactly beating down Connie's door, but still, there was hope for the two of them, wasn't there? She also remembered the stark look on Connie's face when that other guy, that Max Squire, entered Wings of an Angel. Just what was going on there?

But when she compared the type of guy Max seemed to be against Dennis' fame and money, well, she needed to make sure Connie went after the one best for her future.

As Dennis and the woman turned toward the door, Angie bent down, her head lower than the table top.

"Angie, what are you doing?" Stan lifted his side of the supposedly chichi brown paper and peeked under the table at her.

"Shush!"

"Why?"

"I don't want some people to see me. They're leaving. Let me know when they've gone."

Stan straightened in his seat, munching on bread and salted olive oil, and Angie stayed under there, waiting and waiting... and waiting.

"Stan!" she whispered. "Stan!"

He stuck his head under the table again. "Yes?"

"Haven't they left yet?"

"Who?"

"The people I don't want to see me. A big guy with black hair and a blond woman."

"Oh, them. Yeah. They've gone. I didn't know who it was you were hiding from."

She sat back up and had to wait a minute before telling him what a jerk he was because bent over that way, the blood had rushed to her head and when she sat back up too quickly, she felt woozy. "You would have just left me sitting under the table, I suppose?"

"I didn't even know what you're talking about, so pardon me for living! I came here as a favor to you, remember."

A favor to his stomach was more like it. Stan loved to eat. Coming with her to this restaurant was no hardship.

"So, what shall we have?" Stan said more to himself than Angie as he drooled over the expensive menu. "Anytime you feel like doing more matchmaking, Angie, keep me in mind."

15

"Angelina Amalfi?" asked a pleasant voice on the telephone.

"Yes." Angie tucked the phone between her ear and shoulder. She'd found the webpage link she'd been searching for and clicked on it.

"I'm Kara Saunders, from KRAK-TV. We were recently talking about adding a cooking show to our Saturday morning local TV line-up, and your name came up as a potential host for it. Someone remembered something you were involved in called... let me see... *Angelina in the Cucina*. Is that correct?"

Despite Angie's concentration on the Internet, she still cringed at the horrible name. The show never got off the ground. "That's right."

Nope. That wasn't the information she wanted. She tried another link.

The woman on the phone continued talking. "We're going to hold some auditions, but I'll be honest, you're number one on our list. Do say you'll come and try out for us."

"What? TV? I don't do TV." Angie murmured. As the web

page unfolded, she smiled. It was exactly what she was looking for, and right here in San Francisco, too.

"You aren't saying you're not interested, are you?" the woman asked, sounding crestfallen. "Don't you want to think about it? Hear the terms we're offering? The benefits? The publicity?"

A knock sounded. "Oh, my! Someone's at the door." Angie used the cursor to save the page to favorites, smiling as she read about leprechauns and shamrocks. What fun! "I've got to run."

"But—"

"Goodbye!"

She put down the phone and stared at the web page a moment longer. Wouldn't Paavo be surprised! She could hardly wait to see his joyous expression, feel his gratitude, his love....

The knock sounded again, jerking her from her reverie. She dashed to open the door. It might be Fed Ex with the books she'd ordered about engagement parties. She'd hunted all over the city's bookstores, but couldn't find a thing that—

"Hi. Excuse me for bothering you. Do you have a moment?" he asked nervously.

Angie stared in surprise at the man in her doorway. He was familiar—tall, blond, muscular, with a craggy face, twinkling blue eyes, and wearing a gray sweatshirt with cut-off sleeves and paint-and-grease splattered jeans. Then she realized who he was...

"You're Connie's ex-husband," she said. "Keith, right? I've seen pictures of you." She knew his name was Keith, but she didn't want to make him think she and Connie had spent much time discussing him, which, of course, they had. In fact, if she thought of all the things Connie had told her about Keith, she'd blush.

"That's me." He put hands on his hips and smiled.

She had no idea what he was doing there, but good manners won out. "Won't you come in?"

"Thanks. I wanted to talk to you about Connie." He slowly entered the apartment, taking in, first of all, the view of San Francisco Bay that stretched from the Golden Gate to the Bay Bridge, with Alcatraz centered like a picture postcard. "Kee-rist!" he muttered under his breath. His gaze then leaped to her antique furniture, entertainment system, and lingered a moment on the Cezanne lithograph. Was Keith an art lover? If half of what Connie had said was true, she should tell him it was only a reproduction—which it wasn't.

None of her art or antique furniture were fakes, and she certainly didn't want him sitting on anything with a light fabric. "How about some coffee?" she asked. "I've got some cheesecake in the refrigerator as well. Why don't we sit at the table?"

She led him away from the living room to her dining area. The table and chairs were cherry wood. He plunked himself down on the chair with all the ease of a man making himself at home. Angie peered surreptitiously at his shoes. Old construction boots. At least he didn't leave a trail of sawdust or plaster of Paris. The building owner, her father, was really going to have to start paying a doorman once again. Doormen were mostly unknown around here, although lately, that was changing.

"That sounds great," he said with a friendly smile. "Connie always liked to eat those gooey, chocolate desserts. Women's desserts, I call them. Cheesecake is a man's food."

"Really? I'd never thought of it that way before."

"Yeah. Lots of my buddies feel like that."

"Interesting." She went into the kitchen and cut a slice of cake for Keith. She'd made it that morning for Paavo, who would come by later if there was a lull in his casework. He liked cheesecake a lot. Maybe Keith was right? But Paavo also liked other cakes and pastries, more elaborate ones, like Italian Rum Cake...

After giving Keith cake and coffee, and pouring herself a cup, she sat down. "So, what brings you here?" she asked.

"I'm worried about Connie." He stuffed a big piece of cake in his mouth and made appreciative noises as he rolled it around on his tongue. *Obviously not too worried,* she thought.

She waited until he'd swallowed to be sure he wouldn't try to talk with a mouthful of mooshy dessert. "What are you worried about?"

"I heard she's been seeing some guy connected with football. The 49ers. Big joke, huh?"

"What's wrong with that?"

He put the fork down, blue eyes widening. "So, it's true?"

"I'm not saying it isn't."

He looked stricken. "Those guys are out of her league. She's just a nice kid. Innocent, you know. I don't trust guys like that."

And Angie didn't trust *him.* "Connie can handle herself."

He finished the cake before asking. "I don't know. Maybe she's turned into a... a football floozie, or, you know, a... a grid-iron groupie?"

Angie nearly spit out her coffee. "She's no groupie!"

Keith folded his tanned and tattooed arms. "It wouldn't be the first time."

"I can't imagine it!" Angie said indignantly and suppressed the urge to stab him with his own fork. "Anyway, you just said she was an innocent."

He stood, sliding his fingertips into his back pockets, and strode to the window. "So, the story I heard is true. She *has* met someone who's a big deal." He stared at the bay a long moment. "I didn't think it'd happen."

Angie felt a twinge, a small twinge, of pity for him. She made no reply. Was Keith actually remorseful about the way he'd treated Connie? She knew Connie had been crazy about him, but when given the choice between his wife and heroin, the drug won out. Angie wondered if he'd cleaned up suffi-ciently, and for long enough, that Connie would be interested in him again.

On the other hand, Connie had given him plenty of chances, and each time, he'd failed her. Now, she had a chance with Dennis Pagozzi, who was just about perfect in every way—except that he might be two-timing her. Or, he could have been breaking up with that other woman so that he could be free to be with Connie. Angie had no idea.

"I guess you miss her," Angie said finally, not quite sure what to say or why she suddenly felt any sympathy for him. Was she turning into a total marshmallow because of love?

His mouth tightened. "Could be." He did another once-over of her apartment. "I guess she'll be getting a place as nice as this, if she stays with this guy. Maybe even a house. She always said she wanted a house—just a little house to call her own, nothing more. Now, she'll be able to afford a mansion, if she can pull it off." He chuckled morosely.

"Pull what off?"

"Make the guy think she's in love with him. I know how she feels about me...how we feel still about each other." He smirked, on sure footing once again.

What little sympathy Angie had felt vanished. She didn't like his words or his attitude. "Connie doesn't have to pretend anything. I've seen the two of them together. This guy worships the ground she walks on. He treats her like a princess, and she adores him."

His smile disappeared. "The hell with her, then. Who cares, right? Well, I'm outta here. Thanks for nothing!"

Angie escorted him to the front door and opened it, glad to see the back of the loser. How had Connie stood him?

He stepped out into the hall, then faced her once again. "Say, when you talk to her, ask her if she could rustle up a couple of 49ers tickets for me, okay?"

"Dennis Pagozzi?"

Bleary-eyed, Pagozzi stood in his doorway in his robe and pajamas, trying to focus on the identification presented by the round, balding man: Chuck Lexington, State of California, Division of Adult Parole Operations. "Yeah?" Dennis muttered. He'd been up most of the night drinking and making love with Veronica until, both drunk, they began to fight. Finally, she left in one of his many cars, a Prius that didn't have as much power as he would have liked, so he rarely drove it. He had no idea where she'd gone.

Lexington stood tall. "I'm looking for Veronica Maple. Our records indicate that you are a long-time acquaintance of hers."

Pagozzi rubbed his face, wanting nothing more than a shower and a shave. Veronica was the last person he wanted to talk about. Or even think about. "That was ages ago. I don't know anything about her."

"Mr. Pagozzi, we have reason to believe she's armed and dangerous. A danger to you, and to others."

He frowned. Even with his hangover, he'd heard the words "armed and dangerous." He had no idea about the armed part. "What do you mean?"

"It appears that she killed a man soon after getting out of prison. She failed to report to my office as required, which lends credence to her having perpetuated the crime. She was tracked to San Francisco, but we don't know where she's gone from here."

Pagozzi was suddenly wide awake. "Veronica? A killer? No way! She was always just interested in money."

"People change in prison," Lexington explained. "They go in as white-collar criminals and come out hard, willing to do anything for a buck. She robbed the pawn shop along with killing the owner. A handgun was taken from the shop."

Pagozzi's nerves felt ready to snap. He didn't think Veronica could commit murder, but it wasn't the first time he'd been wrong about her. This time, he could be dead wrong.

His mind raced. "Thanks for letting me know. I'll contact you if I see her."

"Just what was your relationship with Miss Maple?" Lexington asked.

"Nothing. We hung out when we were young, that's all."

Lexington nodded, peering intently into Pagozzi's eyes. "For your sake, I hope it wasn't anything more than that. Here's my card. We have to get her before she kills again. Once a person like her starts, it can lead anywhere."

Dennis had to swallow a couple of times before he replied. "That's exactly what I was thinking."

Connie glanced at the clock. 5:55 p.m. Five minutes more and she could lock up shop, thank goodness. The day began much too early at six-thirty, in time for the New York Stock Exchange's opening bell. Stockbrokers were already at their desks in San Francisco—not a good way to live in her opinion, but she was glad she could immediately get the answer to the question that had plagued her all night.

"I'm interested in buying a stock," she said to the Merrill Lynch broker who answered her call, "but I want to know the price first."

"Great. I can help you," the enthusiastic voice responded. "What is it?"

"Geostar Biotechnologies."

"Okay." In a moment he came back. "Are you sure of the name? I checked the New York, NASDAQ, even American exchanges, but I don't see it."

So he *had* lied! "That's what I was told. Oh..., wait. He said something about over the counter and GBST. Does that help?"

"It sure does. One moment." He found it selling at two dollars a share. The broker nearly choked as he asked her if she wanted to "actually" buy any of it.

With a shudder, she said no.

What kind of fool did Max Squire take her for?

She'd fumed about him all day and maybe that was why she'd only sold a single item—a twenty-dollar porcelain flower and vase to a woman looking for a small gift for a hospitalized friend allergic to real flowers.

Not only that, Dennis hadn't called either. What was with him? He should have at least apologized for not saying goodbye when he ran out on the dinner they were having, sticking Angie with his bill. He was making it mighty hard for her to keep him from sinking fast on her stud rating chart.

A minute before closing time, the shop's bell rang. Connie froze. If the customer was returning the vase, she'd run into the back room and hide until she gave up and left again. That sale was important. She needed to eat.

When she gathered her nerve and glanced up, Max stood in the doorway.

"What are you doing here?" she demanded. She could feel her face redden—God, sometimes it was awful being blond—as anger and frustration warred. "Looking for more money?"

"I was desperate, as I told you," he said, approaching her. He hesitated, then said gruffly, "I'm sorry about the way I treated you yesterday. It was uncalled for. I also want to thank you for not saying anything about it to Dennis. What I did was embarrassing enough without him knowing."

Now he wanted to apologize? She folded her arms. "It embarrassed me, too, to have been such a patsy!"

"I've known Dennis a while," he continued, his voice calm. "He's a good guy. A good woman is exactly what he needs, and you're a good woman, Connie. I feel bad about involving you in my problems at all. I promise I'll do something, when I'm able, to remedy it."

None of this made any sense to her. "You feel bad about me?"

Dark eyes captured hers. "Hell, woman, do you think I'd be here if I didn't? I couldn't get you out of my mind, even though I tried. Believe me, I tried hard."

That gave her pause. She swallowed, then asked, "Why?"

"Why couldn't I forget you?"

"Why did you want to?"

He shook his head, eyes downcast and looking more embarrassed than anything. Then he lifted his chin. "Your kindness. Your trust. I didn't think women like you existed anymore."

She didn't know what to make of him, only that he was hurting and desperate. She'd been there herself at times. Slowly stepping around the counter toward him, she lifted her hand to touch his arm, but then dropped it again and drew in her breath. "We met, we talked, and to my amazement, we seemed to enjoy each other's company. You were hurt, and I helped you. It was all good... until you made it turn ugly."

"I know," he said, his voice filled with pain. "I know."

She stamped her foot. "You made me so angry!"

A hint of a smile touched his mouth. "Hit me, why don't you? A slap in the face or a good hard sock in the stomach. Your choice. Just, not the ribs, okay? Still, it's what I deserve, and it'll make you feel a hell of a lot better."

She smacked her arms against her sides. "I can't hit you! I'm mad enough at you, that's for sure, but I can't."

Gently, he touched her cheek. "I'm so sorry, about everything." With that, he turned away. "I'll pay you back when I can, I promise."

She watched him walk toward the door. Under his beaten down, trying-to-be-jaded, trying-to-be-tough exterior, she saw a good man, a lonely, sensitive man, someone who had been damaged badly. She moved toward him. She wasn't sure why; she was never impulsive. Constant Connie, as Angie said. Angie was the impulsive one. Not her; never her.

"Max, wait!" she cried. He turned.

She stopped, unsure what to say. How could she forgive him? But, somehow, she already had. "What would you say to a bowl of Campbell's vegetable soup and a couple of hamburgers for dinner? Chef Connie's cooking might not be exciting, but it's filling."

He blinked as if not sure he heard her correctly. "It would be better if I just left."

"No," she said, despite herself. "It wouldn't."

<hr>

With the engine running, Veronica sat in Dennis' Prius, parked in a truck loading zone and watched Max enter Everyone's Fancy. She couldn't imagine why he'd taken an Uber to a cheap little gift shop. She hadn't intended on following him, but merely to check up on him: to keep him in her sights, so to speak.

But curiosity had gotten the best of her.

That afternoon, she'd gone back to Dennis's house to try to make up to him for their fight after reminding herself that Dennis was the type of guy you could sweet talk into doing almost anything for you, but push him, and he'd get stubborn.

But when she saw him, he was a wreck. He told her a parole officer was looking for her, that she'd killed a shop owner, stole a gun, and now was "armed and dangerous." She tried to tell Dennis that was ridiculous.

It did no good. He believed the PO. He also said Butch had let Max know that she was in the city and Max didn't take it well at all. From his expression, Dennis figured Max would like nothing more than to make her pay for embezzling from him, for destroying his life. He might even want to kill her. She had to leave town. He also suggested she stay away from him, his house, even Wings of an Angel, because Max was so down on his luck, he was living in a homeless shelter near it. He had watched Max enter the place after he bought Max lunch a few days earlier.

She didn't know what to make of this. Although she didn't trust Dennis, something about his words, the fear in them, rattled her. And, strangely, she *had* felt watched; as if someone, something, was moving ever closer to her. Something dark and deathlike. Perhaps, death itself.

She hated such thoughts, didn't believe in them. They meant nothing. Shoving them aside, she concentrated on Max. She talked Dennis into letting her continue to use his too-small car and went in search of Max.

It didn't take long to locate the homeless shelter Dennis told her about.

She was stunned Max had sunk so low. He used to be a Hugo Boss suit man, his casual wear nothing less than Armani or Polo, with five-hundred-dollar loafers and ninety-dollar haircuts. He liked imported wine, gourmet meals, classical music and Broadway shows, and had treated her to the same when he could get away from his job and customers. Too much work had been Max Squire's biggest problem. He had spent so much time involved in his business, expanding it and finding new clients, that to say it made Max a dull boy was an understatement.

At first, he'd considered himself far above her. Eventually, he swore undying love for her, but when it came to a choice between his money and reputation or her, he'd chosen the former.

He could have let her get away with her scheme. It would have been a lot better for everyone if he had. He was smart enough to make back the money she'd taken and no one would have been the wiser. Instead, he had turned her over to the police. That wasn't love. It was betrayal.

She'd gone to jail. But Max, instead of working harder than ever, had obviously spent the last three years wallowing in self-pity. What a loser!

Now, she was stuck in this city with another loser. Dennis Pagozzi. As soon as she got her hands on the money, *her* money, she'd be out of here. No one was going to get in her way this time.

She sat a little higher in the seat when the "Open" sign on the door of Everyone's Fancy flipped to "Closed." A moment later, the door opened, and a blond woman, a bit too heavy in the waist and hips, stepped out of the shop, Max right behind her. Veronica had seen the woman before... with Dennis. Who was this two-timing broad?

The blonde locked the door, took Max's arm, and they walked down West Portal Avenue.

Max always was a sucker for blondes. She touched her hair, the long strands brushing her shoulders, as she studied the woman.

Veronica's hair had been short, just like *hers*, when she and Max had their affair. He liked it; used to riffle his fingers through it. She wondered if he was pretending the blonde shopgirl was really her when they kissed, when they made love. Max had sworn his undying love for her, and now was proving himself to be as fickle as all men. It was good the only lust she ever felt around him was for his client's money.

Veronica abandoned the car and followed them to a corner, up one block and onto Wawona street. Two blocks later, they entered a building. She crept close and managed to grab the heavy main door before it locked again.

She waited a moment, then entered. No elevator; the stairs carpeted. A woman's hand glided along the banister near the top, three flights up. Silently, Veronica also climbed the stairs. Those prison workouts had paid off well for her.

On the top floor a door opened and then a light came on. She angled herself to see which apartment they'd entered. Soon, the door closed again, and all was quiet.

She paused on the stairs, remembering the many times Max had taken her to his home—an immense, professionally decorated place that he had lived in alone. He'd been a good lover; one of the best, in fact. Much better than Dennis, who was more in love with himself than anyone else. *Too bad things went so wrong, Max.*

It was tempting to simply burst into the apartment and have it out with him. To think, that while she rotted in prison, he was out enjoying life. Bad enough that he was rutting, but doing it with women whose resembled her in so many ways infuriated her even more... although this one had a good twenty or more pounds on her.

Her breathing grew heavy as her fingers twisted in her hair and she tugged on it hard. Damn them both! If her hair was short, her eyes blue...

An idea, a wonderfully pleasing idea, struck her. Could she do it? Tomorrow was the big day. But if she hurried, she would have time.

As she faced the apartment door, her plans for the next day's adventure grew a bit more complicated... but far, far more satisfying.

16

Max sat in Wings of an Angel, the income and spending records in shopping bags all around him. It was morning, so he had a few hours to work before the restaurant opened for the lunchtime crowd. He'd never seen such a mess. All of them, Earl, Butch, and even Vinnie, thought nothing of reaching into the till whenever they needed cash, mixing tips with receipts, credit card payments with cash, even payables with receivables in ways he never imagined were possible. He didn't even want to think about what they'd done about state sales tax, let alone liquor and cigarette taxes.

Where to begin puzzled him. He might not have taken the job at all except for Butch's statement about too many from the past showing up, first *her*, then him. Had Butch meant Veronica? In the context spoken, who else could he have meant?

If she'd been to Wings of an Angel, that meant Dennis had lied to him. Max needed to stick closer than ever to Dennis and Wings of an Angel both, and this job was a great way to do it.

He was trying to decipher scribbles on a receipt when Earl called him to the restaurant's phone. "For you."

Assuming it was Dennis, Max answered.

"I'd know that voice anywhere," a woman said.

His blood turned hot, then cold. He'd know *her* voice anywhere as well. "Veronica."

"You remember. How sweet. I was sure you'd forget after you sent me away. Three years, Max."

"It was your doing," he said, trying his best to keep his voice hushed and steady. And more than anything, he wanted to ask, *Why?* Why had she chosen his clients to embezzle from? How did she not know how much he had loved her? Why had she caused his love to turn to black, soul-crushing hatred?

"I'm out now," she said. "It's over."

His hand gripped tight on the receiver. Nothing was over as far as he was concerned. "I want to see you." He struggled to keep his voice soft and friendly, but he could hear it quiver.

"Why? Do you think I want to share?" She laughed.

"I know you better than that," he said. "I just... I want to see you again."

"I'm sure you do. Maybe we can pick up where we left off, is that what you're thinking? I don't think so! After all, you're broke."

Every word was another stab to the heart. It was already broken. How could it continue to hurt? "But you have the money, I suspect."

"How could I? I served time. You don't think they let you keep money you've embezzled, do you?"

He knew she was toying with him, the same as always. He'd followed the case as closely as humanly possible. No one knew where the majority of the money she'd taken from his clients had gone. She claimed it went to gambling and drugs—all eight million. He knew, though, that she didn't gamble and rarely touched the hard stuff.

He knew far too much about her.

His entire history with her raced across his mind like a

movie fast-forwarded on warp-speed, beginning with the day she first walked into his financial consulting business office. In her hand was a folded *San Francisco Chronicle* with his help wanted ad circled. It was four years ago. His business was growing more quickly than he and his secretary, Mrs. Hendricks, could handle. He needed a part-time office aid.

She looked like a schoolgirl, her hair pulled back into a ponytail, face scrubbed and make-up free, wearing a sweet dress buttoned up to the neck and hemmed below the knees. Her intelligence had shown through, and she quickly learned and understood everything Mrs. Hendricks explained to her.

Even then, behind the innocent smile, there was a knowing-ness, a sexiness, that Mrs. Hendricks didn't recognize, but his male hormones did.

Before long, Veronica would stay at work after Mrs. Hendricks went home for the day. She would then enter his office and point out how incompetent his secretary of the past seven years had been, and how much more efficient she was. During those times, they'd relax, and she often unbuttoned the top few buttons of her dress or blouse to breathe more easily, or remove the band from her pony tail so her long blonde hair could swing freely.

When confronted with such "inefficiencies," Mrs. Hendricks' protests sounded weak, and the more she complained about Veronica, the more Max found himself defending her. Three weeks after Veronica began working for him, she came into his office after hours and didn't stop with unbuttoning just a few buttons. Their affair began, and soon after that, Mrs. Hendricks quit.

Veronica took over her job. She was amazingly intelligent, and Max had trusted her completely. His little protégé, he'd called her, and promised to teach her all about financial coun-seling. They had dreams of her bringing in her own clients, and having the business grow larger and more prosperous than ever. She made a goal for herself—a goal to hire a secretary for them both.

They say love is blind, and he was more blinded by Veronica than ever a man should be. She cut her hair short and sophisticated—much the way Connie wore hers. She threw away her cotton dresses for business suits, and got to know his clients' affairs as well, or better, than he did.

A few times he walked in unexpectedly to hear her talking cheerfully to one of them. He didn't question her though, and pushed aside his suspicions, especially when she'd tell him how magnificent he was and that the luckiest day of her life was when he hired her.

He wanted to get married, practically begged her, but she had refused. He didn't know why. Only much later did he learn she'd had lots of lovers, including several of his clients. Ironically, if she had married him, he wouldn't have been able to testify against her.

It was his deposition that had caused her to take a plea bargain, resulting in a three-year prison term with five additional years of probation.

He'd been furious. Three years was a slap on the wrist for the damage she'd inflicted on him, on his business and reputation. On his heart. He'd love her with a passion and intensity he'd never felt for anyone before and hadn't felt since. The day he realized she'd betrayed him was the day he'd lost interest in life, along with his faith and self-respect.

Although she was the embezzler, and he wasn't criminally guilty, since she'd been his employee, the civil lawsuits against him were very real. At first, he'd cared about his clients, even though they were so rich their losses wouldn't have mattered that much. Hell, with the tax write-off it gave them, for all he knew, they might have made a profit off his problems. But instead of showing him support or understanding, they sued him. They ruined him. He would have worked hard for them, too, had they not been like sharks at a feeding frenzy, taking all they could, destroying any sense of regret, obligation, or even basic humanity he'd felt for them.

Everything he'd worked for, everything he owned, went to pay his lawyers and pay off the clients. He'd been insured, but what he owed, including massive legal bills, was far more than the insurance and much more than he had saved, so a lien was placed against his future earnings as well. Since his capital would be taken away from him the minute he amassed any, he soon realized he would never be able to build up his assets. He was, in a word, screwed.

A few of his clients, like Pagozzi, stuck by him for a while. But long before the creditors lined up at his door, long before the last of his clients took their business elsewhere, he'd ceased to care. Some days, he would find oblivion in a liquor bottle so that he didn't have to wonder why she'd done it, and if she'd lied about *everything*, including her feelings for him. For months after the betrayal, he would wake up out of a nightmare with her name on his tongue and tears in his eyes. He hated her then as he hated her now. It was the only honest emotion he'd felt for the past three years.

The life he'd known, his business, his love, were gone, all destroyed by the woman on the telephone. His hand tightened on the receiver because, damn it, as much as he wanted to kill her, he also wanted to see her again.

"If you don't have the money," he asked, forcing himself back to the here and now, "where is it?"

"I didn't say that, exactly. In fact, that's what I want to talk to you about."

"I'm ready."

"Good. Let's meet at Ghirardelli Square, under the clock tower. Be there at two o'clock on the dot. If you're late, I won't wait for you. And no funny business."

"That's a great one, coming from you."

"It's *perfect,* coming from me," she said. "And I suggest you don't tell your new girlfriend anything about this. I'd hate to fill her in on what you're really like. It could ruin a good thing for you, don't you think?"

He hung up the phone, hating her even more than he thought possible.

Was she referring to Connie? Who else could she be talking about? But how could she know anything about Connie? Maybe her taunt was just a stab in the dark.

He would meet her all right. He'd arrive early to be sure he saw Veronica before she saw him, just to get ready to face her again.

He didn't want her spooked; didn't want her to do anything other than trust him and talk to him about where she'd put his damned money!

Just the thought of getting some of it back, to be able to live somewhere that wasn't squalor, was more than he would allow himself to hope for. He deserved a few crumbs, at least, didn't he? Well, didn't he?

But why had Veronica contacted Pagozzi when she got out of jail? What had they meant to each other?

Suddenly, he staggered as a new thought struck him. How had he not considered it before?

Was it mere chance that Veronica had walked into his office when he needed clerical help some four years ago, when they first met? Or had something been going on between her and Pagozzi—his client—before he and Veronica had ever met?

Paavo tried to bury himself behind his computer and ignore the chaos going on around him as Elizabeth and Bo Benson made lattes and cappuccinos for homicide, robbery, and any other inspector who wandered into room 450, following their noses and the aroma of good, strong espresso coffee. Angie had bought a fancy espresso machine for the staff and sent it over, along with biscotti and cannoli, as afternoon coffee break treats.

"Inspector Smith."

Paavo started at the sound of Lt. Hollins' voice. Hollins was the head of Homicide. Age fifty-plus, gray-haired, heavyset, and usually found holding or chewing on an unlit cigar. Right now, his tone was harsh, and his expression a severe frown. And he never used his men's title unless there was a problem.

Paavo jumped to his feet. "Yes, sir."

"Come into my office." He marched off, and Paavo followed.

The office was no more than a partitioned section in the corner of the homicide bureau. For several years, the lieutenant had been promised a real office, but whenever he'd get one, the mayor would create a new commissioner or department, and the boss—usually the mayor's friend—would, of course, need his own office. People would be juggled around to accommodate the political appointee, and Hollins would be booted out of his new office, and sent back to the supposedly "temporary" partitions in Homicide.

"Have a seat," Hollins said.

Paavo sat down.

"I don't know quite how to put this." Hollins didn't sit, but walked around the little space, then stopped in front of the window. "I appreciate that you've just gotten engaged, and that your fiancée is thrilled by it, and she has money... but she's going too far."

"She is?"

"Nothing's getting done. The inspectors are all hanging around the office waiting for their daily delivery of food rations." Hollins' face began to redden. "Is this an office or a soup kitchen? The problem is, the food she's sending is great. I can't pass it up either. It's delicious, and fattening. I've gained five pounds just this week!" Each word was more agitated than the last. "I can't keep this up. I won't be able to fit into my clothes. My wife is wondering why I don't eat much dinner anymore. She thinks I'm stepping out on her or something. I can't take it!"

Paavo did his best not to gawk. "I'm sorry. What do you want me to do?"

"Stop her!"

Paavo kept silent. He'd have more luck locating Jimmy Hoffa. He wondered grimly what would happen when the lieutenant found out that Angie also had matchmaking plans for his fellow inspectors.

"You don't understand temptation!" Hollins cried. "That's what's going on. Many of us, er, them, are weak around such temptation. Especially the pizza and the pastries." His eyes rolled heavenward. Instead of agony or anger, he almost seemed to be in bliss. "And the Italian deli foods—the coppa, galantina, Gorgonzola, pepperoncini—"

"I understand, sir," Paavo said, standing. "I'll talk to Angie soon."

"The caponata, dry olives, bruschetta." Hollins raised his handkerchief to the corner of his mouth, aware that he was starting to drool. He blinked, forcing himself back to the task at hand and gruffly added, "Good, Smith. I expect you to take care of it."

17

Sid Fernandez sat in a dark blue commercial van's passenger seat and watched as a young, female Courier's Unlimited driver steered the company truck into the Franklin building's underground garage and stopped in her usual spot near the elevator. She looked bored. This was just a job; one she'd done over and over, despite the supposed danger of it, and the danger in becoming blasé about it.

She should have listened to her boss' warnings because, as she shut and lock the truck's door that particular afternoon, Julius Rodriguez sprang from the commercial van and hit her on the head with an iron bar. He caught her as she crumpled.

In under ten seconds, Julius had lifted her into the back of the van. While he broke the courier's neck to make sure she wouldn't wake up and cry out, Veronica, who had been waiting inside it, quickly changed into the uniform she and Julius stripped from the dead woman.

Fernandez sat in the passenger seat and watched as the two double-checked the company's ID to confirm that the one made for Veronica was the same as the ID's currently being used by Courier's Unlimited. It was.

Veronica took the courier's package, carefully removed the mailing label, and taped it onto a large padded envelope with heavy cardboard inside. They had to be sure Isaac Zakarian would need to open the door to receive the package he'd been expecting.

Zakarian's, a very exclusive diamond jewelry shop, was located on the second floor. It had a small public area, where customers could view the unset diamonds and settings, and a back room where the diamonds were stored in locked cases. The storeroom also had a bulletproof window with a slot where jewels could pass through without the need to open the steel door protecting the jewels.

Each day, the office closed between noon and two. Between one-thirty and two, when his assistant went to lunch, the owner was alone in the storeroom. During that time, the only people he would deal with were couriers.

Initially, Julius was going to handle the robbery, but when El Toro learned Veronica would be out of prison, he thought she would be less likely to arouse any suspicions on Zakarian's part. Their scheme required him to relax enough to open the door from the public area to the storeroom to accept the package.

Fernandez and Julius would wait until she was in—giving her exactly one minute from the time she stepped onto the elevator. She'd send the elevator back down to the basement, and they'd hold it there, waiting, until the minute was up, then ride up.

Zakarian had cameras that scanned the hallway outside the shop. If he saw the two men out there, no way would he open the inner office door for a courier. Once she got inside to the area where the diamonds were stored, she needed to stop Zakarian from calling for help, pressing an alarm, or anything else, by whatever means necessary. The two men would show up soon after, in case she was having a problem with Zakarian.

Once in the room, they would "neutralize" Zakarian, clean out the store, take out the cameras, and simply ride down in the elevators and leave the way they got in.

They'd burn the van with the courier in it, and be on their way, richer than their wildest dreams.

It was a straightforward, but carefully timed plan. In Fernandez's experience that was the kind that worked best. Too many of his compadres came up with complicated robberies only to have some little something go wrong and end up in jail. Much like what had happened to Veronica three years ago.

Once, he thought he could trust her with this job. But after seeing her and Julius, he was having second thoughts. For some reason, that very morning, she'd changed her hairdo—cut it short and dyed it a light blond color. Plus, she'd put blue contact lens over the gray of her eyes. She said it was to make it less likely she'd be identified in case anyone did happen to see her in the courier outfit.

He didn't like to wonder about the loyalty of his people. He didn't like it at all, but the robbery was set, and to change plans now would only create more delays.

Delays always brought bad luck. El Toro hated delays.

He'd also lined up an airtight alibi and made sure his fingerprints would be nowhere at the crime scene. Afterward, if she and Julius were being as disloyal as he thought, as he'd seen with his own eyes, he'd take care of them both. Permanently.

They waited until they saw Zakarian's assistant walk through the garage to his car and drive off. Zakarian was now alone. It was time to move.

Veronica gave Fernandez a backward glance, then stepped into the elevator.

Veronica walked into Zakarian's customer room and rang the bell. An older man with a round face atop an equally round body, receding gray hair, and oval glasses perched on the end of a nose with enormous, fleshy nostrils came to the bullet-proof window.

"Delivery," she called.

He didn't say a word, but opened the slot. "Give it here," he ordered gruffly.

When she placed it against the slot and it wouldn't fit, she tried to fold it with no luck. "What the hell did they send me?" Zakarian complained. "Let me see it."

She held it up to the window so he could read the label. "Okay, okay! Bring it to the door." He stood. "Hold it, you! Show your ID. Don't you know procedure?"

She held the ID against the glass.

"Hmm. You cut your hair," he said, eying the photo. "Looks better now."

She kept her expression taut as she tucked the card into her back pocket.

He opened the door just a crack and was waiting for her to slip the package through when she hit the door hard, knocking him backwards onto the floor. As soon as she did, she drew her gun. "Don't touch a thing!" she ordered, knowing there were panic buttons all over, on the floor as well as the walls. She grabbed the shoulder of his shirt, lifting and spinning him around so he didn't face her while she pulled him to his feet. "Keep your head down. Don't look at me!"

He raised his arms up even though she didn't tell him to. He'd seen lots of movies. "What the hell is this?"

"Unlock the cases and grab those trays." She handed him a pillowcase to put them in. "We're going out the back way. Fast!"

"Okay," he squawked. "Anything you say."

She knew he was thinking about the alarm on the back

door which, if opened when not deactivated, would cause the office to be surrounded with security and soon after, the police.

It was all right. She'd be out of there by then. With the diamonds. And if Fernandez and Julius were caught lurking around the hallway, so be it.

He stuffed several trays into the pillowcase. She looked at the time. Fifty seconds had gone by.

"That's enough. Move it!" She shoved him toward the back of the store. "Listen, old man. My friends expect me to kill you then let them in, but I'm not. I'll let you live. Got it?"

He nodded, quivering.

"I want you to run right down the stairwell to your car. If you don't run fast enough, my friends might catch us. Then, we're both dead. Understand?"

He turned a pale shade of green and nodded again.

"Now. Run!"

He ran, faster than she thought he could, literally jumping from stairs to landing as he descended the three flights to the garage. She stopped him as he got there, stuck her head out, and didn't see El Toro or the others. They should be riding up on the elevator by now; maybe they had already reached the second floor.

"Now!" she ordered, and he ran, dripping sweat, to his car, a blue Buick.

They jumped in, and he tore out of the garage, using his key card to open the door and get out.

One good thing about silent alarms even in jewelry shops was that so many people tripped them by mistake, nobody took them as seriously as they should. There was always a delay, an "is-it-real-this-time-or-just-another-false-alarm?"   moment, which she was counting on to give her the additional seconds she needed to escape.

"Hey!"

She didn't know if it was a security guard or one of El Toro's men who yelled, but she ducked, and told Zakarian to head for Ghirardelli Square.

He kept staring straight ahead, gripping the steering wheel, his foot heavy on the gas pedal. "Slow down!" she yelled. "Do you want to get a ticket?"

"You've got the diamonds. Let me go," the old man pleaded as they neared Ghirardelli Square.

"Shut up and drive."

As they reached Ghirardelli Square, she saw Max standing beneath the clock tower, just as he said he would. "There. Stop the car in the bus stop," she ordered.

"The bus stop? But what if a bus comes?"

She waved at Max, and he nodded back. She watched Zakarian stare unblinking at Max while not daring to glance at her again. He remembered her warning. His voice quaked as he whispered, "Please let me go."

"Ask him. He's the boss." She then swiveled toward the jeweler and smacked the butt of her Smith and Wesson hard against his temple. He slumped against the driver's door.

Clutching the bag with the diamonds, she jumped out of the car and ran down the hill, away from the clock tower.

People in the busy tourist area began to put together what had happened, and some began yelling and screaming. Veronica reached the spot where she'd left Dennis's Prius and in seconds was pulling away. She wove around the busy traffic, ran a red light, and somehow managed to find enough space open on the roadway to quickly leave. In the rearview mirror, she could see Max's diminishing figure as he ran after her. She smiled. *Perfect!*

18

Julius kept his head facing straight ahead, only his eyeballs swiveled toward Fernandez. Once again in the limo, they'd ridden around endlessly for hours as El Toro brooded over the disaster the diamond heist had been.

That afternoon, as planned, exactly one minute after Veronica rode up the elevator and then sent it back down to the basement, they had held the elevator doors open and waited for the exact right time. When it came, they'd stepped onto the elevator and hit floor two, where Zakarian's Jewelers was located.

They had expected to ride up to the second floor, but the elevator stopped on the ground floor. Someone in a wheelchair wanted to get on, but the person pushing the chair kept getting the wheels skewed in the wrong direction, and the chair didn't roll properly. It was half in, half out, when El Toro and Julius yelled at them that there was no room, to back up and wait until the elevator was empty. By the time they'd pushed the wheelchair out of the elevator car, the security guards had reached it and stopped the elevator, shouting that there had been a robbery attempt on an upper floor of the building, so no one could go up there.

El Toro and Julius simply stepped off the elevator, thanked the security guards for warning them and, as nonchalantly as possible, walked out of the building.

They abandoned the van they'd stolen in the garage and hurried to the end of the block where Raymondo was circling the streets in the limo in case he was needed. Fernandez and Julius jumped in the limo while keeping an eye on the building they'd just left, expecting to see Veronica brought out, under arrest.

It didn't happen. As time passed, the realization struck that somehow Veronica had gotten away. She might also have the diamonds. El Toro's diamonds.

Julius feared Fernandez's reaction and was trying to think of how to get away when Fernandez suddenly turned red-faced and began to shout expletives. He was all but out of control, pounding his fists against the limo's interior when he realized Veronica had double-crossed him.

But as terrifying as Fernandez's anger was, his ensuing silence was worse. He refused to go home or to let Julius out of the limo. He refused to talk, or to allow Julius to talk, saying he needed silence to think.

Finally, after the sun set, Fernandez ordered Raymondo to head for the southwest section of the city, and once there, he told him to drive to the "special" place he liked.

Julius had no idea where they were going.

As they drove along the highway that edged the Pacific, Raymondo took a nondescript turnoff onto an unpaved road, and then stopped the car by the sand dunes.

El Toro faced Julius. "What do you think of this spot?"

Julius looked around nervously. It was desolate, quiet, except for the sound of ocean waves on one side and cars zipping past on the Great Highway. "It's peaceful out here, isn't it, Toro?"

"Peaceful. Yes, that is one word for it."

"We'll find her," Julius added quickly, sure Veronica was still on Fernandez's mind. "She can't hide from us."

Fernandez's fists clenched, his face darkening. "She can't hide. That's true. Not from me. And you can't either."

His nerves jumped. "Me? What do you mean?"

Fernandez's eyes were harder and blacker than coal. "Where are you planning to meet her?"

Sweat beaded on Julius's forehead. "Boss, what do you mean? I had nothing to do with this!"

"Get out of the car, Julius."

He quaked. "No! I mean, Toro, you've got to believe me."

"You *will* tell me where she is. Don't doubt it for a minute."

"But I don't know! I swear to you, I'm as shocked by her actions as you are!"

"Why, Julius, don't I believe you?"

Raymondo opened the door beside Julius and waited for him to step out of the limo.

"No," Julius cried. "No, please. Wait! I just remembered. One day I followed her—spying, you know. I never trusted her. Anyway, she was hanging around a small gift shop on West Portal. A place called, uh, Everyone's Fancy. Yeah, that's it."

Raymondo screwed a silencer onto the barrel of his Sig Sauer. Julius saw the look in El Toro's eyes. "Toro, please! I told you what I know!"

Fernandez stared straight ahead, no longer looking at Julius.

Hopeless, he got out of the limo and walked with Raymondo toward the water, a sand dune blocking the two men from the cars on the highway. Julius listened to the sound of waves, breathed in the fresh scent of the sea air, and stared at the beauty of the nearly full moon casting a beam of light onto the ocean. He'd watched this scene play out in the past. He knew that fighting, running, would only make things much, much more painful and would end with the same result.

And so he got down on his knees, his back to Raymondo, as silent tears fell from his eyes.

Keith Trammel rang the bell to Connie's apartment. He had to see her, to talk to her alone, and she should be off work by now. It couldn't really be over between them. She'd give him another chance; hell, she always had before.

If not, having an ex-wife who hung out with a 49er team member might not be such a bad thing. She always did have a soft spot for him, and if suddenly she was rolling in dough, she wouldn't be too selfish. It wasn't in her nature to be. She was a surprisingly good-hearted person—too good for him, if he were being honest. But he'd learned that honesty wasn't always the best policy.

He waited at the door. No response. He rang again.

Maybe she was out with her jock. He probably had a fancy car, fancy house, fancy servants. He wondered if the guy had learned yet how much Connie enjoyed making love in the morning, when the house was chilly, but the bed toasty warm? Or the way nibbling on her ear and neck turned her on?

Hell, but he missed her.

Still no answer. Damn it!

Deep in his pockets, he pulled out a key ring. He tried a couple before finding the one he'd been looking for. He unlocked the main door, then quickly climbed the stairs to the third floor.

Keith Trammel wasn't born yesterday. The last time the two of them tried to save their marriage, he'd stayed with her over a week and had copies made of the keys she'd given him. In the end, she decided it just wasn't working out.

But he'd kept the copy of the keys, not telling her about them. He knew they might come in handy someday. Like today.

He let himself into the apartment.

Nothing had changed since the last time he'd been there. Same old furniture, same pictures on the walls, same old-fashioned dolls junking the place up. She'd thrown out his beer bottle collection, he noticed. He'd been trying to save bottles from all over the world. They looked really cool, or so he thought. What did she know, anyway?

He walked into her bedroom. She'd made the bed. Now, he couldn't tell if it had been slept on just one side, or two. It was the queen-size bed they'd used. Damn thing nearly filled up the whole room.

He turned away. There were some memories he didn't want to have. He walked into the kitchen and found a beer in the refrigerator. Coors Lite. It figured. Connie was always worried about her weight.

When he had money, he was a Heineken man. Today, Coors Lite would have to do.

He picked up the beer, then settled down in the living room to wait for his wife, ex-wife, to come home.

A bit earlier that same evening, Max had dashed into Connie's shop a half hour before closing time. "Are you all right?"

"What are you talking about?" she asked.

"Nothing." He looked around the shop, then stepped outside and searched the street.

"What's going on?"

He tried to appear calm. No sense scaring her more than he probably already had, and no reason to think Veronica or

Dennis Pagozzi or whoever was involved in any of the madness he'd witnessed would come near Connie... was there? "It's all right. Just... I was thinking, why don't I take you to dinner? There's a Chinese restaurant down the block. I was paid a little yesterday for helping with some tax forms."

As she studied him, he was afraid she'd refuse. They had spent a pleasant evening, more than pleasant, together the night before in her apartment. She'd cooked a simple dinner, and they'd talked for a long time. He'd asked about her marriage, and about her sister, and how she'd coped with losing both. She didn't say much about her ex-husband, and that troubled him. He even was surprised at a pang of something—could it have been jealousy?—that made him want to say the guy had been a complete jackass to let her get away.

It had been a long time since he'd sat and talked, as a friend, with a woman. He'd enjoyed her company, her humor, her good nature. He thought she might ask him to stay, but she didn't, and he left a little before midnight.

He wouldn't blame her if she tossed him out now. Who was he to ask anything of her? But then she smiled and his heart lightened and lifted.

He stayed in the shop as she counted her income and wrote up the day's receipts, then locked up the shop. They went to dinner at the nearby Chinese restaurant and then decided to go for a walk. Max mentioned that he had never been to Lake Merced which he guessed was nearby. It was a couple of miles to the lake shore, so Connie drove them over to the lonely stretch of parkland by the sand dunes along the Pacific Ocean. Few attractions were in the perpetually cold wind and foggy area.

The moon was nearly full, and a few street light lit the pathway edging the lake as they strolled along it. He should have felt carefree and happy, enjoying this time with Connie.

Instead, his mind kept going back to the afternoon at Ghirardelli Square. What he saw had worried him.

Although he hadn't seen Veronica in three years, he'd been shocked when he finally saw her at how much she'd changed. She'd lightened her hair a whole lot. She never wore that much eye makeup and rarely put on lipstick. Now, as he looked at the woman beside him, it dawned on him what bothered him so much about Veronica's new look—she actually resembled Connie.

It made no sense to him.

Could it be chance? A weird coincidence? He doubted it, and that worried him even more.

He had to figure out what was going on here. Veronica and Dennis had a lot more going on between them than he had ever imagined, and Dennis knew Connie. Was that the connection? Something involving Dennis?

Still, his instinct told him Connie had no idea about any of this. He took hold of her hand as they walked. But, if Veronica was involved, it meant danger—and he was afraid the danger could extend to Connie.

In the distance, a sound, a "tick-thump," rang out.

Max knew that sound. He knew it from years of practice with a handgun at a shooting range, both without a silencer, and with one. He'd practiced so that, when the time came, he'd be ready. But now, his reaction was to run. His grip on Connie's hand tightened, and he turned off the pathway, plunging into a forest of tall pines and pulling her with him.

"What are you doing?" Connie asked, tugging at him to make him stop. "I'm sure that was just a car backfiring. Nothing dangerous. Stop, Max!"

He did stop and let go of her. She was staring at him as if he'd taken leave of his sense, and perhaps she was right. Although he was pretty sure the sound was a gunshot with a silencer coming from the area near the beach, there was no reason whatsoever to think it had anything to do with him or Connie. "I'm sorry. I'm just a little tense after..."

"After what?"

He ran his fingers through his hair. "Damn her to hell!"

"Damn *who*? What are you talking about?"

He couldn't even look at Connie, knowing the danger he might have brought to her. If Veronica had, in fact, made herself up to look like Connie, and it wasn't simply coincidental... he shook away the thought of what it might mean. "I'll make sure she doesn't get you, or me, if it's the last thing I do," he whispered.

Connie grew even more desperate. "You're scaring me, Max. Am I in some kind of danger? What's wrong?"

He shook his head. "I'm sorry. I'm probably just overreacting. It's a long story. All I can say is, be careful, and don't trust *anyone*, Connie. Do you hear me? Don't trust anyone."

He rode back to her apartment with her, and after seeing her safely inside and checking to be sure the apartment was empty, he left without offering any further explanation for his strange behavior.

When he turned to say goodbye to her, he could almost read the question in her eyes—when he told her not to trust anyone, did that include him?

19

From the moment Connie opened her shop the next morning, she kept one eye firmly fixed on the entrance, wondering if Max would show up, and then wondering why she cared. She scarcely slept last night after his nervousness at Lake Merced and his frightening words about some woman. She didn't need to be Einstein to recognize he thought he'd heard a gunshot and then spoke of making sure "she" didn't get Connie or him.

Who was he talking about? Why was Max in danger, and why was she as well? It was as if she'd found herself in a horror movie. *The Zombies of Lake Merced* or something. What was with the guy?

In the light of day, she decided Max was just being melodramatic. No one was after her, and if Max was in trouble with a woman, that was his problem, not hers. The less she heard from him, the better off she'd be.

Still, she had to admit, two nights ago at her house, and last evening, before her life catapulted into the Twilight Zone, she'd enjoyed his company more than any man she'd met in a long, long time. To begin with, he was a good listener. Sometimes, just having someone listen with no criticism and no advice was of more benefit than all the well-intentioned suggestions in the world.

Curiosity caused her to call another stockbroker. To her amazement, Geostar Biotechnologies was now selling at six dollars a share, a three hundred percent increase over the last report.

If she'd put two hundred dollars into Max's recommendation, she'd have six hundred now. As she contemplated how many porcelain figurines she'd have to sell to make a four hundred dollar profit, she felt a little queasy.

How could he have known the stock would soar that way?

Helen Melinger stuck her head in the shop. "I'm closing up early today. Got a crick in my shoulder, can't get nothing done. If anyone comes by upset, just tell them to keep their shirt on, and I'll be back tomorrow." She looked from one end of the shop to the other.

"What are you looking for?" Connie asked.

"Want to make sure Angie's not here with any more male friends. The last one should have been pinned like a bug on a display board."

Connie grinned. "Stan's not really so bad."

"Not if you like someone with the personality of kitty litter. Anyway, I noticed your sister hanging around," Helen added. "That must be nice for you."

Thoughts of Tiffany rocked Connie. "What are you saying? My sister is dead."

"I'm so sorry! I had no idea." Helen looked abashed. "The gal I saw looks so much like you, I'd assumed... she's a cousin, maybe?"

"I don't have any cousins either."

"Hmm. Well, whoever she was, she looks enough like you to have fooled me. It's the hair, I guess—exact same style and color. Anyway, like I said, I'm out of here. Stay cool."

"So long, Helen."

The door chimed throughout the day as more customers than she'd seen in ages came in. But Max wasn't one of them.

Paavo couldn't take much more of this.

Angie varied the time of what was becoming her daily food contribution to the SFPD Homicide Division. Today, it was afternoon—around break time.

Paavo would have asked her to stop sending treats to the office the way Lt. Hollins had requested, but it was the sort of thing he needed to explain in person and she'd spent last evening at her parents' house. He passed on joining her, knowing she and her mother wanted to talk all things wedding.

Now, as he and Yosh returned to Homicide from testifying in court, the bureau was empty. On the desk at the front of the room stood an open pastry box and a cake box.

Both had been picked clean. Yosh scoured each one, as if hoping a piece of napoleon had been stuck under the lid or in the folds. No such luck.

Paavo looked around for Lt. Hollins and was relieved when he didn't see him. He quickly broke down the boxes, making them as small as he could and stuffing them into a wastebasket. If Hollins hadn't spotted them, maybe no harm done. Or, less harm.

While Yosh got himself a cup of coffee, Paavo returned to his desk. On it was a slice of a fancy cake in three layers, with almonds on the side and chocolate on top. The layers looked more like meringue than regular cake. The thought surprised him. He'd obviously paid more attention to Angie's talk about desserts than he'd ever would have imagined. With a shake of the head, he pushed the cake aside as he picked up a message from the Robbery detail.

The counterfeit autographed sporting goods they'd found matched items Robbery had gotten complaints about. A number of people had been scammed by the fakes. Finger prints had been lifted off the boxes and Robbery would soon go after whoever was behind the ruse.

"Good news," Paavo said, giving a quick rundown to Yosh. He realized that not only was Yosh paying little attention, but that his head had bobbed from his desk to Paavo's at least three times. No fancy meringue based cake graced his desk.

Yosh, who loved sweets more than anyone he knew—except maybe Angie's neighbor, Stan—looked so crestfallen Paavo wouldn't have been surprised to see tears start to roll down the big man's cheeks. "You take it, Yosh," he said, handing Yosh the cake and a plastic fork.

"No, Paav," Yosh said with forced dignity, raising his hands so Paavo couldn't hand him the cake. "It's your engagement. She sent the cake to you. Gee, I wonder what else she sent."

"I'm too full to eat any cake now." Paavo placed the slice on Yosh's desk. "No sense letting it go stale. Enjoy it."

"You sure?" Yosh asked, his eyes bright.

"Positive."

Paavo was relieved of any more argument when a call came in. A young woman's partially clad body had been found in a van parked in the basement garage of the Franklin office building, the same building where, the day before, Zakarian's Jewelers had been robbed. No one knew, yet, what the connection was.

Connie was glad to be home after her day at Everyone's Fancy. All afternoon she'd felt a strange nervousness in her stomach, a prickling on her neck, as if something terrible was about to happen. A couple of times she thought someone was watching her. Thank God, no phantom stalker came in search of porcelain figurines or stuffed toys.

Now, she locked the apartment door, checking the deadbolt to make sure it was strong and secure. Damn that Max Squire! He'd done this to her with his creepy ways. And Helen the shoe repairer's words about her "sister" lurking around only added to her uneasiness. Why did she have to get involved with Max, anyway?

At least she'd had the good sense not to let her feelings about him cause her to move too fast. A couple of times, she'd been tempted. He was the type whose looks grew on a person over time, especially when one got to know his personality, and how thoughtful and well-meaning he actually seemed to be.

But she'd been taken in by charmers in the past, which made her glad common sense prevailed.

For dinner, she dished out a big bowl of cherry-vanilla ice cream. Too much common sense was no fun.

She curled up in front of the TV and streamed a Hallmark love story, which she paid scant attention to, while scarfing down the ice cream with Oreo chasers.

Her mind wouldn't let go of Max. He was making her crazy. If she didn't watch out, she might become as insane as he was, then what would she do?

On an impulse, she went to the window and looked out. But there was nothing out there in the dark. She sighed and turned back to the coach.

That was when she realized that one of her best dolls, one with a hand-painted porcelain face and that had been her grandmother's from the nineteen-thirties, wasn't on the shelf near the front door. What had happened to it?

She remembered showing Max some of the most intricate and oldest of the dolls, but she thought she'd put them all back where they belonged, or close to it. He couldn't possibly have—

A loud knock sounded at her apartment door. That was strange because normally, she had to buzz people in.

Her heart pounded as she stepped slowly toward the door. "Yes?" she called, praying the deadbolt was as secure as she believed.

"Connie? Open up. It's me, Mrs. Rosinsky."

She recognized her landlady's voice and, relieved, unlocked the door.

Her landlady huddled on one side of the door opening, and two uniformed policemen stood in front of her. "Constance Rogers?" one asked, to her surprise.

Surprise immediately turned to fear as thoughts of all the horrible things that could possibly have happened to someone she was close to, assailed her. Her mouth dry, she said, "Yes."

One of them lifted a pair of handcuffs. "You need to come with us. You're under arrest."

20

Paavo had been working late on the murder of the woman found in the van. It didn't take long at all to determine she was the courier who had gone missing at the time of the Zakarian diamond robbery.

When Angie's phoned him with the shocking news that Connie had been arrested in connection with that same robbery, Paavo left Yosh at the murder scene to rush to City Jail to meet Angie and find out exactly why Connie had been arrested. Angie's version from Connie was muddled, to put it mildly.

Angie waited in her car until Paavo arrived, and then she got out and hurried with him to the jail. "I called my father's attorney right after talking to you. Maybe he's already bailed Connie out," Angie said, huffing a little as she kept pace with Paavo's long-legged strides. "What in the world is going on?"

"We'll know soon enough." Paavo showed his ID to the night guards and then he quickly located the clerk for the night magistrate.

"She's here," the clerk said, checking his logs. "In fact, if you hurry, you'll catch her in a lineup in 7-C."

"*What!* A lineup?" Angie glared at Paavo as if it was his fault. "What are they trying to do to her? Let's go get her out of here!"

"The arrest came out of the Robbery unit, so I'll need to talk to an officer there. We'll know more in a while," he said.

"I want to see this lineup." Angie whirled on the clerk. "Which way is 7-C?"

He pointed toward the right, down a long hall.

"Angie, why don't you wait here?" Paavo suggested, ushering her toward one of the benches lining the hallway.

"No!" She glared at him and the clerk still hovering near. "Connie's my friend and I want to know why the police arrested her. It just doesn't make sense."

Paavo led Angie near the room where the lineup was being held, explaining that she couldn't go inside. He could, and would let her know all about it.

She didn't like it, but there was nothing she could do.

Paavo turned to enter 7-C when Robbery Inspector Vic Walters stepped out. He looked at Paavo and a smug expression plastered across his face. "Hey, you Homicide boys are fast. Guess you heard we might have solved your case for you."

That wasn't what Paavo was expecting. "My case? What do you mean?"

"The courier. Hold on a minute." Walters began to make a call on his cell phone.

A sick feeling gripped Paavo at Walters' words. A thought struck him, but it was impossible. "I'm going into the line-up," he said.

"It's already ended. Cut and dry. Just a sec." Walters quietly said a few words into the phone. As he spoke, a man in his sixties or so, with a thick, gauze bandage on one side of his head, was led out of the line-up room, accompanied by a uniformed cop. Walters ended his call then quickly thanked the man for his help and said he'd be in touch. The uniform led the older man from the area and would see he got home safely.

As soon as the door opened, Angie was on her feet in search of Connie, trying to see around the men leaving the room.

"Isaac Zakarian, the jeweler, viewed the lineup?" Paavo asked Walters.

"He sure did."

Paavo's impossible idea was beginning to look more probable. "And the lineup was for him to identify the woman who stole his diamonds?"

"You Homicide boys sure are smart," Vic said.

"What makes you think the woman you arrested is the right one?"

Vic pushed back the sides of his jacket and put his hands on his hips, his chest puffed up like a peacock's. "Other than the fact that Zakarian made a positive ID right now, you mean? She killed the courier, dressed up in the courier's clothes, and stole half a million worth of diamonds."

"Impossible!" came a furious shout behind them. "Connie's no murderer!"

They spun around as Angie stormed toward them. "She's no thief either! Anyone with half a brain can see that! What's wrong with you?"

Vic raised his eyebrows at the angry woman, then faced Paavo. "She must be your fiancée. I've heard a lot about her."

Paavo scowled at Vic as he said, "Angie, this is Vic Walters, Robbery. Vic, meet Angie Amalfi, my fiancée." As the two warily shook hands, Paavo couldn't help but think how incongruous it was to be introducing Angie to a peer as his fiancée, while her best friend was being charged not only with a robbery she didn't commit, but possibly of a murder he was investigating.

"Connie Rogers is my dearest friend," Angie explained to Walters, visibly trying to calm herself. "This has got to be some horrible mistake!"

"I'm sorry." Vic's expression said he'd heard that one before. "But since the lineup confirmed our case—"

"Angie's right," Paavo said coldly. "Connie doesn't have it in her to do any of this."

"There's a man involved," Vic said out of one side of his mouth, angling his shoulder to try to cut Angie out of the conversation. "You know how nutso some dames get around a guy. She might be one of them."

"No way!" Angie said, once again proving how sharp her hearing was. "Not my friend." She was so annoyed she was practically hopping.

"Who's the guy?" Paavo asked.

"The jeweler called it. Six one or two, thin—hundred seventy or so, sandy hair, longish, wavy, too far away to see eye color. His clothes apparently seemed pretty grubby—jeans and an old overcoat."

Paavo turned to Angie. "Does Connie know anyone like that?"

She paled and then shook her head. More subdued now, she slid closer to Paavo as if for protection. "Let's talk to Connie, see what she says."

Paavo told himself she couldn't be hiding anything, but his suspicions rose. He turned again to Vic. "How bad is it?"

"Other than the positive I.D., you mean?" Vic asked with a smirk.

"You know how unreliable eye-witnesses are. Any evidence?"

"We're sending a team over to search her place right now for the diamonds."

"You have people going through Connie's things?" Angie shrieked. "And she's not even there to watch them? Paavo, you've got to stop them! What if they break something?"

"Angie, they're cops," Paavo said with a you've-just-gone-too-far warning tone to his voice.

"I don't care who they are! She has rights. Cops can't just go barging into her place and—"

"We got our search warrant approved when Zakarian ID'd her. That was the call I just made," Vic explained.

"You did?" Angie quieted down considerably.

Paavo asked, "What evidence led you to Connie Rogers?"

"A phone tip went into the jeweler's office, a message on his phone. Anonymous, from a phone booth downtown, next to Union Square. The caller, a woman, told us the apartment to go to, said we'd find the robber, her lover, and the diamonds there. But, so far, no diamonds and no Casanova. We already had a description of the robber from Zakarian, and Connie Rogers fit it to a T."

"So, you had nothing until an anonymous call to the robbery victim? That's strange," Paavo mused.

"Look, Rogers told Zakarian she didn't want to kill him, which goes along with you saying she's actually an okay sort," Walters pointed out. "She also said the guy standing under Ghirardelli's clock tower was the boss. Right after that, she clocked Zakarian with her gun."

"No way!" Angie muttered.

"Zakarian doesn't seem like the type who'd say something and not mean it," Walters said, addressing Paavo and ignoring Angie's comment.

Paavo shook his head. "Knowing Connie, this simply doesn't make sense."

Walters shrugged. "Maybe we've got something more."

Just then, the lawyer Angie had hired approached them. When he noticed Angie, his expression echoed the grimness of Connie's situation.

Paavo had heard of Luciano Matteo. He knew the attorney often worked for Angie's father and had known Angie from the time she was a little girl. A meticulous dresser, even at nearly ten o'clock at night, his suit showed no wrinkles, his shoes were glossy, and his shirt fresh and starched.

He held his arms out to Angie, and they hugged. She quickly introduced him to Paavo. "I'm so sorry this is happening to such a nice young lady as your friend," Matteo said.

"Can you get her out of here?" Angie asked, worried. She read the answer on his face, and her stomach sank.

"There will be an arraignment soon, but until then, there's no bail. I'm frankly out of my league here. I do corporate and family law, civil cases, people suing each other, that kind of thing. She needs a good, criminal lawyer. I have some people I can recommend."

"This case isn't going to be over quickly, then?" Angie asked.

He shook his head sadly. "Not without a break. Let's go see Connie. I'm sure she'll be happy you're here."

Paavo signed in Angie to join him and Matteo to the visiting room. Connie had already been made to change into an oversized prisoner's orange jumpsuit and paper slippers. She looked pale, confused and frightened. When she saw Angie, she flew into her arms with a sob. Angie's eyes teared up as well.

"I don't understand any of this," Connie said as they hugged. After a moment, she backed away and turned to Mr. Matteo. "Can I go home, yet?"

His gaze was gentle. "The jeweler identified you as the robber."

Angie was holding her hand, and Connie nearly crushed her fingers at this news. "How could he do that? I was at work!" she searched their faces, bewildered. Tears spilled down her cheeks.

"Let's all sit down," Matteo said, "and discuss this calmly."

Except for a wooden table and four chairs, the beige-colored room was bare. Wired glass faced the hallway, allowing the guard to view everything that happened inside.

"Since she's got to spend the night here," Paavo said, "you need to request that she be put in administrative separation. I don't know how she'd handle general population in the state she's in."

Matteo nodded. "Right. I do know about that, at least."

Connie and Angie both blanched and scooted closer together.

At the lawyer's tacit consent, Paavo asked Connie, "Do you have proof you were working yesterday afternoon between one and three p.m.?"

"Yesterday? Today I had a lot of customers, but yesterday... The store was open. I was in it," Connie said helplessly.

"Did anyone see you there? Any customers who could testify for you? Any cameras in your shop?"

"No cameras. My tchotchke aren't high on thieves' lists, so I never spent the money. But what about later? Around six o'clock, does that help?"

Paavo shook his head.

She thought a moment. "Anyone walking by could have seen the Open sign on the door."

"What about Helen Melinger?" Angie asked. "Did you have the door open? Did you talk to her?"

"Actually, the door was shut. The heating system isn't working well, and I was freezing."

"Connie, how many times have I told you that you need to make your shop inviting for people to walk into?" Angie cried.

Connie looked at her as if she'd lost her mind. "And find me sitting there blue with my teeth chattering? I don't think so!"

"Now isn't the time for this," Paavo interrupted. "What about the phone? Did you make any phone calls?"

Connie nervously flexed her fingers. "Between one and three? I doubt it."

"Do you have a computer in the store that shows you were on it doing some work during that time period?" he asked.

"I look at emails in the morning, and do accounting at the end of the day. I basically use my phone the rest of the day—mainly listening to podcasts if I don't have customers to talk to."

"How can you run a business without using a computer all day long?" Angie put her hands to her head in frustration. "What about your inventory?"

"What am I supposed to use a computer for? And if I don't have customers, my inventory isn't about to change!" Connie was growing more hysterical with each question she couldn't answer.

Angie rolled her eyes. Paavo frowned at her to keep quiet.

"What about this fellow who was supposed to be with you in this?" Mr. Matteo asked.

"Why do they keep asking me about—" Connie abruptly shut her mouth.

"About who?" Paavo asked.

Connie faced Angie, her eyes wide. Angie faintly shook her head. "No one," Connie said.

"Do you know what's going on, Angie?" Paavo asked, his jaw tight.

Angie stared at Connie, desperate for her to say something. She didn't. Angie glanced at Paavo. "How could I know?"

He faced the attorney. "Miss Amalfi seems to have lapses of memory at times."

"Yes." Matteo stroked his mustache. "It runs in the Amalfi family. But always for a good reason, of course."

Paavo made no comment about that, but turned to Connie. "You need to think twice before protecting anyone, because in the course of the robbery, the female courier was killed."

"Killed? You mean I could be tried for murder?" Connie's voice rose so high she could have broken the sound barrier. She looked ready to pass out.

"I didn't tell my client that part of the proceedings yet." Matteo sighed. "She was already so upset, I didn't think it would help matters any if she fainted."

Paavo was not so sympathetic. Both Connie and Angie were hiding something. They had to know how serious this was. "She had to find out sometime."

"I suppose she did," Matteo responded, eying Paavo with new respect.

At this point, Connie was crying harder than ever, and Angie burst into tears with her. The two men escaped.

Once outside, they stood in the hallway in mutual sympathy. The nature of the charges against Connie Rogers meant that if she were convicted, she could spend the rest of her life in jail. The only thing Paavo was sure of was that she was innocent.

"There's nothing we can do tonight," Paavo said. "I'll talk to the DA first thing in the morning."

"Then?" Matteo asked with some professional curiosity.

Paavo looked at the closed door of the waiting room. "Then, I'm going to take apart the case point by point, and find out who really stole the diamonds and killed the courier."

21

The San Francisco District Attorney's office was located on the third floor of the Hall of Justice, right below Homicide. The DA had a walnut furnished office to the right of the reception area, and the assistant DAs—the ones who handled 99% of the casework, were in a cubicle-lined room to the left.

The Zakarian robbery and Janet Clark murder case had been assigned to Assistant DA Hanover Judd.

Paavo had worked with Judd on many occasions and knew him to be a hard-nose, by-the-book guy. File folders, message slips, briefs, and a half-eaten bagel with cream cheese cluttered his desktop. After shared greetings, Paavo said, "I'm here to talk to you about Connie Rogers."

Judd offered a chair. He didn't answer right away. Handsome, ambitious and in his early thirties, a few years out of Hastings Law School, he was cautious to a fault, seeing the D.A.'s office as his most promising route to a political career. "We'll be pressing charges for the Zakarian robbery," he said to Paavo. "I assume you'd like to add in the murder of the young courier as well. You weren't thinking special circumstances were you? To go after a woman with the death penalty—"

"I'm asking that you take a little time before you indict her on anything," Paavo replied. "I know Connie Rogers. I have no idea, yet, what's going on here, but there's no way she could have been involved."

"She's a friend?" Judd looked surprised and put his pen down on the desk. "Sounds like some guy took part as well," Judd offered, tapping his fingers. "Maybe he masterminded it and she just went along. An accessory to murder, though, is equally guilty."

"Did Robbery find any diamonds in her apartment?" Paavo asked.

Judd's face closed, but meeting Paavo's direct look, he relented. "No. But that means nothing. She could have easily stashed them somewhere else. Or the guy kept them or got to them before we did."

"The jeweler's identification was weak," Paavo added. He was only guessing, but based on past experience, that was true in about two-thirds of the cases. "He 'thought' she looked a lot like the robber, but he couldn't say positively, right?" When Judd didn't protest, Paavo added, "Something about her face or her build bothered him, perhaps?"

Judd didn't deny it. They were both old hands at this, and there was little need for subterfuge or mind games. "What do you expect? Zakarian has a slight concussion from where she clobbered him. Plus, he was under stress." He sat back, and eyed Paavo a long moment before he decided to be completely open. "There's a possibility—although Zakarian wouldn't admit it—that his vision isn't the best. His glasses were knocked off when she pushed him to get into the room where he kept the diamonds."

The identification sounded even weaker than Paavo had imagined. He pressed his point. "Connie Rogers is as clean as they come. She's never been involved in any crime. Probably not even a traffic ticket. I'll bet she doesn't even fudge on her tax return. You're saying someone like that committed murder and a diamond heist?" Since Judd didn't stop him, he pulled out the big gun. "Someone whose own sister was murdered, by the way. Tiffany Rogers. You remember the case. It involved our very own former district attorney, Lloyd Fletcher."

Paavo watched the ADA's face turn gray.

"She's that sister?" Judd's voice cracked. He remembered the case. He should. It had rocked City Hall and San Francisco politics.

Paavo would never forget the case. He and Angie were in the early stages of dating—he had expected her to dump him after she was killed in the course of it. The only good thing for her was that the investigation had led to Angie and Connie meeting and becoming close friends.

"That's right," he said to Judd. "That case has no bearing on this what we're facing now, except for me to tell you that Connie has always been a law-abiding citizen."

"There's the phone call—"

"Called in anonymously. How much can you rely on it? A good lawyer could say she's being framed, being used to throw off a bunch of cops too eager to close a case."

"But if so, he'd have to answer why is Connie Rogers the one being framed?" Judd mused. "There's got to be something going on there. Her name wouldn't have come out of a hat."

"She looks like the real robber, obviously."

"Hmm. Next thing I know you'll tell me the robber is a third sister. Or maybe Tiffany, come back from the dead. Look, Robbery had enough on her to bring her in and the victim ID'd her."

"I don't know what the connection is." Paavo tried to hide his frustration and feared he was failing. "I'm working on it. The courier's death is my case. I'll find out who killed her, but I don't want my investigation stalled or the whole case going off on the wrong track if you indict Rogers and only later learn it was a mistake. I'm here to stop you from ending up with egg on your face."

Judd smirked. "Nice guy, aren't you?"

"We're on the same side in this." Paavo's words were firm and deadly serious.

"I know. Hell. Let me think about it."

Paavo wanted Connie out of jail. She was separated from the other prisoners, but the segregated area was no picnic. "She's not a threat to run, Judd. Let her go. She's innocent."

Judd's secretary buzzed him, and he picked up the phone. "It's Robbery with some new information," he explained to Paavo. "I'd better take it."

Paavo waited, listening to Judd's "yeses" and "I sees." Finally, Judd hung up and cast a stony glare at Paavo.

"Well, well." He rocked back in his chair, one foot up on the edge of his desk. "Robbery just got the security tapes from the basement parking area under the building."

Paavo stared at him.

He dropped his foot and jumped to his feet. "Damn it, Paavo! You wouldn't have come to plead for Rogers' innocence if you'd waited until you saw those tapes. They show Connie Rogers leading the jeweler to his car at gunpoint."

"Paavo will get you out of here," Angie said tearfully that same morning as she visited Connie. Angie sat at the visitor's chair on one side of a glass partition with Connie on the other, a small mouthpiece embedded in it for them to converse. This was much worse than the lawyer's meeting room, which had been fairly decent and Connie could freely move around. Here, armed guards watched them and Connie, her sweet friend.

"I hope so," Connie said. Glassy-eyed, she appeared numb with shock.

"He's at the district attorney's office right now. It should be only a couple of hours." Angie prayed her words would be prophetic.

Connie nodded glumly. She seemed to have aged ten years over night. "He believes I'm innocent, doesn't he? He looks so hard sometimes."

"He knows you. He gets that stone face when on the job. Don't worry. We're going to find out who's behind this. That's the best way to clear your name."

"If anyone can, it's you," Connie whispered.

"Connie, I need you to be honest with me. From the description of the man involved, he sounds like Max Squire," Angie said sternly. "I want to know what this is about. Who is he and what's going on between you two?"

Connie slumped in the chair, as if she could scarcely hold her head up. "There's nothing going on, not really. I thought he was a nice guy. Troubled. Interesting. What can I say?"

"You can say he's no good for you! You can tell Paavo about him!" Angie waved her arms with frustration. The guard noticed and stepped closer. "It's okay. I'm Italian." She smiled demurely, then quickly sat on her hands. The guard didn't smile back.

"Do you think he pulled this robbery?" Angie continued.

"I'm sure he didn't," Connie said.

"Why?"

"I've gotten to know him, that's why!" Connie cried.

Angie lowered her voice. "Then tell me more about him. Why is he hiding? Why doesn't he have a job?"

Connie thought a moment, then told Angie everything she knew about Max, including the money he took from her and his reaction to the backfire... or possible gunshot... near Lake Merced just hours after the robbery and murder took place.

Angie couldn't believe what she was hearing. "He stole from you when you tried to help him, and later you saw him, scared and nervous, just hours after someone had been murdered, and you still don't believe he was involved?"

"He's hiding something, yes, but I don't think he committed those crimes," Connie said, not sounding wholly convincing herself.

Angie sighed in exasperation. "The jeweler who was robbed identified Max as an accomplice of the woman who looked like you," she repeated, and then firmly stated, "You've got to answer Paavo's questions about Max."

Connie pressed her hands to her temples. "I'm so confused. None of this makes sense. He seemed troubled, as I said, but honest. A good man."

"You could be wrong about him, Connie," Angie urged.

Connie nodded, even more dejected. "Okay, I'll tell Paavo whatever he wants to know. But I still think Max is innocent."

The guard moved closer. Visiting time was over.

Later that same day, when Paavo stepped off the elevator on the fourth floor of the Hall of Justice after his meeting with the Assistant DA, Angie stood in the hallway waiting for him. She looked worried and scared and terribly sad.

"There you are!" she cried as she rushed toward him. No kiss, no flowers, no caffe lattes or French pastries. He almost wished them back. "Where have you been? Can we get Connie out of here yet? I can't bear the thought of her having to spend another minute in that jail! It's so depressing a place, Paavo! I feel so bad for her."

"Calm down." He held the door open and drew her into the elevator then pushed the button on the first floor. No sense taking her into Homicide with him. Not with the mood Lt.

Hollins was in. "I was just talking to the ADA. He's not willing to let her go yet."

"So he doesn't believe it's simply mistaken identity? That Connie and the robber look a lot alike?"

"Not yet."

They stepped off the elevator on the ground floor, but Angie stopped walking. "I just talked with Connie. There is a man involved. Max Squire. She swears he's innocent but something is strange about him. She's willing to tell you about him now."

"Finally!" he said. "Okay, I'd better go see her before she changes her mind. Now, you should go home and try not to worry. We'll get her out. We know she's innocent. I'll call you as soon as there's a break in the case."

After a quick goodbye kiss, Angie headed for the parking lot.

But she couldn't simply go home and bake cookies while her friend was in jail. She drove to Wings of an Angel. Earl stood by the entry stand. "Earl, I've got to find Dennis's friend, Max. I need to talk to him. Do you have any idea where—"

Earl pointed toward a far corner. Max sat at a table with piles of paper around him. "He's doin' our books. Tax time. Butch said he's good at dat stuff. An' Dennis is givin' us da money to pay him a good wage. Too good, if ya ask me."

"Thanks." She marched past Earl and got in Squire's face. "All right, mister. You tell me what's going on, and I mean now."

He jumped to his feet, standing nearly a foot taller than her. "Now? I don't..."

"Connie's been arrested," she shrieked, making up in volume what she lacked in height.

He sank back into the chair. "Arrested? For what?"

"Murder! And robbery!"

He looked dumbfounded. "Is this a joke?"

Angie folded her arms and glared hard at him. "I wish! She

supposedly killed a female courier and then robbed a jewelry wholesaler. She nearly killed him—she hit him on the head so hard she caused a concussion."

"She... oh, my God!" He said nothing for a moment as he seemed to ponder her words. Then, his voice hushed, he asked, "Why do they think Connie did it?"

Angie grabbed a chair, pulled it to the table where he worked, and in a lowered voice told him about the jeweler's identification.

"Don't they realize there can be other women who look like her?"

Yes! Angie thought he knew more than he was letting on. "Who?" she asked, leaning close.

"Well... anyone," he muttered, then fell silent.

"No. You're thinking of someone in particular, aren't you?"

"I was just speaking in generalities," he replied quickly.

"The jeweler said Connie had an accomplice—a man who fits your description exactly. He claimed she said he was her boss, right before she hit his head with her gun, knocking him out." At this news, Angie gave him a smug look.

"What?" His eyes widened.

"Now, frankly," she continued, "I don't think you'd be here shuffling papers if you'd just stolen a half million dollars in diamonds, but the police might not be so logical. Tell me what you know. Work with me on freeing Connie, or I swear, I'll call them and tell them you're here."

"The police mentioned an accomplice? My God! I think it makes sense now." He was ashen, his hands shaking as he rubbed his chin.

"What makes sense? What do you mean?" Angie was so frustrated she could have clubbed him with the receivables register.

Suddenly, he stood and piled his papers into a stack. "Give me time, Angie. I know who did it. I'll get Connie out of there."

Angie jumped to her feet. "You know? You were involved?"

"No! Not me." He shook his head, put the papers into a small cardboard box, and placed the lid on it.

"Why should I believe you?" she cried.

"Good question." As he grabbed his overcoat, he added, "Because I want Connie free." Then he rushed out the door, leaving Angie gaping.

She found Earl. "Have you ever talked to Butch or to Dennis Pagozzi about Max Squire?" Angie asked.

"Butch don't talk to me," Earl answered. "And Dennis says even less."

"What about Vinnie?"

"Vinnie had to go down to China... I mean, to da bank. Nobody knows nothin'."

Another stall job, and she wasn't about to put up with it. "Well, Butch will talk to me." She headed toward the kitchen.

"Stop! Miss Angie, you can't go in dere!" Earl's stubby legs pumped fast as he ran to the swinging double doors that led to the kitchen and hurled himself, arms stretched out wide, in front of them.

"Why?"

"Uh... da Board of Health says we can't let nobody in but da cook and da waiter."

"I've been in a number of restaurant kitchens. Besides, who taught Butch how to cook half the items on the menu?"

"I know, an' we 'preciate you. But you still can't go in dere. Anyway, you're a customer!"

"Not now. Now, I'm a consultant. Dennis has asked for my help, you may recall. I suggest you let me in there or I'll help Dennis expand this place to the size of the Moscone Center! And you'll be out of a job!"

He dropped his voice to a whisper. "I'll tell you da trut'. Dere's a problem."

"Do tell!"

"We got a couple cockroaches, and Butch put powder all around to kill 'em. He don't want nobody to see what's going on. Not even you. I'm sorry."

She put her hand to her throat. "Cockroaches? In the kitchen?"

"Shhh! He just saw a couple, so he's actin' real fast. He's standin' dere wit' a can of Raid and if he sees one, he shoots it. *Bam!* We don't want 'em to tell deir buddies to come over. An' you don't wanna see dem layin' on deir backs, wigglin' deir little legs in da air, an' strugglin' with deir last breaths."

Her mouth curled in disgust. "This is the truth?"

"Miss Angie, would I lie?"

"Then ask Butch to come out here and talk to me. It's about Connie. She's been arrested, and I've got to help get her out."

"Miss Connie? Arrested? Wait here."

He was back in a minute looking worried. "Butch is gone. He put all da pots on simmer and took off."

2 2

Paavo lived in a bungalow in San Francisco's Richmond district, a neighborhood of small, middle-class homes, not too far from Ocean Beach, but without the ocean view that would have raised the prices of the homes even more astronomically than inflation and lack of expansion space in San Francisco had already done.

Paavo had bought his house some years earlier, when the economy took a slight dip, and he could afford it. It was also affordable because it consisted of only three rooms and one bathroom, needed work, and didn't have a garage, which wasn't too bad since neither rain nor snow nor sleet nor hail could do any more damage to his Mustang than old age had already done to it. Nevertheless, he loved the house. So did Angie.

To an extent.

Angie's biggest concern about their marriage was where they were going to live. She wouldn't be able to fit her clothes into Paavo's place, let alone anything else she owned. And she knew Paavo wouldn't want to move into her penthouse apartment, which she was able to afford only because the building was owned by her father so he kept the rent "reasonable."

They had time; they'd work it out... somehow. Paavo's home had a good-size backyard. The house could always be expanded into it. Or, have an entire second floor added. Or possibly raise it to fit in a garage and basement room or two. Or do all three.

But now, Angie sat and watched while Paavo stirred and seasoned. She was so upset about Connie, Paavo had offered to cook dinner for them at his house.

He was cooking a Finnish dish for her called Karelian Hot Pot. It was a simple stew made with equal parts chuck steak, pork shoulder and stewing lamb, onions, salt, and allspice. It traditionally cooked in the oven for several hours. He fudged by putting it in a crock pot when he left for work that morning, and now was adjusting the seasonings.

Over the year they'd known each other, he had told Angie what little he knew about his family and that, despite the name "Paavo," which was Finnish for Paul, he wasn't sure what his ethnic background was. All he knew was when his mother went out, she often left him and his sister in the care of a neighbor, an older Finnish man named Aulis Kokonen. One of those times, she didn't come back.

Paavo was only five years old and his sister, Jessica, was nine when their mother vanished from their lives. Ten years later, Jessie was dead from a drug overdose.

Jessica knew more about their mother than Paavo did, being five years older. But she never told him anything about their mother or about Paavo's own father. All she confirmed was that the two of them had different fathers. Jessica's father was African-American. No one would say who or what ethnicity Paavo's father was. Jessica's only comment was that he definitely was not Aulis Kokkonen.

As Paavo got older and learned more about the world, he decided his mom probably made money walking the streets, and one night was either killed and her body was somewhere under the bay or ocean, or she met someone who convinced her there was a better way to live than to be tied down with a couple of kids and no money.

At this point, he didn't care which story was the true one. His birth certificate showed his mother as Mary Smith and his father as "unknown."

Aulis was the only parent he really knew, and since Aulis was Finnish, he decided that was good enough for him. Eventually, Paavo put his past behind him, except when it came to making a few Finnish dishes, like Karelian Hot Pot.

As he checked on their dinner, he began talking about Connie's situation. Although she had given him a complete description of Max Squire, she had no phone number, and could only tell him the homeless shelter she'd once gone to. But Max had left the shelter and so far, Paavo hadn't been able to locate the guy.

He also requested a search be made of the sand dune area where Connie and Max had heard what might have been a gunshot. Paavo held little expectation that anything would be found there, however.

Paavo also told Angie he had seen the surveillance video that showed the courier being hit by a figure wearing gloves and a black sweatshirt with a hood. That was probably a man, one strong enough to lift the courier into the blue van where the police later found her.

But the video also showed a woman getting into the van, and then, a bit later, that same woman, now wearing the courier's uniform, leave the van for the elevator bank. The video never got a clear look at her face, but what he could see did resemble Connie. Yet, to Paavo's eye, she looked thinner and more athletic than the Connie Rogers he knew.

A couple of minutes later, the Connie look-alike appeared again coming through the door from the stairwell while holding a gun on a scared Isaac Zakarian. The two got into his car and he drove them both away in an obvious panic.

Finally, Paavo declared his Karelian hot pot should continue to cook at least one more hour for the meat to become even more tender.

His work done, he put his arms around Angie, studying her face and the unshed tears he saw there. "Relax, Angel. We'll get her out. She's innocent. Once we find the woman who looks like her, we'll be able to prove it." She shut her eyes and leaned into him. As much as she wanted to enjoy the comfort he offered, all she could think about was the fear and loneliness Connie was enduring at that same moment.

Veronica walked toward Wings of an Angel. She was feeling good. Connie Rogers hadn't shown up at work that day. A little birdie told Veronica why. A carefully worded phone call to the cops from one of the few remaining phone booths in the city had clearly done its job.

Now, all she had to do was get the police off their fat asses and arrest Max. If he was at Wings of an Angel, she'd call them now. If not, she'd check the homeless shelter where he'd been staying. They could pick him up there.

Footsteps were fast approaching. She turned but saw no one behind her. Odd.

She kept going, suddenly irritated when she thought of the stupid cops who hadn't yet managed to pick up Fernandez or Julius. The robber and murderer were at the scene of the crime and they had somehow just walked away!

Now, she had those two losers to worry about. But she could handle them. No problem.

She thought she heard a noise. Stepping into a doorway, she

reached into her purse to assure herself her gun was in easy reach. But, still, the street was empty.

Nerves. That's all it was. Maybe because Fernandez had to be looking for her. She chuckled at how furious he must have been when he realized she had the diamonds and he didn't. She knew he would try to hunt her down. But he wasn't clever enough to find her.

More likely, her nerves were because of the courier. When she'd put the woman's uniform on, it was still warm from her body. She'd never worn a dead woman's outfit before—not knowingly. And she hadn't known Julius would kill the woman like that. Tying her up should have been enough.

She shook away the image and proceeded down the block. Some cars went by, but no other pedestrians were near. This wasn't a touristy area, but usually a person or two could be seen.

She concentrated on her situation. Dennis was the one who bothered her the most. She had to come up with a way to—

From the corner of her eye she saw a hand reach for her. She spun around fast, and he ended up with only the strap of her shoulder bag.

"You!" she yelled, jerking on it. He didn't let go, and the bag flipped over. The clasp opened, and the contents fell to the sidewalk.

The gun! She fell to her knees and lunged for it, but he was faster. In one quick movement, he picked up the Smith and Wesson and pointed it at her.

Drawing herself to her feet, she saw the cold, icy fury in his eyes. "You can't be serious," she said. She glanced from side to side, thinking that he would back off if she could get someone to notice them, but the streets were empty. Even the cars seemed to have vanished. Her heart pounded, and her throat went dry. "Put it down!"

He slowly neared, and she backed up, scared now. "Hey, let's talk about it, okay?" She tried to modulate her voice, make it low and husky, the way he liked it. "I know you're disappointed. In me. Us. We can fix that."

She looked around, searching for some means of escape. Behind her was an alley and what looked like an open door at the bottom of a flight of stairs. She needed to get down there, shut the door and lock it. She could do it.

"Talk to me," she said. "We were always able to talk." As she began stepping backwards, he followed.

He was blinking fast, and tears filled his eyes. A cold certainly descended on her. He was going to kill her. "You wouldn't do this to me. Not to me," she whispered.

Veronica's hand touched the railing that ran along the steps to the basement door. She grabbed it and spun around, starting to run.

He fired once, and then once more, even after she fell.

At first, Angie thought the ringing she heard was the oven's timer, but then she realized it was a phone—Paavo's phone, on the nightstand by his bed. She unwrapped her arms from his chest as he rolled to one side, grabbed his phone, and sat up. "Hello."

He glanced at Angie. "It's okay, Rebecca. What's up?"

Angie raked her fingers through her hair and fluffed it as she listened.

The shocked look on Paavo's face made Angie's blood run cold. Quietly, he hung up the phone.

"What is it?" she asked, imagining the worst.

"Probably just a false alarm, but I've got to go." He got out of bed and quickly began to dress. "If all goes well, I'll be back in an hour. If not, I'll give you a call."

"You have to go?"

"Yes." He buttoned his shirt.

"But what about the dinner you worked so hard to prepare?" Angie protested.

He picked up his shoes and socks and padded out to the kitchen. "How do you put the crock pot on 'pause'?"

Paavo hurried into the morgue on the bottom floor of the Hall of Justice. He didn't want to tell Angie why he'd been called here until he was certain about the information Rebecca had given him.

Rebecca and her partner, Bill Sutter, were the on-call inspectors that evening, so they got called to any suspicious deaths. Rebecca had phoned to tell him that the victim of a shooting, a woman with no identification on her, looked an awful lot like Connie Rogers.

Paavo knew Connie's lawyer had been working on getting her bailed out as soon as possible. He could have just called the jail, gone through a lengthy rigmarole, and found out if Connie was still there. But he didn't want Angie asking questions. Also, he needed to see the victim for himself.

If his worst fear was true, however, he'd return to Angie immediately. He didn't want her to hear it on the news or to be alone at such a time.

Rebecca saw him and waved him over. "Thanks for coming by. I hope I'm wrong. I've only seen Connie in passing a time or two."

He nodded.

"She was still alive but unconscious when the cops found her. She died on the way to the hospital, so the paramedics brought her here. She'd been shot twice in the back."

The body lay on a gurney awaiting autopsy, covered by a plastic sheet.

As Rebecca glanced at Paavo, she took hold of the edge of the sheet, and slowly, carefully slid it back to reveal the face.

Paavo's heart nearly stopped when he saw the short, blond hair. "Good God!"

The lowered sheet showed a face that was slack and colorless in death. "Is she Angie's friend?" Rebecca whispered.

He let out the breath he'd been holding as he saw the jaw line, the shape of the brow. The victim wasn't Connie, but someone who bore an unsettling resemblance to her. "It's not her."

"Thank God!" Rebecca answered, also sighing in relief. "We've got her prints. If they're on record, we should have a match soon."

The woman's clothes were askew and bloodied, as were her hands, and her face smudged from lying on the street. "Any evidence?" he asked.

"Nothing much. The CSI has already bagged what they could. The only strange thing was in her hand. It might be a factor, though it could be just trash found on the street, and she clawed at it just by chance."

"What was it?" Paavo asked.

"A matchbook. It was from a restaurant I've never heard of."

"Do you remember the name?"

"Sure. A weird name for a restaurant, frankly. Bill Sutter said it reminded him of an old, old song about prisoners wanting to escape. I don't know if you've ever heard it. It went something like, 'if I had the wings of an angel, over these prison walls I would fly.'"

Paavo nearly choked. "Yes, it's familiar."

23

When Paavo returned to Homicide in the morning, the fingerprint identification Rebecca had requested on the murder victim had come in. Rebecca placed a photocopy on his desk as well as her preliminary homicide report on the victim and the victim's prior file. Paavo turned to the prior file first.

Veronica Maple. Ex-con.

He studied the mug shot taken three years ago when she was arrested. An attractive woman despite her hard, cynical smirk, with features somewhat similar to Connie's except that her hair was longer and darker, and her eyes gray. He quickly read through her record. She'd been sent to prison on a three-year term because of embezzling from her boss, Max Squire. She'd recently been released, on parole, from the Women's Correctional Facility at Chowchilla.

He called over to Benson. "Where's Calderon? Your partner has been making himself scarce around here lately."

Benson grinned. "Last I heard, he was going to lunch with that tall, skinny blonde Angie brought over here. She calls every hour on the hour to talk to him. He's either fallen for her or he's going to kill her."

Paavo cringed. Knowing Calderon, he had an idea which it was. Calderon was divorced. His wife took the kids and moved to New Mexico, saying she couldn't handle being married to a cop any longer. He was bitter about life and everything in it, but Paavo couldn't say that bitterness came about because of the divorce. He'd been bitter before the divorce; after, he turned completely toxic.

Paavo turned back to the reports on his desk and read Rebecca's findings. At times, handling a homicide investigation was like putting together the pieces of a jigsaw puzzle. This was one of them.

Maple's eyes were gray, but she wore blue contact lens. Her natural hair color was a dark shade of blond, yet she'd dyed it light ash. Making herself resemble Connie Rogers, as far as he could tell, was no accident. The obvious connection between the two women was Max Squire— Connie met and liked the guy, once again showing there's no accounting for taste, and Veronica had embezzled from him.

So why would that lead Veronica to want to look like Connie?

But then, a woman who looked like Connie had robbed a jeweler. That was almost certainly Veronica Maple.

According to the jeweler, a man was also involved in the robbery—a man whose description fit Max Squire. Had Squire managed to fool Connie, and to an extent Angie, about his character?

Paavo rubbed his head. It just wasn't making sense.

Connie had met Max Squire at Wings of an Angel. The victim was found with a Wings of an Angel matchbook in her hand when she died.

A parole officer had shown up in Homicide looking for a

woman who'd skipped and allegedly killed a man in Fresno. The woman's name was Veronica Maple.

His jigsaw puzzle seemed to have all the pieces on the table and showing, but he couldn't yet see how to put them together.

Continuing with Veronica's file, he turned to her younger years. One of her cohorts, back then, was Sid Fernandez.

Paavo knew about Fernandez from the Gang Task Force. They'd come to him a couple of years ago, hoping to find a way to pin a homicide on El Toro since they'd so far failed to tie him to any drug dealings. Fernandez was smart, though. He'd covered his tracks well and scared his underlings into keeping their mouths shut.

Paavo also noticed that, back in those early days with Fernandez, Maple sometimes stated she was married but separated, and other times that she was single. Nowhere in the file did she give her husband's name, if there ever was a husband.

Maple was her maiden name.

Strange. No one had questioned her about it; no husband ever showed up.

Whoever shot Maple probably ran, but also might have hidden and watched as the paramedics picked her up. They would have realized she wasn't dead at the scene, and they might not yet know she had since died.

A strange cat-and-mouse game was going on. If the cat knew the mouse was dead, it would go away, but if it didn't, it just might hang around to finish the job.

Paavo walked into Wings of an Angel.

"Hello, Inspector," Earl said. "Would you like a table?"

"No thanks," Paavo said. "I'm here on business." He took out a photo, Veronica Maple's mug shot, and handed it to Earl. "Do you know this woman?"

Earl looked at it and swallowed. "Who is she?" he asked, not meeting Paavo's eyes.

"I was hoping you could tell me something about her. We were given information that she had some connection with this restaurant."

"I see." Earl swallowed even harder as he studied the photo a little longer. "If you got da case, it must mean she's dead, right?"

"Not everyone I investigate is a victim." Paavo carefully chose his words.

Earl grew increasingly nervous and handed the photo back. "I don't know her."

"I'd like to go back and talk to Butch and Vinnie," Paavo said.

"Wait, Inspector. You don't hafta do dat. Dey'll come out an' see you."

"No need. It's just a couple of questions."

"You wait right dere!" Earl dashed away. Paavo frowned and sat down to wait for Vinnie and Butch. When he two men arrived, they didn't look pleased to talk to him.

"I'm here about a case," he began. Although no customers were in the restaurant at the moment, he added "If you'd rather go into the kitchen, or someplace more private, that would be fine."

Vinnie glanced balefully at the other two. "Right here is okay." The three eyed each other, then each took a seat. Earl wiped a drop of perspiration from his temple.

"Do you recognize this woman?" Paavo asked, showing them the mug shot. "Her hair is now lighter and much shorter."

Butch was the first to back away, followed by Vinnie, then Earl. "Is she dead?" Vinnie broke the team silence.

"We're investigating her," was as far as Paavo would go.

"I already tol' him I ain't never seen her," Earl said quickly.

Vinnie scowled at him, then at Butch. "I've never seen her neither," he responded.

"Ditto," Butch added. "Why you askin' us, Inspector?"

"Something was found at a crime scene that might link her to this restaurant. We're trying to find out why."

"Sounds like a coincidence to me," Butch said, standing. "We don't serve no criminals here. An' if a dame what looks like her came in here, Earl would remember, right Earl?"

"Sure," Earl said, also getting to his feet. "Sounds like one of dem coincidences, don't you t'ink, Vinnie?"

"Sure. It's a big coincidence. Nothin' else." Finally, Vinnie also stood. "If that's all you want, Inspector..."

He stopped talking as he watched Dennis stride into the restaurant.

"Hey, looks like the gang's all here!" Dennis chuckled and patted his uncle as he traded hellos, then looked at Paavo. "I believe we've met—you're Angie's fiancé, right?"

"Right." Paavo half stood as the two shook hands.

"We ain't got nothin' for you today," Butch frowned at Dennis. "You may as well go home. *Now!*"

"Go? I just got here. I'm hungry." Dennis said, then paid closer attention to the expressions of the three owners and Paavo. "What's wrong? You guys look like you lost your last friend."

"I'm trying to find out about a woman," Paavo said.

Dennis froze.

"Here's her picture."

As Dennis looked at it, his face drained of color. "Did... did something happen to her?"

"I'm just asking about her. Do you know her?"

Dennis's smile was sympathetic, but without any warmth or brightness now. "Can't help you, I'm afraid. Well, I, uh... I better be going," he said, backing up. "I didn't mean to intrude. I was just going to say hi to my uncle. In the neighborhood and all. Later. You'll be around, Butch?"

"Sure, kid. I'll be here for you."

Paavo didn't answer. He watched the escaping Dennis with cold speculation, then said a quick goodbye to the three owners huddling nearby.

Dennis had just reached his Jaguar and was lighting a cigarette when Paavo caught up to him.

Dennis frowned as he watched Paavo approach, and he was the first to speak. "What brought you to Wings of an Angel looking for information about that woman? My uncle and his friends aren't connected with anything illegal, are they?"

"Just following-up," Paavo said. "You had an interesting expression when you looked at the photo."

"It's not every day I look at a mug shot. She a felon or something?" Dennis asked.

Paavo stared hard at Pagozzi. "If you know anything about her, now's the time to speak up."

"Why? What's it to you?"

"I don't want to see your uncle or his friends get hurt," Paavo said.

Dennis took a drag from his cigarette. "Some years back, a guy I know had a girlfriend. I think it was her. She ended up doing time. Some kind of money scam. Embezzling. I didn't really understand it."

"And?"

"And... nothing." He shrugged. "If it's her, it doesn't mean Max is involved. He's not that kind of guy."

"Max Squire?" Paavo asked innocently.

"Yeah." Dennis looked at him curiously. "I thought you knew him. Angie and Connie both do."

Paavo ignored the comment, and said, "Tell me about Squire."

"He's a good guy. Down on his luck right now, so I helped him out, got him some bookkeeping work with my uncle, a few free meals, that kind of thing. In fact, the woman in the picture not only ruined his career, but ruined his whole life. If it's her, she's bad news. Real bad. I don't know why a guy like Max got involved with her."

"What does Max look like?"

"Tall, medium build, I'd say. Dark sandy-color hair, long—needs a cut bad, brown eyes." The description was familiar—he needed to be sure Connie and Dennis both 'saw' Max Squire the same way."

"How did you meet Squire?"

Dennis sighed heavily and gave Paavo a you-aren't-going-to-believe-this look. "He was my financial advisor."

Angie had spent the entire day hovering near her telephone waiting for Paavo to tell her Connie was being released. When she heard a knock at her door, even though lighter than Paavo's usual hard rapping, she hoped it was him with good news.

Instead, she found Nona standing there with a glass bowl filled with chocolate-orange trifle. Nona was blinking back tears.

"What's wrong?" Angie asked.

Nona shoved the trifle at her. "You and your big ideas!"

They went into the living room, where Angie tried to calm her sometime friend down.

"It's bad enough that I once went to meet Luis for lunch—"

"Inspector Calderon?" Angie asked, stunned.

"That's right, and he showed up reeking of disinfectant and god-only-knows what from an autopsy room. Everything I ate tasted like formaldehyde. Then, when I thought he'd invited me to go on a hot date, we ended up at the morgue because he had to witness someone identifying a body. It took so long and was so sad, I excused myself and went home. But, I decided to forgive him, and invited him to my house for cocktails. Today, I worked so hard to make this trifle dessert—I wanted to feed him something that would put him in a good mood—but he showed up just long enough to say he couldn't stay because he had to go to question some people about an old woman found dead in her bathroom! She'd obviously died of natural causes. I mean, she was *old!*"

"That's the life of a homicide inspector," Angie said.

"His questions could have waited until after he ate dessert. I told him so—me or a meaningless investigation. And"—she sniffled—"he said, '*Hasta la vista,* toots.' Can you imagine?"

Angie just shook her head.

Nona threw her arms wide. "How could I have wasted my time with a man old enough to be my father—almost—with creaky knees, overly pomaded hair, a cranky personality... and who uses a word like 'toots'? This is just too mortifying."

Angie got out a couple of bowls and spoons. They drowned Nona's sorrows with layers of chocolate custard, whipped cream, orange slices and chocolate génoise.

But not even Nona's trifle could take away Angie's constant worry about Connie and the heaviness in her heart.

24

"I need to ask you a few questions about the day of the robbery, Mr. Zakarian," Paavo said after introducing himself as he stood in the doorway of the jeweler's home.

"Of course. Please come in."

Paavo walked into a beautiful Presidio Terrace home, in one of the most exclusive parts of the city—the area where U.S. Senators, a chain of former mayors, and other top politicians lived. It was a part of the city that Angie had her eye on to buy a house big enough for both of them as well as her clothes and shoe collection.

He couldn't see living in a place like this. He'd probably feel he should wear a powdered wig and brocade jacket just to go to breakfast.

The opulent living room was a riot of gaudy French furniture and oversized gilt-framed paintings and mirrors. Angie's parents also liked this very ornate style of furniture that cried "money." Paavo, on the other hand, preferred rustic and comfortable. Right now he liked Angie's taste: refined and not overblown. He hoped it stayed that way.

Zakarian showed Paavo to a sofa framed in cream-painted wood and upholstered in beige with gold thread embroidered in the pattern of leaves. He was unsure if he should sit on it until Zakarian plopped himself into a matching armchair. Between them was a delicately carved coffee table that looked like it might buckle if heavy cups were placed on it. "I want to know if this man is familiar to you," Paavo asked, placing a mug shot of Max Squire on the table.

After talking with Pagozzi, Paavo had pulled up the embezzlement case Veronica Maple had been charged with. It had a lot of information about Max Squire. He'd gone on a couple of rampages and had even threatened to kill Maple. No charges were ever brought against him.

Pagozzi had lost money when Max was embezzled by Veronica, but had recouped most of it. Squire's finances, though, were a different story. The guy went from affluent to homeless. Paavo wondered if he had come face-to-face with the women who had ruined him, and seeing her again drove him over the edge.

Now, Zakarian crossed the room to a cream and gold-edged sideboard, and pulled a pair of reading glasses from the drawer. "I need these, I'm afraid."

Sitting back down with the wire-frame glasses perched on the end of his bulbous nose, he studied the photo a moment. "Yes. I'm quite sure that's the man I saw. He looked a bit shoddier—his clothes were close to rags, and his hair was long and shaggy. When he and the robber nodded at each other, I was shocked."

"They nodded?"

"Yes. As if they were expecting each other. She said he was her boss. That was when I relaxed, and I thought she'd just get out of the car to meet him. Instead, she knocked me out. I never even saw the blow coming." He complained and touched the bandage still around his head.

"You identified a woman in the line-up as being the robber."

"Yes," he said hesitantly.

"I want you to look very carefully at this next picture, and tell me what you think."

Paavo handed him Veronica's death photo. It was the only one he had showing her with short, dyed hair. Zakarian stared at it a long moment, then handed it back to Paavo with a shake of his head. "She's dead?"

"Yes."

Zakarian drew in his breath. "She doesn't quite look like the one in the line-up. Are they the same woman? Of course, since this one is dead..."

"What do you think?" Paavo asked. "Is this the woman who robbed you?"

Zakarian grimaced and stared hard at the photo. "I'll admit, the two look much alike."

"What are you saying?" Paavo asked. "They can't both be guilty."

Zakarian placed the photo on the table, removed his glasses and rubbed his forehead a moment. "There was something about the woman in the lineup that made me hesitate. I don't know why, really. I was pretty much convinced it was her. But now that I see this one, I don't know anymore. My eyesight isn't that great without my glasses, so I mostly went by hair and general looks."

"Are you unable to distinguish between them?" Paavo eyed him closely. "This is a murder case, remember, as well as a robbery."

"I was scared." Zakarian rubbed his hands as if they were still chilled from all he'd been through. "The woman ordered me not to look at her. She had a gun! I tried not to, but there were flashes. But... but when I saw the young woman in the lineup, she looked scared. That jarred me. The one who robbed me didn't have a frightened bone in her body. So, I don't know.

It might not have been her. I just don't know for sure. I'm sorry."

"It's okay, Mr. Zakarian. We'll get back to you. Thank you," Paavo said as he stood to leave.

With this latest information, Paavo decided to go back to Wings of an Angel with Yosh. They had the good cop/bad cop routine down pat. All he knew was that something strange was going on in this restaurant. He hoped it wasn't murder.

Paavo didn't like the increasingly complicated Squire-Maple connection he was learning about, nor did it make sense that Butch didn't know about Max's background. At minimum, he would have heard if his nephew's finance counselor had lost a bundle of his clients' money due to an embezzling employee. Butch had to know a lot more than he admitted to. This time, Paavo was determined not to take "No" for an answer.

The lights were out as Paavo and Yosh passed by Wings of an Angel in Yosh's Ford Galaxy. It was eight o'clock on a Wednesday night. The restaurant was usually more than half filled on a night like this. Now, a closed sign hung in the window.

Paavo got out and checked the door—locked, and then the flat over the restaurant where the three owners lived. No one answered there, either.

Yosh decided to call it a night, and Paavo realized that, more than anything, he should be with Angie. She was home alone, worrying about Connie, and he hated that she was anything but happy during this special time in their lives.

Right then and there he decided the hell with Lt. Hollins' concerns about her gifts to the homicide squad. Hollins would have to deal with his inspectors enjoying the treats Angie sent to them. Paavo wasn't about to stop her; he was proud of her, her generosity, her good heart, and her fine taste.

She was the woman he loved; and she had actually agreed to marry him. He should have been used to it by now, but he wasn't. Each time he looked at her, the wonder of it filled him all over again.

But before going to see her, though, he needed to talk to Hanover Judd. The ADA was still in his Hall of Justice office and agreed to meet.

Paavo filled him in on everything he'd turned up since Veronica Maple entered the picture. Veronica was a known thief and felon who had made herself up to look like Connie, even to the point of wearing blue contact lenses. She knew Max Squire, who Zakarian had identified as an accomplice, and knew Sid Fernandez, who could easily have been the fat guy on the security camera tape. And she, herself, had been murdered. On top of that, Zakarian was now admitting he couldn't be sure if the robber had been Connie or Veronica.

The evidence they'd amassed made a lot more sense if it pointed to Veronica, not Connie.

Judd agreed. If no new evidence against Connie showed up, he would let her go in the morning.

Paavo called Connie's attorney and Angie with the news. Then, he drove faster than the law allowed to Angie's apartment.

"I knew you could do it!" she cried, throwing her arms around him and kissing him as he walked in the door.

He held her tight, enjoying the way she felt in his arms. "She's not out yet," he cautioned.

"She will be." She stepped back. "Stay right there. Don't move. I'll be back, and we'll talk."

He sat on her yellow petit point sofa in shirtsleeves, his jacket, tie and shoulder holster discarded on the antique

Hepplewhite chair, waiting for her to rejoin him. Talking was the furthest thing from his mind at the moment.

She walked into the living room carrying a big, colorfully wrapped present. "For you."

"A present? But why?"

"Just for fun. I ordered it before Connie's troubles began, and it arrived today. Anyway, it's just a little thing until... or, I should say, I'm having a such good time buying you things, in case you hadn't noticed, I couldn't pass it up."

He tore off the fancy gift-wrap. Inside was a football. He pulled it out and saw it had been autographed. "What does it say? It all looks like consonants."

"I think it's upside down."

He turned the ball over and studied it. "Elvis Grbac?"

"Remember when he was a 49er quarterback?" Angie said enthusiastically.

"No."

"That's right! Apparently, few people do. He backed up Steve Young, I've been told. Anyway, that's why this autograph is so rare."

Paavo was confused. "I see."

"That means it's quite valuable!" she explained. "Joe Montana and Steve Young autographs are a dime a dozen. But how many Elvis Grbac autographs are there?"

"Probably not many," he said.

"That's right. And this is a genuine 49er football."

"I see. This didn't happen to be from Dennis, or was it?" Paavo asked, carefully inspecting the ball and the signature.

"Yes! Did I tell you Connie once met his partner, Jonesy, in what Dennis hopes will be a lucrative business? I don't know, though. He knocked off over fifty percent for me. Not a great way to make money, though it still wasn't cheap, but I know the 49ers are your favorite team. Anyway, he said he was quite sure my fiancé would be stunned and amazed by such a gift."

Paavo immediately wiped the frown that filled his face. "He's right about that." Then he smiled at her. "Thank you, Angie. This gift was quite thoughtful."

25

Angie raced to City Jail first thing in the morning. Two hours later, Connie's lawyer walked into the waiting room and joyously waved a sheet of paper. "She'll be out any second. I've cleared her record. But she has to stay in town in case they want to talk to her again."

"Wonderful!" Angie cheered.

As promised, the door opened and Connie stepped into the room, a free woman once again. Angie gave her a crushing hug. Connie thanked her lawyer, holding Angie's arm like a lifeline.

Just then, Paavo entered. Connie's face fell when she saw him.

"Don't worry," he said. "I just want to explain to you and Mr. Matteo what's happening."

In a private interview room. Paavo told them about Veronica Maple's murder, and that he had gotten Hanover Judd to agree to keep her death from the press as long as possible.

Judd was a man with good law-enforcement instincts, and he trusted Paavo's judgment on this. Unfortunately, he had bosses, and newspapers could get nasty if they thought the news was being covered up, so the story could leak at any time.

"That woman looks like me?" Connie asked, incredulous.

"She dyed her hair, cut it like yours, was even wearing blue contacts," Paavo said.

"That's creepy." Angie shuddered.

"I have a picture of her," Paavo said to Connie. "It's a mug shot from some years back, but I was hoping you might recognize her and give us some idea why she wanted to look like you."

Connie took the photo he handed her. "I don't get it. And I don't think she looks at all like me!"

Angie took the photo from her. "I've seen this woman." She glanced from one to the other. "She was at dinner a week ago with Dennis Pagozzi."

"You're sure about that?" Paavo asked, remembering Dennis' denials about knowing Maple.

Angie looked at him as if she couldn't believe he was questioning her knowing exactly what the woman with Dennis Pagozzi would look like. "Of course."

"Did she have her hair like Connie's at the time?"

"No. It was long, like in the photo. A dirty blond color. She could have used a good haircut and stylist, frankly. And... I guess she got one."

Without another word, Paavo put the photo back in his breast pocket and stood. The others did as well. "Listen carefully, Angie," he said, "do not go near any of these people. Connie, you stay at Angie's place until this is over. Don't go home."

Connie gasped. He didn't have to explain.

"Before we go to your place," Connie said to Angie after Paavo left, "let me just stop at my store a minute. I've got some money in a safe there, some extra checks, and a change of clothes."

"I'll lend you money," Angie replied. "Aren't you tired?"

"I'm exhausted, but I need to make sure everything is okay at the store."

Angie could understand that. Connie was a businesswoman, the store her livelihood. Of course she'd want to check on it, and Angie couldn't deny her that.

Unlocking the shop's door, Connie stepped inside, Angie behind her.

Connie froze. "My God!"

The first thing Angie saw were rows and rows of empty shelves, followed by shattered figurines on the floor. Stuffed toys had been shredded, and the stuffing lay in clumps throughout the room.

"Oh, Connie!" Angie whispered. She grabbed her friend's arm, but Connie shrugged her off and walked directly to the phone. Somehow holding herself together, she called the police first, then her insurance agent. That done, she stared numbly at the mess around her.

Angie chewed her bottom lip, unsure what to say or do. Connie was emotionally and physically exhausted. This was sure to drive her over the edge to a hysterical, blubbering mass.

Amazingly, it didn't. By the time the police arrived Connie was furious at whoever had trashed her shop. The insurance agent soon joined them. Reports were made and pictures taken, the only snag coming when Connie told them she'd been mistakenly jailed at the time of the robbery. Angie practically dared them to make an issue of it. They didn't, and all but backed away from the two murderous sisters-in-arms as they left the store.

"Why do I *know* this has something to do with Max Squire?" Connie fumed when she and Angie were alone again. "First, he stole my money, then I was thrown in jail because I resemble some floozy he knew, and now the shop I've put years of sweat and blood into has been destroyed. I've had it with him!"

"That's the spirit!" Angie affirmed. "You have two choices: to cry, or to kick-ass."

Connie's eyes narrowed. "Where can I find a pair of combat boots?"

Angie high-fived her. "Watch out, Max Squire. We're coming, and we want answers!"

"Answers, hell." Connie put hands on hips. "I'm going to beat the crap out of him!"

They tore out of the shop, commandos on a mission, and jumped into the Lexus. "Put your seatbelt on, girlfriend," Angie said through gritted teeth as she cranked the motor. "This is going to be a bumpy ride."

Forty minutes later, they shuffled back toward Angie's car. Max hadn't used the Vallejo Street shelter's facilities for several nights.

"Now where?" Angie asked.

"I'm not sure." Connie sulked, disappointed, while Angie phoned Wings of an Angel.

"Earl said Max hasn't been there for a few days," Angie reported.

"If I find him and kill him," Connie spat out the words, "it'll save the taxpayers all kinds of time and money."

They got into the car. "All right, let's go through this," Angie said and then ticked off the items on her fingers. "First, someone called the police and said you robbed a jeweler. Then, two, the police searched your apartment looking for the diamonds, but found nothing. Now, three, someone has rifled through your shop. What if whoever did that is looking for the diamonds you supposedly stole? That would make sense, wouldn't it?"

Connie glanced at her. "Max? Could he have done that?"

"It goes back to the woman, that Veronica Maple," Angie said. "And she knew Dennis."

Connie yawned, and Angie could see that the adrenalin that kept her going up to now had fizzled. She needed rest, but Angie didn't. As she drove in the direction of her apartment, where she hoped Connie could finally get a good sleep, she vowed to help her friend no matter what it took.

The two women sat up for hours and talked deep into the night. Between having been in jail and then finding her shop trashed, Connie was too upset to fall asleep quickly. Eventually, talking relaxed her enough she was able to head off to the day bed in the den.

When Angie woke up that morning, she found that Connie was still sleeping. She guessed her friend would sleep quite a while and left her a note saying she'd be back "soon."

Connie's situation so bothered Angie, that she'd awakened in the middle of the night thinking about it and couldn't go back to sleep for a long time. She knew that Dennis lying to Paavo about having known Veronica Maple was important, and as she dwelled on that, inspiration struck. Finally, she was able to go back to sleep.

In the light of day, her plan did have a few holes in it, but since she had no other, she decided to give it a try. Luckily, Stan hadn't gone to work that day, because she couldn't have managed alone.

"What do I know about cleaning carpets?" Stan whined as he sat in the passenger seat of Angie's Lexus and pouted over her idea. The big coward didn't want to get involved, but Connie needed their help.

"You don't have to know anything," Angie said as she drove. "Put water in the tank, cleaning solution in the dispenser, flip on both the brush and suction switches, and then push the machine around the room. Just remember, you have to do the talking. He might recognize my voice."

"Well, I doubt he'd recognize you in that get-up," Stan griped.

She glanced at herself one more time in the rear-view mirror and shuddered. She'd wrapped a dark blue satin table-cloth over her head, shoulders, nose and mouth. She'd learned some time back from a Muslim girlfriend that the mouth-covering style was called a "niqab." She also knew what she was wearing wasn't correct, but she doubted Dennis Pagozzi would know the difference. She then left off her mascara but heavily colored her brows and eyelids with a thick black eyebrow pencil. As a final distraction, she made a big, black beetle-like mark by her left eye.

Under the niqab, she wore a long-sleeved black blouse and an old, full-length, baggy black cotton skirt that she'd borrowed from her neighbor, Mrs. Calamatti.

"If he were to recognize me in this getup," she answered finally, "I'd have to shoot myself."

"Maybe he won't be home," Stan said asked hopefully.

"All I can say is, I doubt he's an early riser. We take our chances. But this is the only way I can think of to get inside the house and look for evidence of what he knows or doesn't know. You clean the carpet. I'll do the rest."

"I don't know, Angie..."

She parked down the block from Dennis's house. She didn't think it would be believable for carpet cleaners to drive up in a new Lexus. Besides, veil-wearing women didn't usually drive their men around, but there was no way she'd let Stan behind the wheel of her new car.

"This is heavy!" Stan complained as he lifted the Bissell out of the trunk and onto the sidewalk.

"Don't put it down! We don't want the wheels and brushes to get dirty."

"Maybe you don't…"

Angie grabbed a couple of old sheets she'd put in the trunk and then picked up two handfuls of dirt from beneath a Japanese maple near the sidewalk. "Shut up, Stan, and follow me."

Dennis answered the doorbell.

"It's Happy Carpet Time!" Stan said, handing Dennis a business card Angie had run off on her computer. He lifted the carpet cleaner into the house. "We'll be in and out in a jiff, just like we promised."

Angie stayed hidden behind Stan's back, her head bowed, her arms around the sheets.

"Hey, what's this?" Dennis demanded. He was only a few inches taller than Stan, but about twice as wide, and a hundred pounds of pure muscle heavier.

As Stan tried to explain that he was there to improve Dennis's life, Angie darted past them and sprinkled a pile of dirt over the white carpet, then she remembered to twist her engagement ring around on her finger so Dennis wouldn't see the diamond.

"You paid for it, man," Stan said, finally. "Like, I'm just doing my job."

"I didn't pay for this," Dennis shouted.

"Yeah, you did. It's on our records." Stan pointed to a folded up piece of paper sticking out of his pocket. "Anyway, this place is a mess. Look at all the dirt you got in here. You're going to ruin your rugs if you leave it there. Don't worry, we're fast."

Dennis looked where Stan pointed, then up at the Arab-looking woman, standing demurely by the wall, looking at the floor and pulling her headpiece down even further over her forehead.

"I never noticed all that dirt on the carpet before," he said, eying Stan.

"That's always the way it is," Stan added nervously. "You don't notice until someone else points out the filth you've been living with. It's kind of that way in life, wouldn't you say? In and out, twenty minutes."

Angie cringed at Stan's sudden philosophical pronouncements and started to spread a sheet out next to the stairs to the bedroom. Dennis looked at her and scratched his head.

"How long did you say this would take?" he asked.

"Just about twenty minutes," Stan answered.

"You said I already paid for it?"

"That's right."

"I guess, since it's paid for..."

"Good."

As Stan plugged in the machine, Dennis escaped to the den.

Angie continued to spread sheets over the stairs. When her parents had their wall-to-wall carpets cleaned, the place was always covered with sheets so that no one would step on a still-damp carpet. It didn't make sense to put them on top of dirty carpets, but she was pretty sure Dennis wouldn't know that and was definitely sure Stan had no idea what she was doing.

Once upstairs, she snuck into Dennis's bedroom and looked around for anything that might tell her about Max. Nothing.

Another bedroom door stood open. Angie crept toward it, not wanting anyone to suddenly appear and find her snooping.

The room didn't have the unused look or musty smell of a guest room. The closet door stood open, one bureau drawer wasn't quite shut, and the bedspread looked mussed. Could this be Max's room? Was he staying at Dennis's house? Worse yet, what if the two of them had set up Connie?

The closet was empty. Opening the bureau drawers, she saw

they were all empty as well. A bathroom was attached, and she entered.

A hairbrush lay on the washbasin. Twisted in its bristles was ash blonde hair—as short and light as Connie's. She saw some clothing tags in the wastebasket and lifted them out. Two Liz Claiborne tags from Nordstrom's, size six, $149.95 and $79.95.

Connie hadn't worn a six since high school, if then. She was a snug eight on a good day, and generally a ten. What was wrong with all these people who said the two women looked alike?

So, Dennis must have had Veronica Maple staying at his home at the same time as he was making goo-goo eyes at Connie. The two-timing cad! And to think, she'd encouraged the two of them! Why, oh why had she ever meddled in anyone else's love life?

A cordless telephone was on the nightstand by the bed, a pen and paper beside it. Who still used those? But it had a digital display and several special features. When she hit the "last number redial" button, a number popped onto the display. She jotted it down.

A quick look in what would have been a third bedroom revealed a room filled with football trophies, footballs with dates and special achievements marked on them, photos, and memorabilia from Pop Warner to 49ers. Dennis Pagozzi, this is your life.

She pulled the door shut and headed for the stairs.

———

In the meantime, Stan had poured a little water from a glass into the Bissell tank, and then realized he'd left the cleaning solution in the car. Maybe, he hoped, he wouldn't need it. He wheeled the carpet cleaner close to the dirt Angie had put on the carpet, then flipped a switch. The brushes spun, and so he pushed the carpet cleaner over the dirt. Water shot from the cleaner onto the dirt and formed mud. More water, Stan thought, and ran to the kitchen for another glass full.

More water allowed the now diluted mud to spread. As he pushed the carpet cleaner, the once white carpet now had a peculiar brown tinge. Back and forth over the mud-stained area he went adding more water. The mud puddle grew, engulfing even more carpet. The only good news was that the brown tinge had faded to a light tan color.

Frantically, Stan rolled the machine furiously back and forth over the carpet, hoping the carpet cleaner would eventually live up to its name. But the slop—no matter its color—only spread further. His gaze darted every so often to the stairs Angie had taken, knowing she wouldn't be happy with him. With each run of the cleaner, he felt more and more like Cinderella being watched over by her evil step-mother.

Desperate, he now leaned heavily on the machine, hoping that would cause the cleaner to slurp up the mess like milkshake through a straw. It didn't. He must have pressed down too hard because the Bissell suddenly shrieked, gasped, and died, refusing even one more glug of the gelatinous mess.

Now what? Stan wiped perspiration from his brow, then headed for the kitchen, flinging doors, drawers, and cabinets open and shut as he searched for a cure-all. Panic grew.

Angie was going to kill him.

"Finally!" Relief and triumph filled him. He reached for the aerosol can labeled Easy-Off—Industrial Strength.

Exactly what the doctor ordered, Stan thought, snatching the container from the shelf and holding it close to his heart.

He sped back to the mud and sprayed the entire contents of the can onto the tan-colored mess. "Gotcha!"

He waited for the brown color to lift up and away, leaving the carpet clean and new and white again. Easy off, right?

Instead, carpet fibers began to quiver and shake. The mud started to bubble ominously. He watched, aghast, as Easy-Off plus water plus the carpet's poly-this and poly-that fabric, and God only knew what components were in the dirt, created a chemical reaction.

Swallowing hard, he watched a cloudy vapor rise from the swamp. The stench was unbelievable.

Triumph turned to horror.

He'd created a gas chamber.

Holding his breath, he flung open windows and the front door, praying Angie wouldn't come downstairs and the football player wouldn't turn him into a pigskin. Then he ransacked the kitchen for paper towels and anything else he could use to scoop up the toxic dump site.

On his hands and knees, he desperately scooped the molten muck into a light plastic bucket he'd found under the sink.

The center of the rug was gone, and in its place a crater. He peered down it. In some spots it was bare all the way to the hardwood floor.

The few surviving carpet threads at the crater's edge appeared to be writhing.

His hands and knees tingled ominously, and he jumped to his feet and looked down at himself. His shoes were pock-marked with fissures, and his slacks were shredded around his knees. He was being eaten alive!

"Stan!"

Angie's cry barely cut through his shocked numbness.

"What did you do?" she whispered, pulling on his sleeve, and looking toward the den as if praying Pagozzi hadn't heard her cry.

"Thank God you've found me!" he wailed. "Quick, take me to Emergency. I'm rotting!"

"But the carpet—"

"Who cares?" He waved his red, slightly swollen hands.

"Look at my hands! Plus, my pants are disintegrating. My knees are on fire. My shoes are frying off my feet!" He started to cry.

"Okay, okay. But how?"

"I found a spray—Easy Off, it said. I thought that sounded good."

"That's oven cleaner!"

"So?"

Angie didn't answer. Instead, she stared, slack-jawed at the plastic bucket, at the hole that formed at the bottom, and the muck that was starting to ooze out and eat its way toward them.

Just then, they heard movement in the den.

Stan grabbed the Bissell, Angie wadded up the sheets, and the two fled in terror.

26

Paavo arrived at Wings of an Angel when the restaurant first opened. No customers had arrived yet. He marched up to Earl. "I'd like to talk to Butch now. In the kitchen."

Earl looked momentarily stricken, but quickly pulled himself together. "In da kitchen? Sure, t'ing, Inspector. No problem." He waved his arm toward the swinging double doors and pushed one open wide. "Butch! You got company! Go right in, Inspector. It's okay."

Paavo gave Earl an odd look. Butch was stirring a pot of spaghetti sauce.

As Paavo entered the kitchen, Earl following, he and Butch greeted each other. Butch did his best to appear nonchalant, but his movements were beyond tense.

"I want to ask you about Veronica Maple," Paavo said.

Butch flinched. "I already told you, I don't know nothin' about her." He set the wooden spoon on the counter.

"Your nephew knows her," Paavo said.

Earl walked to Butch's side as Butch washed and dried his

hands. "Dennis knows lotsa people," Earl said, not very helpfully.

"He tried to deny it," Paavo added.

Butch's entire body began to twitch as he suggested, "Maybe he forgot."

Paavo wouldn't let up. "She used to work for Max Squire."

"The guy helpin' with our books?" Butch's voice squeaked. He looked ready to faint and turned imploringly toward Earl.

"Can you beat dat?" Earl cried, an over-the-top look of astonishment on his face. "I didn't t'ink Max coulda had somebody woikin' for him. He acted like woik is poison."

"And he ain't been around here for days," Butch added, now that he could breathe again.

"In fact," Earl said quickly. "We'll tell Dennis. We don't want his friend to come back here no more. How's dat? In fact, why don't you go tell him right now, Butch?"

Butch grabbed his jacket. "Sounds good. You hold down the place. I'll go find Dennis."

"Wait a minute," Paavo said. These guys were acting peculiar even for them.

"I'm sorry, Inspector," Butch said, fidgeting and studiously avoiding Paavo's eyes. "I got no information for you. Absolutely nothin'."

Connie was dressed, but looking tense and worried when Angie returned home, pushing the carpet cleaner ahead of her. Connie opened her mouth to say something about Angie's clothes and make-up, but Angie shook her head. "Don't even ask. You're better off not knowing."

Connie snapped her jaws shut.

Angie took a piece of paper from her baggy skirt and phoned the number on it, listened, then hung up.

"I believe Veronica Maple may well have stayed at Dennis's house a while. I phoned the number she'd last called from his phone," she explained. "It was a small hotel called the Madison. Since none of her belongings were at Dennis's—and if we can assume he didn't kill her and burn her things—she might have moved there. If we can get our hands on her stuff, it might have some answers for us."

"How do you propose we do that?" Connie asked with a frown.

Angie pulled a pair of Armani sunglasses out of her handbag and handed them to Connie. "Easy. Let me change and I'll explain everything."

Connie approached the desk of the Madison Hotel wearing Angie's dark glasses, Angie at her side, also in sunglasses, the two deep in conversation. "I think I locked my room key in the room," Connie said, only half facing the desk clerk as Angie blathered. "Can you give me another? Veronica Maple. You know me, don't you?"

"Of course, Miss Maple." He quickly created a new key card.

"You have the room right, I hope?" Her tone was sharp. Angie had convinced her that this was the sort of hotel where patrons expected to be recognized and remembered. So far, she was right.

"Room 15," he said proudly.

"That's right," she muttered, and took the card, pretending to be paying far more attention to Angie than him.

The two women hurried to the elevator and rode up, scarcely able to contain giggles and squeals of joy at how easily their plan had worked.

When they reached the room, Angie knocked. They didn't

want any ugly surprises. After a moment of silence, Connie unlocked the door.

Cautiously, they entered. The place scarcely appeared used, as if Veronica had dropped off her clothes and left. Opening drawers and closets, they began a meticulous search of the few jeans, tee shirts, one blouse, and a couple of bras and panties, plus a new Liz Claiborne outfit.

"Hey!" Angie was on her knees, peering under a dresser drawer she'd opened. Taped to the bottom was an envelope.

She yanked it free. Inside was a ticket from Bay Pawn Shop, plus a torn sheet of paper with about twelve numbers on it. "I wonder what these are?"

"Whatever, they must be important," Connie answered, still rifling through the closet. "Keep them."

"I sure will." Angie put the envelope in her purse. "I wonder what she could have pawned? I suspected Dennis might have given her money for clothes and even a hotel, but what would she need with a pawn shop?"

Connie reached into the pocket of a pair of jeans and pulled out a scrap of paper. A phone number was written on it.

"It was a phone number that got us this far," Angie said, picking up the phone and dialing.

After several rings the phone switched over to an answering machine which gave no identifying information.

"A dead end?" Connie asked, then with a chill, glanced around the too-silent room, remembering who it belonged to. "Sorry." She put the jeans down quickly.

"Where there's a will..." Angie replied thoughtfully, ignoring Connie's sudden squeamishness. "Let's go to the bank."

"Bank?" Connie asked. "What bank?"

Max watched as Angie and Connie enter the Madison Hotel. He knew Veronica's taste, and remembered that she'd always liked the Madison. When he asked the hotel clerk if Veronica was there, he learned she had a room but wasn't in at the moment. He decided to wait for her return and sat at a bus stop where he could watch the hotel's entrance.

But what did Connie and Angie know about Veronica? Why were they at her hotel?

When they left, he walked up to the desk clerk, who drew back at his scruffy appearance. "Is Veronica Maple in? Can you contact her for me?"

"I'm sorry. You've missed her again. Miss Maple just left."

"Was that her? The blond lady? A short brunette was with her?"

"Yes, sir."

Max said nothing more and headed out the door.

Lying at the bottom of the dunes, buried in the sand, was the body of a man, thin with black hair. The medical examiner and her team were already working on him, looking for clues as to the cause and time of his death. The body had been hidden under sand and rocks until a combination of buzzards and bad smells helped the police find the reason for the gunshot Homicide had told them was reported.

When the body was found, word had quickly spread through the nearby neighborhood of upper middle-class homes, and a crowd had formed. A dead body discovered in that part of town was rare, one that had obviously been a murder victim, rarer still. The uniformed cops had cordoned off the hill, and now Homicide, CSI, and the medical examiner filled the area.

Paavo and Yosh had obtained what little they could from

the scene, gave the medics the okay to remove the body, and now climbed up the steep sandy soil to the street above. The man had been killed by a single shot to the back of the head, execution style, and had been dead some five days. The area had no foot traffic to speak of. The crime mostly involved drugs, and the people involved weren't likely to report a dead body.

Disgust marred Yosh's usually cheerful face as he scanned the area, and the crowd. "God, but I'm getting sick of this." When it was clear the victim wasn't known to any of the onlookers, they were able to relax. They were laughing and smiling in a neighborhood block party atmosphere, as if this were a TV show come to life. "Sometimes it seems people are killed faster than we can catch the perps. It's a losing battle, Paavo."

"What choice do we have?" Paavo's voice was coldly rational. "We need to try."

"Maybe it's time for me to quit this job. I think I'd like my next job to be at Disneyland. Someplace where I can work with kids all day long—kids who still believe in joy and fantasy and goodness in life. Wouldn't that be a change? Man, listen to me. I think I need a beer."

Paavo nodded. "You and me both. Maybe after we get through with the prelims."

His partner grumbled grudgingly, but followed him toward the crowd. "That should be about six a.m. tomorrow morning," Yosh said, "the way these things usually go. What a time for a brew."

As the CSI continued their search for blood, hair, clothing fibers, and any other physical evidence, the medics slowly carried the body bag up the hillside.

A hush fell over the crowd.

The time had come for Paavo and Yosh to take names and talk to people. They had to interview the neighbors, on-lookers, and anybody else who might be able to give them a clue as to who had killed this man, who he might be—he had no ID on him—and if they had any idea why he had been targeted to die.

Suddenly, the tune "Here Comes the Bride" began to chime. Paavo looked around, his head swiveling back and forth as if searching for inescapable doom, before he realized the sound was coming from his pocket—from the latest model Apple iPhone Angie had given him. He yanked it out and answered, to the amused curiosity of the crowd.

It was Nona Farraday, wanting to know if Inspector Calderon was with him. He wasn't.

"Would you pass on a message?" she asked sweetly. "Just tell him, I'll try to be more understanding in the future. All is forgiven. Call me." With that, she hung up.

Paavo stared at the phone. Had Angie now turned him into a dating service?

Much to Angie's amazement, Stan Bonnette was in his office at Colonial Bank's headquarters when she and Connie arrived. He had the title of assistant director of supply maintenance, an honorary title if ever Angie heard one because the guy never did any work. His father being one of the bank's top executives, however, gave him job security.

Although there was a secretary's desk in front of his office, it wasn't being used. Angie knocked on his door.

"Come in," he called.

She walked in to find him with his feet on the desk, cleaning his fingernails with a letter opener. His desk was almost as spotless as the secretary's. One manila folder was on it. In back of him, his computer was on, the screen showing a game of solitaire. He had lost.

"Angie!" He jumped up. "And Connie. What a surprise. Did

you two come to take me out for a late lunch?" Suddenly his face fell. "You didn't bring Connie's shoe-making neighbor, Paul Bunyon, along, did you?"

"Relax, Stan. We're too busy to eat. We need your help."

"No one should ever be too busy to eat," he murmured, disappointed, as he sat back down in his chair and indicated guest chairs for them to sit on. "What can I do for you?"

Angie wiped the dust off the guest chair before she sat, then said, "We've got a phone number. I need you to find out who it belongs to."

He swiveled around to his computer. "You can do this on the Internet, you know."

"Not easily," she said.

He tried the Internet first, and sure enough, nothing came up. "You want me to go into bank records to find who this is?"

"Not Colonial Bank records, but whatever the bank uses to make sure a person's legitimate—credit reports—I have no idea. But you should know that much about banking, shouldn't you?" She glanced at Connie, who gave her a firm nod.

"And, after that, I'd like you to do the same for a man named Max Squire," Connie added with a sly smile.

Angie high-fived her.

Stan looked at his computer, then back at the two, and swallowed hard. "I haven't done anything like that... in a while," he said. "So it might take some time."

"Will thoughts of a home cooked meal help your brain to remember?" Angie asked.

His eyes lit up. "Definitely."

Angie and Connie nearly fell asleep as they sat, slumped in their chairs, and waited. But Stan was persistent. He even phoned a person in the technology department for help. He loved Angie's cooking.

Finally, he turned and faced them. They pulled themselves up straight. "The phone number belongs to Sidney Edmund

Fernandez. I've written down his address. The bank gives him a zero-credit rating. He has no bank or saving accounts, but he does have credit cards that he uses infrequently. He pays them off right away, so I suspect the zero-credit rating has something to do with him not exactly being a law-abiding citizen, but I'm not sure."

"Interesting." Angie tried to make sense out of the news.

"What about Max?" Connie asked.

"I have no address for him, zero credit rating here, too. But, if you go back four years, he had superior credit. His bank account had over fifty-thousand dollars cash, plus several two-hundred thousand CDs. He obviously had a lot of stocks, bonds, and real estate. The mortgage on his house was for over nine-hundred thousand, and he never missed a payment. He often put ten thousand on his credit card in one month and paid it in full the next. But then, he filed for bankruptcy, and everything disappeared. I show no credit history for him after the bankruptcy."

"Mercy," was Connie's only comment.

"That explains a bit about his attitude, doesn't it?" Angie murmured.

Stan looked from one to the other. "What time is dinner?"

27

Paavo sat at his desk in Homicide looking over the latest information he'd received. The sand dunes murder victim was an ex-con named Julius Rodriguez. He'd been killed by a bullet to the back of the head. Rodriguez had done time for dealing drugs and was said to have been the right-hand man of Sidney Fernandez.

Looking at the size of Julius, he well could have been the second man—Fernandez being the first—in the diamond heist. If so, who had killed him?

While pondering this, Paavo noticed a bald, stout fellow enter the bureau with Homicide's aide, Elizabeth Havlin. She walked him over to Paavo. "This is Parole Officer Chuck Lexington. He's looking for Inspector Calderon. Perhaps you can help him?"

With that, Lexington held out his hand to shake Paavo's. "I was Veronica Maple's parole officer."

Lexington... Paavo remembered he was the one who'd first talked to Calderon about Veronica Maple. This case was going around in circles in more ways than one.

"Have a seat." Paavo indicated the chair by his desk.

"Thanks," Lexington settled in. He took a breath, then let his words flow. "I talked to Inspector Calderon, but I never heard back from him. I've been trying to find out Veronica Maple's whereabouts. I don't know if you heard, but she got out of prison and, we believe, killed a man."

Paavo looked at him questioningly. "You've been here all this time looking for her?"

"No, not at all. But the case keeps going around in my head. I have a couple days off, so I thought I'd come back to the city and check if anything has been learned."

"Why does she interest you?" Paavo asked.

Lexington shrugged, looking sheepish. "I know it's odd, but frankly, I don't meet many felons like her. We talked a lot before she left prison. I found myself feeling sorry for her. She wasn't a bad person, but she got caught up with bad people, mostly men, who took advantage of her." He shook his head. "If possible, I'd like to bring her in myself. I can't help but think if I'd been there when she was released, I might have helped her avoid whatever caused her to go so wrong. I feel responsible, and I'd hate to see her get hurt. I know, you'll say she killed a pawnshop owner. Still... I don't know if I believe it. I think there's something more going on. Anyway, have you heard anything about her at all?"

"I do have some questions for you," Paavo said. The man sounded sincere, but Lexington had let himself get much too involved. The parole officers he'd met had all learned to keep an emotional barrier between themselves and their parolees. "Let's go to the interrogation room. It's more private." He nodded at Yosh, who followed.

The room had a metal table with two chairs. Lexington took one, Paavo the other. Yosh stood near the wire-glass window at the far wall.

"Why did Veronica Maple come to San Francisco?" Paavo asked.

"I think she had some unfinished business here. Something she needed to take care of. Maybe involving her old boss, Max Squire. The two absolutely hated each other."

"Oh?"

"He came to see her a couple of times in Chowchilla, and the guards said they thought he was going to go through the glass wall to get at her."

Paavo and Yosh's gazes met. "Any other visitors that concerned you?"

Lexington rubbed his chin a moment. "I left a message for Calderon suggesting he look into Sid Fernandez's gang. Fernandez and Veronica went back a long way. I was worried that she might try to contact him since he's in the city. She swore she was through with that kind of thing, but who knows?"

"So it seems," Paavo said. "Anyone else?"

"No. I don't think so." Lexington said with a sigh. "It's weird, her disappearing without a trace. I was afraid she might be dead. I guess I'll keep looking."

"What about Dennis Pagozzi?" Paavo asked.

Lexington looked as if he was ready to stand up and leave, but at the latest question, he leaned back in his chair. "How do you know about him?"

Paavo shrugged. "As I said, we're trying to be helpful."

Lexington gazed suspiciously from one to the other. "When they were young, Veronica was married to Dennis Pagozzi."

"Holy Moses," Yosh muttered. "We never uncovered that about her."

"Are you sure?" Paavo asked.

"They were only eighteen and went down to Mexico. Rosarita Beach. Dennis already looked like he'd be a pro football player and his family threw a fit that he'd tie himself down with a wife. The family first claimed the marriage wasn't legitimate, but the U.S. recognizes Mexican marriages. So then they managed to get the marriage annulled and wiped off the books. After Veronica realized half the money he'd earned playing football could have been hers, she fought the annulment, saying it was invalid, but it didn't work."

"How did you find that out?" Paavo asked.

"I told you, Veronica and I used to talk. I honestly thought she was just misguided, especially about money. Nothing in her background pointed to anything more serious, and especially not her being a murderer." Lexington swore. "If it had, I'd have watched her a lot closer."

Lexington had no further information for them. Since news about Veronica's death hadn't gotten out yet, Paavo and Yosh didn't tell him about it.

Angie and Connie rode to the Excelsior Street address Stan had given them, parked down the block and sat in the car, doors locked.

"What now?" Connie asked as they stared at the house. "We can't just walk up and say, hi, tell us about Veronica Maple. We're running out of time! This day is almost gone. Paavo said by tomorrow, they're going to have to let it be known Veronica Maple was shot to death on a city street. Then who knows what will happen?"

"All we need to do is find out what this Fernandez guy is all about," Angie decided. "We know he's shady and single. And something had to be going on with Veronica if she's phoning him at night from her hotel room. Whatever it takes, we're going to find out what's happening and dispense some justice!"

"That's what I'm afraid of."

Angie gave a long glance in Connie's direction. "Of course! You look like Veronica Maple, and she was his friend, possibly his *girlfriend…*"

"Not again, Angie. No! I won't do it. No way, no how!"

Paavo found information about Dennis Pagozzi on the Internet due to his position with the 49ers. Born and raised in San Francisco, attended Galileo High School, was given a football scholarship to USC in Los Angeles, and signed with the 49ers as a third-round draft pick.

He then turned to Veronica Maple's background. She was born the same year as Dennis, but in Sacramento, California. Moved to San Francisco when she was fifteen. From the address on her juvenile arrest records, she would have been in Galileo High School's jurisdiction. Although it was a good-size city school, the odds were excellent that Dennis and Veronica, both in the same grade, knew each other.

Veronica left San Francisco in her eighteenth year and went to Los Angeles. It would have been the same year Dennis went to USC. And easy enough from there to drive down to Rosarita Beach in Baja California and get married.

But in LA, Veronica's problems with the law began again, and the name Sid Fernandez showed up in her file as someone associated with her.

Five years later, the same year Dennis joined the 49ers, Veronica was back in San Francisco.

It looked like Chuck Lexington was right about Dennis and Veronica, whether they had a legal marriage or an annulled one, they obviously had kept finding each other in their younger years, and still did.

Pagozzi, Squire, Fernandez... and now, Julius Rodriguez could be thrown into the mix. Rodriguez, who was as thin as Fernandez was heavy—again, the feeling hit Paavo that those two had to be the hooded men involved in the Zakarian diamond robbery.

Paavo picked up his phone and called Inspector Vic Walters in Robbery. They needed to talk.

Walters looked over Paavo's information, nodding the entire time. He then showed Paavo his latest finding - a description of the guy who tried to fence Zakarian's diamonds. The man was tall, broad shouldered, scraggly blond hair, wearing ragged clothes. It sounded as if Max Squire had struck again. The usual fences wouldn't touch the diamonds—too hot to handle, they said.

Paavo and Walters looked at each other and nodded. They felt it in their bones; they were close.

28

"I don't like this one bit," Connie said, tugging with dismay at the hem of the two-sizes-too-small-and-therefore-skin-tight glittery purple sweater she was wearing. How did she let Angie talk her into these things? After Angie's latest brainstorm, they'd gone to the Stonestown mall and bought short skirts, tight sweaters, spike heel boots, frosted turquoise eye shadow and bright orange lipstick—the kind that turned practically fluorescent after being worn a short while. Then they drove to Connie's apartment.

Angie ratted her hair so that it stood out from her head in gnarled splendor. Connie's was too short to back comb, for which she was grateful. They then changed clothes, put on makeup with a heavy hand, and leaving Angie's Lexus behind, they now sat in Connie's aged Corolla a half block from Fernandez's house.

"All I want to do is find Max," Connie insisted, "not all this. He clearly had me completely fooled. When I find him, I'll simply beat him to a pulp."

"One leads to the other," Angie insisted, picking lint from the red midriff-baring angora she wore.

"I should be so lucky!"

"Now," Angie began, "remember, all we have to do is saunter up to the house, knock on the door, and say we were told he was having a party, and that we're there to party, *big time*. Got it?"

Connie looked sick. "Yes. Unfortunately."

Angie couldn't be more pleased with her idea. "Well, when he sees a couple of 'ladies of the night' so to speak, and that one of us—you—look so much like Veronica, he's going to be hot and horny and curious, right? So, he'll invite us in."

Connie scowled. "Lovely."

"Don't worry. I'll be right there. I'll protect you. But first, you've got to play up to him, sweet talk him, charm him the pants off him—but not literally. And then just *sli-i-i-ide* in a question here, and a question there, until you have some idea what the connection is between him, Dennis, Veronica, and Max."

"And what if he's trying to *sli-i-i-ide* you-know-what into me while I'm doing all this nicy-nice stuff?"

"If things get scary, I'll just say our pimp is outside, and he's livid. Then we'll leave."

"Angie, I don't think livid is a pimp kind of word. Use 'pissed.'"

"Whatever. Let's go."

"Wait!" Connie said, clutching a door handle with one hand and rubbing her stomach with the other. "I'm scared. I feel sick. I can't do it!"

"There's nothing to be scared of. I'm sure he's harmless. Just some creep Veronica hung out with, a little shady, but aren't most people?"

"What if I throw up on him?"

"That'll work even better than any threat about a pimp."

Just then, a limousine turned onto the street, and the two

stared, their mouths agape, as it pulled onto Fernandez's driveway. The limo looked as big as the house.

A large man, as wide as he was tall, got out and thumped up the stairs to the front door, the limo driver behind him. They went inside.

"Fernandez," Angie whispered. "He must have a lot more money than we thought."

"Why would someone who travels in a limo have anything to do with a deadbeat like Max Squire?" Connie asked, hunkering down behind the wheel. "I think we should forget this and get out of here."

"Chicken!" Angie cried. With that, she was out of the car and sauntering sexily down the street.

With a groan, Connie caught up, and began to saunter as well. They would have gotten there a lot faster if they'd simply walked, but Fernandez might have been watching from the window.

"Let's just take a look at the limo before we knock on the door. I wonder why he uses it," Angie said. The windows were darkened. She and Connie cupped their hands against the glass and tried to see inside with no luck.

"Where the hell have you been?" A voice bellowed. "I'm going to kill you!"

The two spun around. Fernandez huffed down the stairs toward them, waving a gun. It looked like a cannon.

"Don't shoot!" They screamed in unison. This wasn't the kind of greeting Angie was expecting. "We're just looking at your car," Angie explained.

"Yeah," Connie said, too scared to add another word.

"Hey," Fernandez said as he stepped closer. "You're not Veronica." He faced Angie. "What the hell are you two made up for, Halloween?"

Angie was taken aback, and tried not to look at the gun he still held. "We're here to party," she said indignantly. Had she gone a teensy bit overboard with their clothes? Must be the eye shadow.

"Is this some kind of game?" His voice was low, dangerous.

The driver stepped to his side, eying the two women. "Hey, they ain't so bad, boss. Maybe they are what they say. They just wanna see the limo, maybe meet the driver. Party." He faced Angie. "The name's Raymondo."

"You drive this monster? How cool," Angie said. "And you're right. We aren't bad at all once you get to know us."

Like a puppy on a leash, Raymondo's eyes begged Fernandez to let him go play.

Angie peered up at Raymondo and smiled. His tongue was too busy hanging out to form words.

She moved closer to him and turned so that he faced away from Connie. "Why don't you tell me about your drive shaft?" she purred.

This time, Raymondo didn't even wait for Fernandez's okay, but started talking. She paid no attention, simply wanting to get him out of the way so Connie could talk to Fernandez.

Connie's eyes widened with obvious terror as Angie glided away from her. She glanced from Fernandez's gun to his fat face and back to the gun again, and gulped. In a herky-jerky motion, she pointed at the gun. "I'm glad I'm not Veronica," she said with a forced laugh.

His eyes narrowed, but he lowered the gun as his gaze went to her very snug sweater. "You just came out of nowhere to party with me, huh?"

"Sure," she said. Angie's back was to her. "But why do you hate Veronica so much?" she asked. "Is there something I should know?"

Big mistake. She'd tried her best to be saucy, but obviously it wasn't her style because his fingers tightened on the gun's handle. "Who are you two?"

Connie jumped back, grabbed a startled Angie and pulled

her close. "We're nobody. Just being friendly. Forget it, okay? Let's go, Angie."

"Hey, I'm friendly," Raymondo offered loudly.

Fernandez stepped to in front of the women in a way that his wide girth blocked their path to the street.. "How did you two get here?" he demanded.

Connie turned to Angie to answer. It didn't make sense to say they drove there, but if she said they were neighbors, he might ask where they lived, and he might know she was lying. Her lips were dry. "The bus?" she offered.

"Get in the limo!" he ordered.

Raymondo, a lurid sneer on his face, opened a door. "Yeah! Good idea, boss. Come on ladies. After all, you're the ones who said you want to party." He laughed.

"No... no. We're leaving," Angie said. "Our... our pimp..."

Even Fernandez laughed at that statement.

She and Connie backed up, holding each other securely. When Fernandez stepped toward them, they bolted and ran into the street, hoping to get around him, the limo, and the driver.

Raymondo easily grabbed Connie's wrist, and a second later, his arm went around Angie's waist, lifting her off the ground even though her feet kept moving.

They screamed and tried to break free, but he was able to handle both with no problem and tossed them into the back seat of the limo.

The very next instant, the street turned into a sector of hell.

Sirens blared, car wheels screeched, and a force of men wearing black, head-to-toe SWAT uniforms, Kevlar body armor and shields appeared out of nowhere barking orders to Fernandez to drop the gun and freeze.

Feet pounded the pavement, there were shouts and the sound of scuffling, then, all was silent

Angie and Connie untangled themselves from each other

and cracked open the passenger door to see what was going on, Connie's head below, Angie's right above her.

Fernandez and Raymondo stood with their hands up, surrounded by police.

***

"I knew it was a set-up!" Fernandez yelled.

Robbery Inspector Vic Walters walked up to him. "You're under arrest, Fernandez. We've got you this time. Not only for the diamond robbery—"

"What robbery? What diamonds? I ain't got no stinkin' diamonds!"

"Yeah, right," Paavo said with a frown, stepping up beside Walters. "Also for the murder of Janet Clark, a courier employed by Courier's Unlimited."

"Hell. I don't know—"

"And for the murder of Julius Rodriguez."

Fernandez's face fell. "Where'd you get that shit!"

Paavo glanced toward Raymondo, who had also been cuffed. Guilt was written all over the guy's face as he looked at Fernandez. "I'm sorry, boss. They said I was an 'ac-ces-so-ry'. That I could get the chair just for driving you!"

"Shut up, damn you! So this was a set-up! I'll get out, and when I do, you're all dead men! All of you!"

"Did you also kill Veronica Maple?" Paavo asked.

Fernandez's eyes went wide with shock at the news. Paavo doubted he was that good of an actor. "What? She's dead? You can't pin that on me! If you're looking for diamonds, she's the one with them—and Julius was going to meet her, I'm sure. They stole my plan, took the diamonds that should have been mine! I'm innocent!"

"I don't think so," Paavo said, with complete confidence.

Suddenly, Fernandez's mouth began to quiver as the full

import of Paavo's words struck him. His voice was small. "They'd double-crossed me. I thought... I cared about her, dammit! She can't be dead!"

"Take them away," Paavo said to the uniforms who were there with a paddy wagon. He started back toward his car.

"Excuse me, Inspector Smith," Officer Crossen, a young policeman who had helped Paavo several times over the years. "I believe your fiancée is in the limo."

Paavo just stared at him. "What did you say?"

"In the limo." He pointed toward the passenger door. It had been pulled nearly closed, but not latched.

Paavo frowned, walked over to it, and swung it open.

Angie and Connie still cowered on the floor, curled up to make themselves small as possible. But then, big, brown, turquoise-shadow ringed eyes looked up at him.

"Hi," Angie said, her voice as meek as he'd ever heard it.

***

Angie nervously toyed with her engagement ring after Paavo left. She was glad she still had it. She'd never seen him as furious as he was with her and Connie for going to meet Sid Fernandez.

How was she supposed to know he was a murderous gang leader? Nobody ever told her anything! She'd assumed he was rich, had a few dishonest financial dealings, but was basically a harmless guy that Veronica had scammed—sort of like Max Squire but shadier.

How was she to know Robbery and Homicide had, minutes before, worked out a deal with Raymondo on the limo's phone, and that was why he'd brought Fernandez back home, saying the limo was overheating. The SWAT team had been called in just in case other gangbangers were at the house, and Fernandez refused to go quietly.

If a shootout had happened, as Paavo needlessly pointed out several times over, she and Connie would have ended up more holey than Swiss cheese. He didn't know that Angie's imagination, as she and Connie hid in the limo, had been far more vivid and hellish than any words Paavo used. Keeping herself from shattering into a thousand pieces was all she could manage as he ranted.

And Paavo never ranted—except when he'd been scared to death, such as that evening after he realized she'd put herself in what could have been the direct line of fire.

Finally, he left for Homicide to book Fernandez for Julius' murder and to begin some of the paperwork.

Angie was relieved by his departure.

Connie skulked out of the den where she'd been hiding. "Is it safe?" she asked, peeking around just in case.

"For the moment. Men can be so touchy!"

"Well—"

"Don't start."

Angie went to the kitchen and got a bottle of Louis Martini Petite Sirah from the pantry, where she had a small wine collection. She'd been saving it for a special occasion. Surviving a potentially deadly SWAT encounter was about as special as she could imagine.

The first glass was to settle their shattered nerves. They soon discovered it took the entire bottle to settle them. With the second, they were finally able to talk.

"We're two logical, rational people," Angie began, her head whirling. She put her glass down on the coffee table. "Surely, we can figure out what's going on."

"Uh oh." Connie drained her glass and poured herself another. "I don't want to hear it. I simply want to beat the snot out of Max Squire. Is that too much to ask? Nothing else. No more hotels, limos, or shootouts. Got it?"

Angie paid no attention. "You became involved in this

because Veronica Maple made herself up to look like you in the robbery. The question is: why would she do that?"

"She was jealous of my good looks?" Connie took a long drink.

Angie didn't comment on that. "But Veronica also framed Max—assuming he's innocent, which I think is a valid assumption."

"Innocent? Now you're on his side? None of this would have happened to me if it weren't for him! When I'm through with him, his only use will be as a hood ornament! I'll pulverize him. Tony Soprano him. Flat-line him!" Connie hiccupped and held her glass up for more.

"From the pieces I picked up around Paavo—I wish he wasn't so close mouthed—but it seems Max may have once been quite good to Veronica. He fell in love, but she embezzled from him. She went to prison, and when she got out she immediately came to San Francisco, but who knows why? Ah!" Angie sat up tall and faced Connie. "I've got it! What if she was jealous? Not of your looks, but of Max. Of you and Max together."

Connie forced herself to focus. "Helen Melinger told me about a woman she thought was my sister hanging around. That could have been Veronica spying on me!"

"Now we're getting somewhere." Angie staggered into the kitchen and grabbed a box of Godiva truffles. "This calls for the big guns."

They each took a truffle and ate thoughtfully.

"For Veronica, it must have been bad enough that Max was seeing another woman," Angie said, licking her fingers. "Having you resemble her—somewhat—was that much more infuriating."

"But Max and I don't have that kind of relationship," Connie said. "At least, not yet. What am I saying? *Not ever!*"

They both ate more chocolate.

"That aside," Angie said as she knelt down beside the coffee table and poured more wine to wash down the truffles. "Veronica needs money, right? So, what does she do? She finds her old friend, Sid Fernandez. They scheme to steal diamonds. She'll fence her share and get cash, and in the meantime, she'll set up you and Max to take the fall for the heist."

"Me and Max. What might have been. Why do I fall for these losers?" Connie laid down on the sofa, candy in one hand, wine in the other, and her head on the armrest.

"Max seems to think Veronica hid the money she embezzled from him, and that she still had it. But he must be wrong," Angie said. Since Connie took over the sofa, she sat cross-legged on the carpet and munched another candy. "I wonder if, for some reason, she couldn't get her hands on it. I mean, if I stole millions, I'd own a lot more than a couple Liz outfits. And I'd be on the first plane to Rio!"

"You're the big matchmaker," Connie mumbled. "How about a match with a guy who'll take *me* to Rio!"

"I got it!" Angie waved her wine glass. "Veronica was stuck, needed money, and was jealous, so she stole the diamonds, then called the police, and said you had them."

"But I don't have any diamonds. Only a zircon or two. Keith was too broke to give me an engagement ring. That should have warned me." She slugged back more wine. "I'm gonna kick his ass, too!"

"Wait, now we know why Veronica made herself up to look like you!" Angie said. "So Zakarian would identify you at the lineup." She backed up against the sofa, her legs straight out, ankles crossed, and then slid down so that her head lay on the seat cushions. She balanced the wineglass on her stomach, lightly holding it in place with one hand as she groped for the Godiva box with the other.

"Then, somebody killed her," Connie said, generously passing the box over after she plopped another candy into her mouth. "Who would have done that?"

"You mentioned Keith, that reminds..." Angie began, but then noticed the edge of a piece of paper under the sofa. It must have dropped. She pulled it out and saw the letter from *Bon Appétit*. "Hey, look at this. I got a job offer." She sipped more wine as she read. "A good job offer."

"Max might have killed her to get even for ruining him," Connie reasoned, as best she could after so much wine.

The words seemed to jump all over the letter as Angie stared at it. "I kind of remember several good job offers, come to think of it. How strange"—she yawned—"that people seem to want my help now. Where were they when I needed them?"

"Or Dennis," Connie offered, also yawning. "He might have been jealous of her and Max."

"Or, some other man in her life," Angie said, rubbing her eyes and putting down the *Bon Appetit* letter. "But, which one?"

Connie put her empty glass on the coffee table, then lay back and shut her eyes. "How could one woman have so many men, and here I am, dateless? The men in my life are so screwed up. Or, maybe it's me. I think I'll become a nun."

"You haven't met the right guy, that's all." Angie murmured sleepily. "Anyway, you aren't Catholic."

Connie suddenly giggled. "You're Ms. Matchmaker, and you came up with worse losers than I did on my own. No way I'll listen to you again!"

Angie was irked. "I wouldn't say that."

"I would!" Connie muttered, then fell silent.

Angie, thankful she was no longer being laughed at, also set down her wine glass. "I was just thinking, I've got a cousin you might like. He's a little older than you. Single. Good looking. Has money. How does that strike you? Connie?" she murmured.

Connie's answer was a loud snore.

And soon Angie responded in kind.

29

Angie awoke with her mouth dry, her stomach upset, and she had a splitting headache. The one eye she could open read 7:55 on her clock radio. Somehow, she and Connie had made it to their beds after waking up in the middle of the night.

Now, as she lay in bed, wishing her headache would go away, all the ugliness of the past few days rushed at her and she made herself sit up. Connie's situation was unjust, and, in part, she'd gotten Connie into it by her meddling.

The fact that Paavo was furious at her wasn't lost on her either. But she was pretty sure he'd calm down, eventually. Hopefully.

She stumbled down the hall to the den and shook her friend awake. Connie pulled herself up to sit on the edge of the bed in a stupor. Her eyes had dark circles, her skin was green, and her hair looked spiked. "We're going to go find Max," Angie declared. "Time to move it."

"I feel sick." Connie laid back down and pulled the covers over her head. "Anyway, I'd rather hear about your cousin," she murmured, then began to snore again.

"Which cousin?" Angie asked, tugging at the blankets. "Let's go."

Connie held the blankets tight, twisting them around herself. As Angie tugged, Connie slid along the sheets and nearly tumbled onto the floor. "Okay, okay! I'm up already." She stood, blinked a couple of times, then gawked at Angie. "You look like hell!"

"Gee, thanks!" Angie's head felt as if drum majorette try-outs were being held inside it. "I'm just trying to help, here."

"Well, you would have been more help if you'd listened to me earlier," Connie snarled as she headed down the hall. "I told you we needed to find Max, but would you listen? Nooooo. So we nearly got our hair parted by flying bullets!"

Her words stung. "Keep complaining," Angie said, "and I'll cook you some *soft-boiled eggs* for breakfast."

"Yuck!"

"With a great, big glass of *buttermilk.*"

"All right." Connie stuck her fingers in her ears. "I'm sorry."

"Topped with *extra thick whipped cream!*" Angie shouted.

With a groan, Connie clutched her stomach and ran into the bathroom.

Angie rubbed her own stomach. Her irritation had back-fired, and now she felt as queasy as Connie. In the kitchen, she made them both coffee and dry toast. If she never saw red wine or chocolate again, it would be too soon.

After showering and downing several aspirins, they both felt a little more civilized. Each donned a pair of Angie's over-sized, dark sunglasses, more to ease their headaches than to be incognito, and then headed out in pursuit of Max—two slightly *battered* guerrilla fighters.

Three homeless shelters and one food kitchen later, they sat in Angie's Lexus, ready to give up.

"He must have changed his name," Connie said, adjusting

the glasses to better protect her eyes from the sun's glare. "To Max Shithead, maybe."

"He was going to do Wings' tax statements. Maybe they gave him a few dollars in advance to get a room somewhere," Angie suggested. She wondered if wearing two pairs of sunglasses at once would help.

"He might be at Dennis's house," Connie said. "Let's call and ask."

Angie started the engine. "And take the chance he'd lie? No way."

"Go for it, girlfriend. Let's bust balls!" Almost immediately, though, Connie rolled down the window for a blast of crisp air. The rumbling of the car was playing havoc with her stomach. Angie rolled down the driver's side window as well.

By the time they reached Dennis's, both women were hanging their heads out the windows. It made driving difficult, but not as hazardous as the alternative. Anyway, their temporary misery would be well worth it if they could confront both Dennis and Max.

Their spirits sank when they found the drapes closed at the house. It was nearly noon. Dennis might still be asleep, Angie thought. He seemed to keep pretty late hours.

She rang the bell, and after a wait, knocked on the door. No answer.

She and Connie stepped out onto the street. The windows were all shut tight. Left of the house was a gate to the backyard, but it was solid wood and five feet tall. Neither was good at pole vaulting.

"We can come back later," Connie said, rubbing her temples. "And try again."

"That means we'd have to ride all the way back here," Angie wailed. Carsickness was nowhere on her how-to-have-a-good-time list. The potted ferns that adorned the front entryway gave her an idea. "Start looking," Angie said, lifting one plant and peering under it.

Three plants later, Connie found a key. She waved it at Angie. "Let's see if it fits."

"Try it." Angie watched Connie slide the key in the lock. "Only don't—"

She froze as Connie pushed the door open. "Don't what?"

Suddenly a loud shriek sounded, lights flickered, and an alarm clanged making their already aching heads jangle so badly a guillotine would have looked like an angel of mercy.

"Don't set off the house alarm!" Angie cried, too late, as the two clutched their heads and scrambled to her car to make a fast getaway.

"Have a seat," Robbery Inspector Vic Walters said as he sat across from Dennis in Robbery's interview room, a plain, windowless rectangle with only one four-by-eight table and four aluminum chairs around it. Paavo was seated beside Walters as an observer.

"We have a few questions," Walters said.

Dennis's face went white. "About what?"

"We want to ask you about Wallace Jones."

"Jonesy?" Dennis's Adam's apple worked and sweat broke out on his brow. "Why? What's wrong?"

"A stash of sports memorabilia was found not long ago in an old garage—signed baseballs," Walters explained. "Checking on them led us to other things, signed jerseys, footballs, and the like. Everything was traced to Wallace Jones. Mr. Pagozzi, did you know his stuff was all counterfeit?"

"My gosh!" Dennis cried.

Paavo had seen bad acting before, but this guy was beyond

dreadful. "He was going to be your supplier for the sports bar you were talking about opening," Walters stated.

"Hey, I wouldn't try to sell fakes in my uncle's restaurant, would I?" Pagozzi was all wide-eyed innocence. "I didn't know it was fake! If I ever found out, I wouldn't have gone through with the deal, all right. It's not against the law to trust a friend, is it?"

"That's what we're asking you," Walters said.

"But first, why don't you tell us about your marriage to Veronica Maple," Paavo suddenly interjected.

Dennis's head whipsawed between the two inspectors, his forehead glistening. "Christ! Why do you want to know about ancient history?"

"Why did you lie about knowing her?" Paavo asked.

"Is that what this is about?" His eyes clung to one, then the other. Finally, he sighed. "It meant nothing. I've forgotten her over the years. We were kids, in Mexico. It was for fun, that's all."

"Not if there's a valid Mexican marriage certificate," Walters said.

"It was annulled, all right?" Dennis cried. "It meant nothing. Nothing! I was only eighteen. I had a football career ahead of me. What would I want with a screwed up pot-head for a wife?"

"She did drugs?" Walters asked.

"Of course! Why do you think she spent so much time in trouble? She got mixed up with Fernandez and his gang. I couldn't handle it. I tried to get her off my back, but she kept coming around, and coming around..."

There was more to it. Paavo could tell he was holding something back. "She got under your skin, didn't she?"

Dennis's lips tightened into a white line. "There was something about her. What can I say? I don't know the word, but she was almost... feral. Yeah, that's what you call it. Like a wild tiger. Or better, a leopard. Sleek, sexy, smart. And when she set her mark on a man..." He shook his head. "I've never met anyone like her."

"Sounds like you still love her," Walters said.

"No!" He answered too quickly, too vehemently.

"You knew what she was up to with Max Squire?" Paavo asked.

"I never imagined she would do what she did! I was the one who told her he was handling my money and that of lots of other guys. Before I knew it, she'd taken him for millions. She was good that way, using men. All men."

Paavo noted that once Dennis started talking, he couldn't stop. It was as if he wanted to get everything about Veronica Maple off his chest.

"What other men?" he asked.

"How the hell should I know? She was in prison for three years. Ask the guards. She had all of them by the balls—literally. The same with Max and his clients." His mouth twisted. "Rich clients. Lots richer than Max, or me. She could have had any of them, but she wanted money and independence. Max saw to it she went to prison."

"She knew how to use you, all of you," Paavo said, pondering Pagozzi's words, Max's reaction to her, even El Toro's admission that he "cared" about her. "And then, she double-crossed all of you."

Dennis nodded, then shut his eyes against his memories.

"When she got out of prison, why didn't she just leave the country?" Paavo asked. "From the reports I've read, the millions she stole have never been recovered."

"How should I know?" With his elbows on the table, shoulders tight, he leaned forward, his hands clenched.

"You spoke with her," Paavo said. The strange way Butch, Earl and Vinnie had acted, it was a good guess that Veronica Maple had spoken with all of them.

Dennis looked startled, clearly not expecting the cops to

know that. "Look, we were kids together. When she got out of jail, she came here for a couple of days. She had to put her feet on the ground, you know? I let her hang out, gave her some money, and then she split. I know no more than that."

"Where'd she go?" Paavo asked.

Dennis chewed his tongue. "Why don't you guys ask Max Squire? Maybe he can tell you."

Paavo and Walters stood. The interview was over.

"Thanks for your cooperation," Walters said.

Paavo was tempted to let Dennis know Veronica was dead, but if anything, that would make the guy clam up even more than he had already. So he said simply, "Don't go too far, I'm sure we'll have more questions to ask you." And then he left.

30

After not finding Dennis at his home, Angie decided to go to Wings of an Angel and ask if Butch had any idea where Dennis might be. She expected that very soon Veronica's death would become public knowledge. She was surprised it hadn't gotten out already.

Connie was so upset after setting off Dennis' alarm system and having to run before the police showed up, she developed another migraine and went back to Angie's apartment to lie down, refusing to listen to Angie telling her she really wouldn't be arrested again for a "little mistake."

At Wings, Earl stood at the maître d's post, but no customers were at the tables. In fact, the tables weren't even set.

"What's going on?" Angie asked, looking around the restaurant.

"Butch is feeling poorly, Miss Angie," Earl said. "We ain't got no food for customers, so we're only doin' takeout, not da full menu."

"What are you talking about? You need a cook for takeout."

Earl blanched. "Well, Vinnie can—"

"No. Vinnie can't," Angie said, brows crossed. "The man has no sense of taste or smell. He'd eat cardboard. I've got to see this." She headed for the kitchen.

"No, Miss Angie. You don' wanna do that." Earl ran in front of her, his arms spread wide across the swinging doors.

She glared at him, but he wasn't about to budge.

She'd had it with people getting in her way, or trying to push her or Connie around. In one fast movement, she ducked under his outstretched arm, shoved the door open and ran into the kitchen. "Hey!" Earl yelled.

On a table were four closed Styrofoam containers of varying sizes, each with a name written on them. No food was being prepared.

"Where's Vinnie?" she demanded, frowning at the containers.

Earl shrugged.

She headed down the stairs to the storeroom. Vinnie was surrounded by several wooden boxes stamped with Chinese characters.

He was picking items out of the boxes and putting them into a Styrofoam container.

"There you are!" Angie cried.

He raised his hands high in the air. When he saw Angie, he lowered them, wearing a sheepish expression. "Miss Angie. You scared me." He put his hand behind his back and casually stepped in front of his worktable.

"What's going on here?" Angie cried, eying the boxes.

"You don't wanna do dis, Miss Angie," Earl said, now that he caught up with her.

"I'm afraid I do, Earl." She cast a steely eye on Vinnie. "Let me see."

Vinnie shook his head.

She pursed her lips hard.

Vinnie and Earl exchanged glances, then Vinnie lowered his head and stepped out of the way.

She opened a box and lifted out a red tube with gold Chinese writing and a long fuse attached. "Fireworks?"

Vinnie and Earl showed no expression.

Suddenly, it all made sense, and she slapped her forehead. "God help me. These are illegal in San Francisco! You three have been selling illegal fireworks from this restaurant. Are you *crazy?*"

"Da restaurant wasn't makin' too much money," Earl whined.

"We didn't do nothin' wrong, Miss Angie," Vinnie said. "I met a guy in Chinatown, and he needed help getting ridda some a his supplies. He bought 'em for Chinese New Year but the city is crackin' down on the firework sales, so his shop and others in Chinatown are bein' watched. But nobody's gonna think a small Italian restaurant is sellin' 'em. So we made a deal and we get twenty-five percent of the profit. We're just helpin' our friend out, and makin' a little extra money. It's not like we're doin' sumthin' wrong."

Angie folded her arms. "It doesn't wash, Vinnie."

He looked downcast. "I was afraid you'd say that."

Angie looked at the six wooden crates, each about two feet across and three feet long. "Hasn't Paavo been questioning you? Walking around back here? How did he miss finding all these?"

"Remember dat night we locked up oily?" Earl asked.

"Yes..."

"We moved dis stuff," Earl explained. "We carried it all back to Chinatown. After he questioned poor ol' Butch, we figured he was done wit' us, and we moved it all back."

Vinnie held his hands out, pleading. "With Butch being too upset about his screwy nephew to cook, how else was we gonna make money? You don't want us ta lose the place, do you?"

Angie looked from one to the other and shook her head.

"Let's get these out of here, right now. This is our little secret, got it? You don't say a word, and you don't ever do this again!"

"But what about makin' more money?" Vinnie bellowed.

Angie could hardly contain her exasperation. "You won't be making any money at all if you're back in prison or have to pay a fine so big you'll need to sell the restaurant!"

"I guess you're right," Vinnie said woefully. "Maybe we can raise prices for our meals."

"Maybe you can add a few more items to the menu!" She began removing fireworks from the containers and putting them back into the correct crate. "We might have to pay more attention to Dennis's sports bar idea, although I don't know how we're going to do that and keep the ambiance."

"What's ambiance?" Earl looked at Vinnie. "Can we eat it?"

Vinnie gave him a shove. "Dummy. She wants to make sure the place stays purty."

Earl harrumphed. "It's already purty. We can't eat purty."

"We'll figure out a way to increase foot traffic to the restaurant, but it'll be a legal way. Got it?" Angie asked, furiously sorting fireworks and putting them back in the proper boxes.

The two nodded, still just standing there.

"Pack!" she ordered.

"Can't we at least sell the ones we already promised people?" Earl asked. "Dey're comin' to pick 'em up—we don't wanna disappoint 'em."

"Get them out of here, right now!" Angie shrieked. The last thing she wanted was any more friends in City Jail.

All three of them were stuffing firecrackers back into crates when they heard footsteps in the kitchen at the top of the stairs, and then Paavo's voice calling out. "Hello. Is anybody here?"

Angie practically flew up the stairs, launched herself at him, kissing him and spinning him as she did, so that he no longer faced the stairs to the basement. Then she wrapped her arms around him again.

When she finally broke the kiss, Paavo was in the dining room. He looked a little dazed—pleased, yet confused—at what had just happened. But it didn't stop him from asking, "What's going on?"

"You need to stay out of the back of the restaurant," she explained, leading him to a table. "They're having trouble. Butch is upset and won't cook. Let's sit down. How did you find me?"

He glanced at the swinging doors, then sat across from her. "Connie told me you were here. I came by to let you know—"

Just then, a customer walked in, and up to the stand where Earl usually greeted people. Angie gasped then jumped up and stuck her head between the doors. "Earl! Get out here. Quick!" she roared before turning back to face Paavo with a sweet smile.

Earl plunged through the doors just as the customer began to speak. "The name's Agnos. I'm here for—"

"Yeah, I know," Earl shouted, cutting him off. "We ain't got no more."

"Oh? But I was told—"

"You was tol' wrong, buster."

The customer gaped a moment. "Will you get anymore—"

"No! Never. Get lost!"

He looked from Earl to Angie, then Paavo, who regarded him and Earl curiously. "Go? But I was promised—"

"Can't you hear? I said out! We lost our cook. No more nothin' here. Leave. *Sayonara! Capisce?*"

"Cook? But I don't need any—"

Earl ran around the stand and grabbed the customer by the lapels. "I said I want you outta here, mister. You got a problem wit' dat?"

The guy raised his hands and backed up. "No, no problem. I'm going. See." He ran out the door.

Paavo was now standing. He stared at Earl as if he'd just lost his mind.

Angie tugged on his jacket sleeve. "I told you, nerves are a bit frayed."

He looked at her, his brows crossed. Earl straightened out his suit and waddled over to them. "Some people really like Butch's cookin'."

Vinnie, who'd been peeking out of the swinging doors the whole time, came out when Paavo sat back down. "I'll lock the door," Vinnie said nervously. "We don' want no more disappointed customers. They might decide to torch the place."

Angie gazed at Paavo, all wide-eyed innocence. "You wanted to talk to me?"

***

Whatever was going on at Wings of an Angel, Paavo advised Angie to have no part of it. He walked her back to her car after getting a promise that she would go home and stay there. After yesterday's near disaster around Fernandez, he would tolerate no more ugly surprises. "You and Connie need to keep away from Max Squire and Dennis Pagozzi, both, until we figure out exactly what's going on."

"Dennis? Why?" She held his hand as they walked.

"Dennis was once married to Veronica Maple."

"They were married?" Her voice rose higher with each word.

He quickly told her the story. "They were just kids at the time, but still, it means he could be more involved in this than he let on."

"Wow. That's amazing," Angie said. "How did you find out?"

"Veronica's parole officer told me. He's in the city trying to find her for a murder down in Fresno. Also, Dennis was involved with fake autographed sports memorabilia. He swore he didn't know it was fake, but guys in pro sports are well aware of the problem. A dealer was arrested—Wallace Jones, a friend of Dennis's."

They reached the car and Angie touched the door handle to unlock it, then turned and faced him. "What do you have on Max?" she asked.

"He may have been trying to fence the stolen diamonds." He told her diamond seller gave a description of a guy that sounded like Max Squire. "If so, he's most likely Veronica's murderer."

"My God," Angie whispered.

He drew her close and tilted her head towards his. "Be careful, Angel. And keep Connie away from those guys as well. I'll take care of this, all right?"

"I feel so badly for Connie," she whispered.

"I know," he said as he pulled her closer for a kiss. But then, his cell phone began to ring.

He answered, and she stepped back with a goodbye wave.

He didn't like the disquieting feeling that struck him as he watched her drive away.

"Where the hell is everybody?"

Calderon looked up at the gruff-voiced woman who had just walked into Homicide. He scowled, then said, "Probably working. Ever try it?"

Helen Melinger stomped toward him, hands on hips. "Listen you fatheaded bastard, I work harder than most men and women I know, so watch your mouth."

Calderon's thick eyebrows nearly reached his pomaded pompadour. Nobody talked to him that way. He scowled at her. "What do you want? Somebody die or you here to confess to murder? Maybe with an ax?"

Helen put her fists on her ample hips. "If you must know,

I'm trying to find a wimpy little gal named Angie Amalfi. She skedaddled after leaving a shoe to be fixed. She hasn't returned for it. But her fiancé works here, so, since I was in the area, I thought I'd drop it off with him and try to find out what the hell's going on. Connie's shop has been closed up, and I'm worried about her."

Calderon's eyes narrowed. Was the battleax showing a hint of human compassion? He jutted his chin toward the right. "That's his desk."

He watched as she swiveled her wide hips to fit through the narrow walkway between cabinets, chairs and drawers left open. He had to admit that a fit, full-bodied woman was a vision of beauty to him.

He scowled even harder. "Is there a charge?" he demanded.

Helen snorted. "No. It'll be payment enough if she keeps her single male friends out of my shop." She gave a little shudder as if remembering something unpleasant.

It made him curious. "Oh? Such as?"

"She called him Stan something-or-other."

Calderon, who never laughed, suddenly burst out in a loud guffaw. "Stan Bonnette? She brought Stan Bonnette to meet you?"

"Most sickening experience of my life," Helen said, then she, too, gave a full belly-laugh at the thought.

"You should have seen the anorexic blonde she brought to me." Calderon shook his head, chuckling to the point tears came to his eyes, as if his entire body wasn't used to laughing anymore.

Helen met his gaze, and then she, too, laughed hard. She touched her throat, so unaccustomed was she to the sound.

The two stared a moment at each other.

Calderon gave a little cough. "Since you came all the way here just to deliver a shoe, I don't suppose you have time for a drink across the street? I got off work ten minutes ago, just fiddlin' around here before going home to an empty house."

Helen eyed him up and down, then cocked an eyebrow and gave a little nod. "I might have time. No one's at my place waiting for me, either. But you should know, I'm not one for wine or anything sweet and bubbly."

He grinned. "How does a boilermaker sound?"

Her lips spread wide. "Sounds like just my style."

31

"You can't imagine what I just learned." Angie ran into the den. Connie was lying down, an ice pack on her head. "Thank God you didn't get any more involved with Dennis Pagozzi. The man was married to Veronica Maple!"

"Married? And Butch wanted me to meet him?"

"It was annulled. Still, Dennis lied about her!"

It took a moment for Connie to absorb all this. She struggled to sit up, then put the ice pack aside. "Does this mean Dennis is now a suspect instead of Max?"

"No, no, that isn't what I'm saying. Paavo is still convinced Max has the diamonds, and that would mean Max murdered Veronica to get them."

"What makes him think that?" Connie asked.

"Someone tried to fence them." She told Paavo's story.

"But—"

"Max is the only one involved in this case who fits the tall, blond, and scraggly description," Angie explained.

"A lot of men fit that description, and Paavo knows it," Connie said.

"Why are you so ready to defend Max? The guy's scum."

"You're right. Still, when I think back on what he was like when I was with him, it's hard to believe I was so fooled by him. Here, I thought I was a good judge of character. Boy, am I wrong."

"Maybe you're just not a good judge of men to fall in love with," Angie said jokingly, trying to lighten the mood and get Connie away from feeling any sympathy toward Squire.

"Isn't that the truth! Look at Keith, and I was married to him." Connie shook her head, her expression filled with disgust at her bad taste. "Come to think of it, Keith would fit the fence's description, too, yet he and Max are nothing alike. So Paavo might be blaming Max unjustly."

"That reminds me," Angie said. "I meant to tell you about it, but with everything else going on... Anyway, Keith actually came to my apartment one day. He'd heard about you seeing a 49er player and wanted to know how serious you were about him."

"Are you joking?" Connie stilled, her voice low. "Keith wanted to know that?"

"He sounded very upset," Angie said. "I suspect he was jealous."

Connie's eyes widened at the possibility. "When did that happen? I haven't heard from Keith in ages."

"I'm surprised I didn't tell you.... Oh, I know why—it happened the day before you got arrested! When you were in jail, I'm afraid Keith was the last thing on my mind."

"The day of the diamond robbery, in other words," Connie said quietly.

"That's right. And as I recall, you were with Max—dinner and Lake Merced." Angie couldn't help but puzzle over Connie's statement that whoever was fencing the diamonds looked like Keith as well as Max. "Can Keith get into your apartment?" she asked.

"Well, I did give him a key once when we were trying to get back together. I wouldn't put it past him to have made a copy."

"Hmm," Angie said, trying to put all this together. "Okay, let's look at this. We know that someone tipped off the police that the diamonds were at your place, but the police didn't find them. But why would someone tip off the police unless they were fairly certain the diamonds were there?"

Connie stared at her a moment, trying to figure out what Angie was suggesting. "Are you saying, the diamonds were hidden in my apartment, but before the police got there, someone else took them?"

"That's what I'm thinking. Especially since Keith matches the description of the guy trying to fence them," Angie added.

"And if he was watching my apartment, saw someone go in, and he had a key..." Connie mused. "Oh, my!"

"Do you know where he lives?"

Connie nodded. "We can be there in ten minutes."

Keith was home in his upper Mission district apartment when Angie and Connie arrived. The area had once been incredibly cheap, filled with warehouses and shabby apartments, until rents throughout the city grew astronomically, and ugly warehouses suddenly became advertised as artsy lofts. There was nothing artistic about Keith's apartment however, starting with the battered door Connie knocked on.

"Who is it?" he called.

"It's me," Connie answered.

They listened as a series of chains, slide locks, and finally a deadbolt clicked open. When Keith opened the door, he looked even shabbier than the apartment building—thin and unshaven, wearing a dirty tee shirt and grease-soiled jeans, generally a lot worse than when Angie last saw him.

"Were you inside my home last week?" Connie demanded as she marched into the apartment nose-to-nose with him. Keith kept backing up. A haze of cigarette smoke overlaid a sour smell coming from the tiny kitchen. Cheap, lumpy furniture reeked of a mixture of tobacco, beer and sweat.

"Good to see you, too, wife." Reaching a wall, he had no choice but to stand his ground. She stopped short of bumping into him.

"Ex-wife, and don't forget it!"

"Won't you sit down?" Keith asked.

Connie stepped aside, letting him dash over to the sofa. He sat in the center of it, leaned over the glass-ring stained coffee table and lit a cigarette. Angie and Connie remained standing.

"You got yourself into some deep shit this time, Connie," he said, his narrow blue eyes giving her a once over and seeming, almost despite himself, to like what he saw. "And now, you've dragged me into it as well. What's wrong with you, woman?"

Connie's eyes shot daggers. "I've dragged you in? What the hell are you talking about?"

"Keith," Angie said, trying to intervene before the conversation spun into a litany of age-old recriminations, "will you please tell us what happened?"

"You tell me." He glanced bitterly from one to the other, then for some reason, decided to plead his case to Angie. "Here I was, concerned about Connie being with some rich dude who was going to break her heart. I wanted to warn her, to tell her I'd be there if she needed me. And you will need me, babe. Believe it."

"You broke into my apartment, didn't you?" Connie screeched. "You prick!"

"I had a key." He glared defiantly.

"How the hell—"

"Go on... please," Angie said to Keith.

Eying Connie warily, he proceeded to tell how he was in the

apartment, heading for the kitchen when he heard a scratching at the front door. Connie wouldn't have to do that to get into her own place. Suddenly uneasy, he hid behind a maroon easy chair in a dark corner of the living room. "It's a big, ugly sucker, not even comfortable," he said. "Nobody ever liked it."

"Screw you," Connie said.

Keith told them about the "chick" who entered. At first, he thought she was Connie. He almost stood up, planning to scare her and get a good laugh, but then he saw that her build wasn't Connie's. Neither was her walk. "You can't have been married to a woman and not recognize her walk or her shape, even in the dark."

"Cute," Connie sneered.

"You always thought I was," he said, catching her eye.

She rolled her eyes and turned away from him.

"Connie," he said, softly this time, his cocky expression suddenly vanished. "I'm sorry. You know I was just kidding around. I'm working fairly steadily; I've been clean for over a year. I'm trying, babe, but without you... what good is it?"

She pursed her lips and stared resolutely at the wall.

"Shit," he murmured, "why do I even try?" He gritted his teeth and faced Angie, a determined look in his eyes. "Okay, here's what happened."

He told of the intruder looking around, sneaking, peering at shelves, in closets, then sticking her hand behind the TV. There was something about her that spelled danger. She poked around a bit more, and as she was going out the door, she grabbed one of Connie's dolls.

After waiting a good five minutes to be sure she wasn't coming back, Keith looked to see what was so interesting behind the TV and found a small velvet sack. Inside were stones that looked like diamonds. He wasn't thinking clearly—only that he held a small fortune in his hand. He stuffed them in his pocket and ran.

"In your pocket? I heard about a hundred diamonds were stolen," Connie said.

"You're dreaming. There were ten. They were beauties, big and crystal clear. I tried to fence them, but no one would touch them. Something bad about them. I could see the fear in the fences' eyes."

"So you still have them," Angie asked, excited.

"That's why I'm staying locked in here. I don't know who wants them, but if they learn I have them..." He took the black velvet out of his pocket, opened it, and dropped the diamonds into his hand. They were eye-poppingly huge—three carats, easy.

"Give them to me," Connie said. "They aren't yours, and they're causing me all kinds of trouble."

"Give them to you?" Keith looked shocked. "Do you know the trouble they've caused *me*?"

"Do I care?"

He glared at Connie, fuming. "Right. Why start now?"

"I want those diamonds! They're going back to the police!" Connie yelled, marching up to him.

"What are they worth to you?" Keith hollered right back, his nose nearly touching hers.

Instead of answering, she kneed him, and as he cried out, bending forward in pain, she shoved him, making him topple over. The diamonds went flying.

Connie and Angie scooped them up, and the two dashed out of the apartment.

Paavo was at work when Angie called on her cell phone to let him know she and Connie were heading for Homicide with ten of the stolen diamonds. She explained that Keith was the one who'd taken the diamonds and tried to fence them. They took them from him.

"You did *what?*" Paavo felt his blood pressure soar, and caught himself, biting his tongue. How many times could he warn her?

She gave him Keith's address, then gleefully added that the thief wasn't Max after all. Max was innocent.

"Don't be so sure about Max," he cautioned, working to keep his voice calm. "You said you have ten diamonds. A lot more are still out there."

"I think the ten stones were planted in Connie's apartment as evidence she was involved in the jewelry theft. I'd say everything points toward Dennis now. He must have been working with his ex-wife. Maybe he still loved her."

"Maybe," Paavo said skeptically.

"That could mean Dennis has the rest of the diamonds," Angie offered. "Butch didn't like Dennis's idea to expand the restaurant, and if Dennis doesn't play football, he'll need money."

"It still doesn't fit," Paavo said. "Go straight home now. I've got a lead on Squire's whereabouts, and Yosh and I are just leaving. I'll come by later to pick up the diamonds."

"Can I leave them with Lt. Hollins?" she asked.

"Hold on." He made a quick call and got back to her. "Vic Walters is at his desk, Robbery is down the hall from Homicide. Room four-eighty. He'll be waiting."

"Great. Be careful."

"Promise me you and Connie will go straight to your apartment after you drop off the diamonds."

"Of course," she said. "Love you! Bye!"

He shut his eyes a moment. Why, he wondered, didn't he believe her? Experience, maybe?

He was on his feet, putting on his jacket to find Max when a small man wearing a green jacket, vest, shirt and trousers, with green face paint, green pointy ears, a green bowler hat and green suede shoes with upturned pointed toes, sprang into Homicide. A small group of people from offices on the same floor chortled, clapped and murmured behind him. "Paavo Smith?" he trilled.

Calderon pointed at Paavo.

The green bean suddenly began to cartwheel down the aisle between desks, cabinets, and chairs to land on one knee at Paavo's feet. With his arms outstretched like someone about to propose, he announced, "I'm Larry the Leprechaun from Shamrock Motors. I'm here, Paavo Smith, because this is your lucky day!"

Paavo looked at him as if he was a giant green bug that needed to be stepped on.

"No, it isn't." Paavo barreled past the guy and marched out of the room daring anyone to say a word.

No one did.

***

I don't believe it. Veronica. Alive.

He watched her leave the Hall of Justice and get into the passenger side of a white Lexus.

They had tricked him. All of them. He thought she was dead, but she wasn't. That was why there was nothing in the newspaper, no word of looking for her killer.

Was she working with the cops now? With Homicide? She must be.

The Lexus pulled out of the parking lot.

He had to follow.

I thought I'd killed her once. I won't miss this time.

onnie didn't know what to do. While Angie had delivered the diamonds to the robbery inspector, she'd stayed in the lobby and used her cellphone to check for messages on her shop's landline.

When she heard Max Squire's voice, she nearly fainted.

She returned his call. He'd gotten himself a pre-paid cell phone and was currently at the Main Library at the Civic Center. He quickly told her he'd begun earning fifty dollars an hour to straighten out the accounting books for the organization that ran the homeless shelter where he'd been staying. It was a bargain for them—a professional CPA could well charge ten times that amount—and it meant desperately needed money for him.

He said he was worried about her and had checked her apartment and business many times, but she seemed to have vanished. He wanted to see her, to try to explain, and to return at least some of the money he'd taken from her.

Despite his explanation, she remained angry with him—beyond angry. "Meet me," he said, "let me explain as much as I can."

The Main Library was a busy place. She was sure she'd be safe meeting him there—and she wouldn't let him sweet talk her into going anyplace where they'd be alone. This girl was no fool! She'd seen lots of TV shows and movies about murderers. No way was she going to let herself get into a dangerous situation.

She glanced over at Angie. Not most of the time, at least.

Why should she meet him? What she should do was call the police and have them arrest his ass! He was a sitting duck.

He'd trusted her, though; maybe that was why she couldn't turn him in. And she'd love to hear his explanation.

She told him she just didn't know if she'd be there.

He said he'd wait all evening.

More trust.

God, but she hated it when people she hated decided to be nice. What was with that?

"Angie," she said as they neared the Library. "I need to be alone awhile. Would you drop me off at the Main Library? I'll take an Uber back to your place later."

"The library? Are you joking?"

"No. I want to think. A lot has happened."

Angie studied her. "You want to think about Keith, don't you? There's still an undercurrent between you two, you know."

Connie didn't want to hear that. "It's ancient history, nothing more. When I see him, the only undercurrent I feel is one of disappointment."

"Maybe this time he's straightened himself out," Angie suggested.

"Sure—like trying to fence diamonds he stole from my place? If that's straight, I don't know crooked." Connie turned away, staring out the window. "I'm tired of hoping."

Angie nodded. "Are you sure you wouldn't rather come back to my place with me?"

"I need to do this. Let me out at the corner."

Angie peered quizzically at her, but did as directed.

"Don't worry about me," Connie said. "I'll see you later."

"Be careful."

Connie headed into the building and went straight to the reading room. She almost didn't recognize Max. He'd gotten his hair cut short and was wearing gold-rimmed glasses. Even his clothes were fresh and clean. Hints of the high-powered financial adviser were before her, a man he'd kept well-hidden up to now. Had he kept the side of himself who might be a killer hidden as well?

He stood as she approached. "Shall we go outside so we can talk?" he asked.

"No," she said too quickly. "No one is using the table and chairs in the far corner. Let's go there."

He nodded, his gaze telling her he understood why she didn't want to be alone with him.

They sat catty-corner on wooden chairs at a wooden table, and Max slid his chair closer to hers, his demeanor sad. "You don't trust me at all, do you?" His voice was just a little above a whisper.

He was right; he seemed like a stranger to her now. "My store was trashed," she murmured.

His brow furrowed at the news. "I'm so sorry. Do you know who did it?"

She shrugged. "Probably someone who thought I had the diamonds. Maybe you."

He shut his eyes a moment. "Connie, I had no idea about any of that. I'm really sorry you're involved in this."

She didn't want his sympathy. She was barely able to contain her anger. "Tell me what the hell this is all about."

He relayed the story she already knew about Veronica embezzling from him.

"So what?" she demanded. "You aren't the first guy who's

ever trusted the wrong woman. She embezzled, she went to jail. Case closed. There's got to be more."

"She still has the money," Max said. "I thought that if I could get my hands on it, I could get the lien against future earnings lifted off my back, and have a life again. I kept trying to find her."

"Why?" She spat the word at him. "Did you think if you asked, she'd just turn the money over to you?"

He shook his head. "No. But I thought that if I threatened, she might."

"Threaten to do what?"

"To kill her."

Connie felt as if her heart sank to the floor. Her voice became a whisper. "And did you?"

"No! Of course not. I never saw her—except once. Under the clock tower at Ghirardelli Square—the time she used to frame us both. I still don't know where the money is. Or, where she is."

She wondered if he was telling the truth—and if he really didn't know Veronica was dead. She wanted to believe him, and yet, strangely, in cleaning himself up, he was no longer the scraggly, vulnerable man she'd been attracted to. He was more in control, more self-contained, and seemed more calculating. She was always a beer and pretzel kind of gal, and he was suddenly chilled white wine and baked Brie. An absurd sense of loss surrounded her, and she rubbed her arms.

"If she had those millions," she continued, deciding she shouldn't mention Veronica's demise to him since the police wanted to keep it quiet as long as possible while they investigated, "why didn't she just leave the country once out of prison?"

"That's what I can't figure either. I believe it has to do with Dennis. She was hanging around him. He must know, but he pretends he hardly knows her."

She drew in her breath. "I've learned that when they were teenagers, they got married. But then Dennis's family made him get it annulled."

Max stared at her a long moment, then he laughed bitterly. "Wouldn't you know it? God, what a fool I was."

"Do you think she gave Dennis the money? And now, he won't give it back? Could that be why she's here?"

"She wouldn't give it to him. I can't imagine her trusting anyone enough to give it to, but then"—another sullen snort rippled from him—"I'm the last person to try to figure her out. I never could."

"If you had the money, how would you have hidden it?"

He picked up his pencil and tapped it, point, then eraser, then point again. "In offshore banks. That's what I did with a lot of my clients' money. That was the system she broke into."

"So, she understands offshore accounts?" Connie asked. "That sounds safe. What would have stopped her from setting up one of her own?"

He nodded. "I expected that's exactly what she did, but I couldn't find any trace of one. Believe me, I searched."

"How would she get into it? Could there be someplace in the city that she needs to go to?"

"It's easier than that. She could get in via the internet. It's just a string of numbers—a code."

"Numbers? Like, twelve or so?"

"Even longer. Plus, a couple of passwords."

Connie remembered the string of numbers she and Angie had found hidden in Veronica's room. It had been torn in a way that some of the numbers might have been removed. "A string of numbers," Connie mused. "Is it possible she didn't have all the numbers needed?"

His gaze hardened. "What do you know?"

"Nothing!" she cried. "I'm trying to figure out what's going on. Why I'm involved; why some fiend is trying to ruin my life!"

He stared at her suspiciously a long moment, and his expression relaxed. He tossed aside the pencil and rubbed his forehead. "You're right. I've let myself to be consumed by her for so long, I can't think straight. You know what's the most ridiculous part of all?"

She shook her head.

"I don't even care anymore. Seeing her again, in that quick moment when she hit the old jeweler in the head, knocking him out cold, I realized the woman I loved never really existed. I imagined her as I wanted her to be, not as she was. The part that makes me the angriest is that I've wasted more than three years of my life over her.

"I could have been working to pay off the liens against me, I could have gone back to court, had changes made in the judgment after the insurance companies paid off my clients, done something more than to sit around brooding and feeling sorry for myself." He caught Connie's eye. "I could have tried to find a good woman to love and worked to make myself worthy of winning her love in return."

"Nothing's stopping you," she said. He bowed his head, and again, the thought struck her that he might have killed Veronica. "You could have been a fine man, Max. A wonderful friend, and a thoughtful lover."

"Not the way I was, not before I met Ronnie... and not after."

Ronnie? Her heart clenched. The night they'd first met, when he'd called out a name, she'd thought he was calling to her and she'd simply misheard. But he wasn't. It was Veronica he'd called. It was always about Veronica. God, but she'd been such a fool!

She tried not to let her disappointment show and folded her hands. "I'm so sorry you had to go through all this, Max."

With great tenderness, he leaned across the library table and gave her a quick kiss on the lips. She stared at him in shock, and he gently brushed a lock back from her cheek, his gaze studying her as if burning her face into his memory. "If I can ever become the kind of man you deserve, and if I'm lucky enough that you haven't found someone else—or, if that ex of yours who you still care about despite your denials, hasn't straightened himself out—I'd like to see you again, Connie. You've touched me more deeply than you know, with your serious ways and your good heart."

She wasn't sure how to answer, and the silence grew awkward.

He stood then, as if her lack of an answer told him all he needed to know. "I have a business I need to get off the ground once more. When I've done it, whenever that might be, I'll come back. Maybe, then, your heart will be free."

She still said nothing as she watched him leave.

Max had last been seen at a skid-row hotel on Third Street. When Paavo and Yosh got there, the room he'd been given was empty. It looked like he wouldn't be returning.

They were headed back to Yosh's Ford Galaxy when the walking split-pea soup guy appeared. "Larry the Leprechaun at your service, Inspector Smith. I'm here to give you the keys to your dream car." He pointed at a black Corvette parked across the street.

Paavo froze a moment as he stared at the gorgeous car, then he got into the Ford and locked the door.

"I've got to stop her," he said to Yosh, a tremor in his voice. "I didn't want to. I was hoping she'd get over it on her own."

"You got to be careful not to hurt her feelings," Yosh cautioned, salivating over the car.

"It's too much."

Yosh grinned at him. "Remember, your partner gets to ride with you. Do I get a vote?"

"Funny." Paavo said, then gave the Corvette a last wistful glance as Yosh drove off, leaving Larry the Leprechaun standing slack-jawed in front of the car.

In no time they'd gone two blocks to another hotel, one Squire had stayed at a couple of days before. He might have returned.

When they walked into the shabby and urine-stained lobby, they found themselves in the middle of a drug deal. They drew their guns, but the dealer burst past them, hitting Paavo hard and knocking him into Yosh, who also toppled over.

The inspectors were soon running down the block after dealer when Mr. Green Jeans jumped in front of them. "Mister, wait!" he yelled at Paavo. "Before I can get paid, I've got to give you the damned car!"

The drug dealer didn't stop, knocking into the leprechaun who went flying. The collision slowed the dealer down enough for Paavo to tackle him, Yosh right behind him.

A paddy wagon was driving away from the scene before the little green man peered over the trash receptacle he'd jumped into when he realized he was in the middle of a drug bust. He remained hidden there until all the cops drove away.

33

Vinnie stood over a kettle of boiling water. After finding a jar of Prego's Alfredo sauce in the grocery, he decided Fettuccini Alfredo would make a nice addition to Wing's menu. Since Butch wasn't interested in cooking these days, he'd do it himself. All he needed was to spoon the sauce over fat fettuccini noodles and add a twelve ninety-five price tag. Voilà.

And if it didn't work, he still had the firecrackers in the basement. He hated the thought of missing out on the profit they were giving him and his pals. He'd just have to figure out a different way to get rid of them, one Angie couldn't know about. He didn't think she'd tell her fiancé about them, but he'd learned over the years, you just can't trust women. Not even the ones you liked. Once they opened their mouths, no telling what might come out.

When the water began to boil, he added a pound of fettuccini. The pieces were long and stuck out over the top. He smashed them down, breaking them into small bits.

He peered into the pot. The noodles were at the bottom and there was a lot of water to spare.

He added another pound of fettuccini. Since the parts not covered by water wouldn't cook—he'd learned that from Butch—he broke and scrunched the noodles so water covered them.

The addition of the noodles caused the water to temporarily stop boiling. He was able to see into the pot even better now. It wasn't even half full! Two more pounds went in before he had to ladle out some of the excess water so the pot wouldn't overflow. Probably, this meant a trip to the store to buy more Prego.

Finally, the kettle was filled almost to the top with noodles.

The water that was there started bubbling furiously, foaming, and boiling over the edge of the pot. He turned the flame down to get it to stop boiling over.

Eventually, it did.

Angie paced around her apartment; her nerves frayed. She tried to reach Paavo, but he wasn't at his desk, and she didn't want to bother him in the field. Connie still hadn't returned.

Angie had watched to make sure she went into the library, then watched longer to make sure she didn't pop right out again, until guilt for spying on her best friend consumed her and she went home.

The phone rang, and she pounced on it.

"Miss Angie, Vinnie's tryin' to cook," Earl cried. "You gotta help."

"Vinnie? You're joking, right?"

"I wish I was. What am I gonna do?"

"I'll be right there."

Before she got to the restaurant, Connie called her on her cell phone, saying she had interesting news. They agreed to meet at Wings of an Angel.

The restaurant was empty once more, Vinnie sitting at a table with a glass of red wine. Angie went straight to him.

"I heard you were cooking," she said skeptically. "Haven't we been through this once already?"

"I'm serious this time, Angie," Vinnie said. "If a bozo like Butch can do it, so can I. In fact, I got something on the stove now. It was a breeze. No funny business this time."

"It's cooking in the kitchen and you're out here?"

"It's hot in there," he complained.

"Kitchens often are," she said. "Where is Butch, by the way?"

"He was wit' his nephew last time I saw him," Earl replied. "Up in the apartment."

Just then, Connie walked in.

"Thank goodness you're safe," Angie jumped to her feet. "I kept imagining things happening to you, and it being all my fault."

"Not this time," Connie said, joining the table. Not exactly the ringing endorsement Angie had hoped for, but it would have to do. "I saw Max."

"My God!" Angie cried. "Where is he? Did you call Paavo? We've got to catch him."

"I don't think he did anything," she said. "He's innocent. He had no reason to kill"—she almost said "to kill Veronica"—"to *do it* other than hatred, and he's well over that."

"Sid Fernandez wouldn't have *done anything* before he got his hands on the diamonds," Angie said. To her, if Max wasn't the killer, it had to be Dennis. She didn't want to say it here, though.

Earl and Vinnie must have read her mind, because they caught each other's eyes and looked downcast. She wondered what they might know. What was she overlooking?

"Anyway, Max told me how Veronica may have hidden the money," Connie said excitedly. "Remember the torn piece of paper we found in her room with all those numbers? Max said Veronica learned about offshore accounts working for him. Many use codes of numbers for security—even longer strings of numbers than we found. And the way the paper was torn— what if someone else has the rest of the code? Veronica could have been here, in the city, trying to get it. Now, we just have to figure out who has it, get the money, give it back, and Max's problems will be over."

Just then, the smell of something burning reached them from the kitchen, followed by a loud thud.

Angie followed Earl and Vinnie as they ran into the kitchen. Black smoke made it hard to see. A strange white glob, like a temple of dough, jutted high over the kettle and then listed to one side. The top of the temple had been broken off, much like a volcanic eruption, and now lay splattered over the stovetop. A part of it was being barbecued by the flame from the burner. At the same time, smoke and the sharp smell of burning noodles were billowing up from the inside of the kettle.

"Turn the gas off!" Angie yelled.

Vinnie did so, then he and Earl each grabbed a potholder and one handle of the kettle. They lifted it off the stove and into the sink where it sizzled.

"What in the world were you cooking?" Angie asked curiously, looking at the peculiar lump.

"It looks like it's alive," Connie said. "Like squiggly brains all mooshed together."

"We ain't never had not'in' like dat on our menu," Earl said.

"What's wrong with you people?" Vinnie cried. "It's fettucini. Why did it stick together?"

"All you have to do to cook pasta is to boil it," Angie said, disgusted. "For ten or so minutes."

"Oh. So, maybe I overcooked it a little. Is that a crime?" Vinnie asked.

"What's a crime is you cookin' anyt'ing. We gotta get Butch back to work!" Earl cried. He spun around to open some doors and vent the room, and when the smoke cleared, he let out a yelp of surprise and horror.

Dennis entered the kitchen, a gun in hand.

"What're you doing?" Vinnie asked, his eyes wide on Dennis's gun. "Whatsa the matter with you?"

"I never wanted to hurt anyone," he said. "You forced me to do this."

"You're da one who's made Butch miserable," Earl scolded. "Why'd you wanna do dat to your own uncle? He was good to you. He didn't even tell da cops what a jerk you are!"

"Will you guys just shut up?" Dennis yelled. Angry tears glistened in his eyes. "I didn't do anything. Don't you get it yet? It was all Veronica. She ruined everything. My football career, my plans for a sports bar, my life. All I needed was some of her damned money. My share, plus a little more to borrow, to get me out of debt and back on my feet. Do you know how expensive it is to live like a football star? To live the way everyone expects? And now, I'm off the team. My contract isn't being renewed. All my dreams, everything I've ever worked for, it's all finished. Give me the code, Angie."

"Where's Butch?" Vinnie asked, as the four of them slowly eased backwards.

"He's upstairs in the apartment. I came down the back way and was going to cut through the restaurant to leave when I heard you talking about finding Veronica's half of the code. I need it—I need those numbers. Give them to me and I'll get out of here." His voice was desperate. "I don't want to use this gun, or to hurt anyone. This is the only way I can think of. I want the numbers, Angie, and then I'll be out of your lives forever.

"You have the other half of the paper?" Angie peeked at Dennis from behind Earl's back. "How did you get it?"

Dennis grimaced and drew his breath a moment before speaking. "I... I saw her working in Max's office and we started talking. I knew a bit about the offshore accounts. We set one up for me—just to see if it'd work. I had no idea she'd go so far." Dennis drew in his breath. "In the end, I couldn't say anything about her because if word got out that I'd taught her anything, even though I was innocent, my career would be over. But also, if she said anything to the authorities about me, I'd tell where the money was. So she kept quiet, and so did I. Then, she came back here, expecting I'd give her my part of the code. She wanted all the money, saying it was payment for the three years she did. But I need it, too! I needed it more than she did!"

"You didn't ask how we got the code," Angie said quietly. "That must mean you know Veronica's dead."

He froze, searching Angie's face to see if this was another sick joke. "She's dead?" he whispered.

They said nothing, and the truth hit him hard. His whole body went limp, the hand holding the gun dropped to his side. "She can't be. Not Veronica. How? What happened to her?"

"Someone shot her," Angie said, studying him.

His shoulders slumped. "Who did it?" His voice was thick with emotion.

"We don't know," Angie said as Earl walked over and gently took the gun out of Dennis's hand and stuck it in a drawer with a bunch of plastic containers.

"El Toro," Dennis whispered. "That bastard! I warned her!" Tears glistened in his eyes.

"He killed his partner, Julius Rodriguez, thinking Julius and Veronica scammed him out of the diamonds," Connie said. "But nobody thinks he killed her—he wanted the diamonds too much to kill her before retrieving them."

"Then who?" Dennis demanded. His face drawn, he seemed genuinely torn up over Veronica's death.

"You knew Veronica," Angie cried. "Who else did she con? That's the murderer!"

"But that means it's someone who didn't take the money or the diamonds," Dennis said. "It doesn't make sense."

"It does," Angie said slowly, testing a theory, "if she was killed out of passion. Because of betrayal, not for wealth. Look at the reactions she's caused in you and Max. She knew how to wrap men around her finger—she acted on pure, gut emotion, and the reaction she solicited was the same."

"You're right," Connie said. "What men did she know? Who was close to her?"

Angie tried to think of every man Paavo had ever mentioned who knew Veronica. Max... Dennis... Fernandez... Julius... Butch...

"Oh, my God!" Angie said. "I think I know who did it."

34

In the lavish Sea Cliff district, Paavo walked up to the door of Dennis's home, rang the bell and knocked, but no answer. He was alone since Yosh had gone back to the flophouse to check on Max's whereabouts.

Paavo stepped out of the front entry to see if he could get to the backdoor, or if there was a sign of any movement in the house, when he saw a figure in jeans and a brown jacket dart from behind a hedge to scramble over a wooden gate to the side yard.

Paavo sprinted after him. The back yard was small, as is typical of even the most luxurious city homes, and the runner realized he had no escape there. One yard backed up to another, and another after that.

He raised his hands and turned around.

"We meet at last." Paavo's gun was drawn.

"You must be Angie's fiancé," Max said. "She talks about you incessantly."

"She does the same about you," Paavo replied, "trying to convince me I was wrong about your guilt, or trying to convince Connie that she was wrong about your innocence."

"I haven't done anything wrong here," Max said. "Except that I didn't want to be seen."

"Why not?"

"I came here to confront Dennis. I was convinced, after you learned he and Veronica had been married—Connie told me, by the way—that Dennis was Veronica's accomplice. I imagined he worked with her to swindle my clients and ruin me. That the two probably laughed together over it. But as I stood here and waited for him to open the door..." Max's voice then dropped and a soulful expression filled his face. "I realized I no longer cared."

Paavo studied the man, taking in the measure of him, of the truth behind his words. "Explain."

"It wasn't worth it. What I did to my life—waiting for three years for Veronica to get out of prison so I could confront her— was pure, self-indulgent idiocy. Her and Dennis—to hell with them both. I want no part of either of them. So, when I saw you pull up, I ran. It was foolish, not criminal."

"A pretty speech, but you could have been running for another reason." He paused and then hit Dennis with the news. "Veronica Maple is dead. She was murdered. And all the evidence makes it appear that you are our prime suspect."

"My God," he whispered. A panoply of emotions flickered across Max's face—surprise, horror, relief, and finally regret. "She was... a force of nature, her mind always racing with ideas, big, exciting ideas." His lips tightened and his voice turned thick. "But selfishness got in her way."

Paavo studied him—another man Veronica had double-crossed, and yet had once loved her. "If you didn't kill her, Squire, who did?"

Paavo's question seemed to snap Max out of his reverie. He shook his head. "I don't know."

"Dennis Pagozzi?"

Max shook his head, then lifted his hands to rub his

temples as he spoke. "Dennis is no killer. And neither am I. The guys Ronnie was involved with, in the jewelry heist—they're killers."

Paavo eyed Squire a long moment, then holstered his gun. Every instinct, every bit of experience he'd amassed told him Angie and Connie had been right about Max Squire. He was innocent. "It wasn't a pro hit, and Sid Fernandez wouldn't have killed her until after he got hold of the diamonds."

Max lowered his arms, then shut his eyes a moment in relief at being believed. "So," he said when he was able to speak again, "the question is, who did it? There's got to be someone... most likely someone else she conned into helping her. That's what she was best at—a real life femme fatale, like the rotten women in the *film noir* of the nineteen-thirties and forties. I've never encountered anyone like her before, and hope I never do again."

"Someone else she conned..." Paavo murmured, and suddenly he realized the suspicions he'd harbored for some time about her murderer were correct. He knew the identity. "You're right. We've been looking at this from the wrong angle. We've been looking at money and diamonds. But greed isn't always the motive for all that's bad in the world. Sometimes it happens for the most unlikely reason. Like love."

"Love?" Max scoffed, but then his expression turned thoughtful and he nodded. "Yes, I suppose you're right. The pursuit of love can make men do all kinds of things quite out of character."

Paavo opened the side gate and stepped out onto the sidewalk with Max. "It can cause them to change"—he gave Max a hard stare—"even cause them to rise above the troubles and injustice society throws at them. But, other times, with other people, it can cause them to simply go bad."

Max said nothing.

"Give it some thought." Paavo turned away.

Just then, the leprechaun drove up in the black Corvette, stopped in the middle of the street, opened the car door and started to get out.

Paavo pulled aside one flap of his jacket so his gun was visible. The Jolly Green Pipsqueak popped back into the car and drove away in a rush.

Paavo got into his city issue Chevy and picked up his cell phone to give a call to the parole office connected to the women's prison in Chowchilla.

As he drove, he could just make out what might have become his very own gorgeous black sports car disappearing in the distance. He couldn't stop a heartfelt sigh.

Sometimes love did turn a man's life upside down.

<hr>

"I think I get it, too," Dennis said to Angie.

"Well, I don't," Connie said. "All I understand is, it isn't Max or Dennis."

"Tell her," Angie said.

Dennis wiped his eyes. "I didn't think I'd be crying to hear Veronica was dead. I thought I'd celebrate such news. She nearly ruined my life. Did I tell you that? All... all because we loved each other. But we were kids, and when I thought about my career, loving Veronica wasn't enough. I chose football. In a way, I guess I ruined her life even worse than she did mine. A lot worse."

The others said nothing as he tried to stop the tears that fell.

"I remember her telling me things, like how she was able to convince her parole officer that she was putting off her release until his day off 'to avoid suspicion.' Can you imagine? She'd told him about the money she'd hidden, and he thought the two were going to go away together, leave the country and live off of it the rest of their lives. She used him the whole time she was in stir, getting him to move her to more malleable cellmates, to get her simple jobs—heck, the last six months she worked in the prison library where he'd 'visit' her in the stacks. She had the jerk wrapped around her little finger. He thought she loved him," Dennis started to laugh, even while he cried because she was dead.

"God, Veronica thought she was such a genius, and she ends up killed by someone who was just plain stupid!" Dennis's sobs and laughter grew louder. "Is that funny, or what?"

A gunshot sounded, and in the shocked silence that followed, Dennis fell to the ground.

Then, amid Angie and Connie's screams, the lights went out.

Max watched Paavo get in an old Mustang. He had seen Paavo's reaction as he watched the leprechaun in the Corvette. Max couldn't help but smile. Connie had told him about Angie's little surprises for Paavo. This one was a more than a little over the top.

Paavo told him he was free to go about his business, whatever it might be.

Max breathed deeply, filling his lungs with fresh sea air.

He was free now. Free for the first time in three years—four, if he counted back to when he first learned of the embezzlement, back to when he refused to believe it. Free of the sickness he thought of as love; free of hatred; revenge; and now, free of the need to hide from the police.

When he was ready, he would return to Wings of an Angel, apologize to Earl, Vinnie and Butch. Even to Angie who, in the way she helped Connie, had showed him what true friendship was all about. And to Connie. Especially to Connie who, despite all she'd gone through, despite how angry she had been, ultimately she had believed in him. He would never forget that about her.

Puffy white cumulus clouds floated in a crystal blue sky. His heart swelled, and he started walking. As he went, his shuffling step turned springy, and soon, he began to whistle.

No need to hurry anymore.

Angie knew the layout of the restaurant like the back of her hand. As soon as she saw Vinnie hit the lights, she grabbed Connie's arm and led her to the stairway down to the basement storeroom, Earl and Vinnie right behind them.

They shut and locked the storeroom door, then switched on the light, while Angie frantically called nine-one-one on her cell phone.

Someone banged against the door. Earl and Vinnie lunged at it, trying to hold it shut.

Another thud jarred the door, and then it sprang open, breaking the door jamb and lock, and pushing the two small men back out of the way.

Connie screamed as she and Angie ran behind the crates of fireworks.

A stocky, bald-headed man carrying a gun entered the room. Lights from the kitchen—he must have found the switch—flooded into the storeroom.

"Put your hands up!" he yelled. "All of you! I know you two women are back there!"

"First tell us," Angie called, cowering ever lower behind the crate as she did so, hoping to throw him off kilter and buy time. "Are you the stupid parole officer?"

"Come out of there, Veronica," he called, ignoring Angie's question. "I won't hurt you. Not this time." He inched closer to the crates while Angie, Earl and Vinnie frantically tried to find something, anything, to use to protect themselves. Connie was too petrified to move.

"Please, Veronica. Talk to me. Tell me you're alive," he said.

"Stop! She's scared of you," Angie hollered. "Leave her alone!"

He froze. "Scared? Of me? Veronica, how can you be scared after all I did for you? After the way I loved you and helped make life easy for you in prison?" His voice choked. "I gave up everything for you. My wife. My job. My home." Tears coursed down his cheeks.

Angie nodded vigorously at Connie, trying to get her to answer him.

"Tell me I was wrong to doubt you," Lexington pleaded. "Tell me you still love me."

Angie gave Connie a kick, but she was too scared to reply.

"Damn you! Talk to me!" He fired the gun at the ceiling. Connie and Angie screamed and cringed. "This time I won't miss!"

"Don't! Please," Connie whimpered.

"Veronica?" he whispered, then stepped closer. "Veronica is that you?"

"Yes," Connie murmured.

"Oh God!" he cried, joyous now. "I thought you were dead. I thought I'd killed you. But then I saw you near the jail, and I thanked God you'd survived. I was so angry, but I didn't really want to hurt or kill you. Just to scare you. I love you. I still love you. We'll go away like we planned. I never cared about the money. I just want you."

As Lexington spoke, Earl and Vinnie quietly eased a package of firecrackers out of one crate, Roman candles and bottle rockets out of another.

"Come on, Veronica. If you love me, you'll come to me."

Suddenly, a man's voice shouted from the kitchen. "Hello?

Is Angie Amalfi around? My God! There's a man hurt here! Hello?"

Angie and Connie exchanged glances. "I'm here!" Angie yelled. "But don't come down the stairs! Run! Call the police!"

Lexington spun around as footsteps hurried down the stairs and a little man wearing green clothes and a sour expression limped into the storeroom. He stormed past Lexington as if the pudgy, bald fellow didn't exist. "Where are you, lady? Is this another one of your stupid charades? I'll call the police all right! I'll call them about you." He walked right up to the crate Angie hid behind. "I see you back there! You can't hide from me!" He smacked the Corvette car keys on top of the crate. "I tried to give it to him, I really did. He won't take it. But I still want my delivery fee!"

Angie gaped at him. She'd forgotten all about the new car she'd ordered for Paavo.

"Shut the hell up!" Lexington roared.

Angie covered her head with her arms.

The leprechaun whirled around. "Who do you think you're —" his gaze dropped from Lexington's face to the gun in his hand—"Ohmigod! You mean that guy upstairs isn't pretending—"

"Get over there!" Lexington ordered, waving his gun. The human pickle turned chalky white.

Suddenly a barrage of what sounded like machine-gun fire erupted. Lexington dived to the ground, firing the gun as he hit the floor.

The leprechaun bolted like a pea pod into a corner. At the same time, Vinnie lit a Roman candle and Earl a bottle rocket.

Connie reached into a crate and came up with a handful of cherry bombs. She grabbed a couple of Vinnie's matches, lit the bombs one by one and tossed them at Lexington.

He crawled from one side of the storeroom to the other to

avoid the firepower, screeching whenever a cherry bomb went off beside him.

Pinwheels skittered across the floor whistling and shooting off multi-colored sparkles. Aerial spinners whirled overhead, missiles and rockets launched, starbursts lit the ceiling, while more packets of firecrackers blasted.

The leprechaun curled up and sobbed.

"You tricked me!" Lexington shrieked. "You don't love me. This is a game." He stood, pointing the gun. "Another of your games."

While Earl and Vinnie tried to figure out how to light a smoke bomb, Angie pulled a can of hairspray out of Connie's purse, then grabbed one of Vinnie's matches.

Earl, Vinnie and Connie saw what Angie was up to, and all began to shout, "*No! Don't!*" as she aimed a plume of hair spray at a box of cherry bombs near Lexington and then held a match to it.

The hairspray mist ignited as she lobbed the hair spray canister onto the crate.

Angie and her friends hit the ground, arms over their heads, as Lexington raised his gun at Connie.

The whole crate exploded, knocking Lexington across the room. He hit a wall and dropped.

Fire from the first crate caused the others to go off and the room soon became a smoke-filled mass of firecrackers, sparklers, whistles and lights. A Fourth of July vision of hell.

When the smoke and ringing in her ears lessened, Angie heard Paavo's voice. "Angie, can you hear me?" Then she felt his hands on her arms helping her sit up. She looked up to see his handsome face.

"Watch out!" she cried. "It's the parole officer! He's here! He's a killer."

"I know. I've got him handcuffed."

At his words and calm tone, Angie let him help her stand.

She looked over what was left of the fireworks crates, then looked down at her hands, arms and clothes—all black with soot. She reached up to touch her hair. The ends felt dry and crinkly as if they'd been singed. "Oh, my God!" she said, all but collapsing in his arms.

Paavo held her and brushed some soot from her nose and cheeks. "I came to tell you to stop sending people in crazy costumes to see me. Also, to warn you to watch out for Lexington, especially after I learned the Chowchilla police now are collecting evidence that makes them believe he killed a pawn shop owner, probably to blame it on Veronica. Payback for dumping him. But I see I was too late to do that."

Lexington, who was sitting handcuffed on the floor, looked stunned and crazier than ever.

As Paavo spoke, Connie, Earl and Vinnie also stood and dusted soot and gunpowder off themselves. As the sound of police entering the restaurant reached them, Paavo left Angie with Connie and pushed Lexington ahead of him up the stairs. The others followed.

In the kitchen, Butch had stopped the flow of blood from Dennis's shoulder, and the former football pro was sitting up and conscious. EMTs arrived as the place filled with cops responding to Angie and Butch's earlier nine-one-one calls, plus several neighbors' complaints about an all-out war having broken out in the small restaurant, describing what they thought were bombs and machine guns being fired.

Paavo turned Lexington over to the uniforms for the trip to City Jail.

"You used me," Lexington yelled at Connie as he was being led out the door. "You deserved to die! I loved you, you bitch! And I killed you! Maybe I'm not as dumb as you thought, *Veronica!*"

Finally, the paramedics took Dennis to the hospital, and Butch rode with him.

Angie, Paavo, Connie, Vinnie and Earl were left alone in the restaurant, shaken and saddened by all that had occurred.

Paavo went back down to the storeroom and looked at the now burned and smoldering crates with Chinese lettering, the firecracker paper, rocket and sparkler remnants laying all over the floor. "What is all this stuff? It looks like fireworks, but all of you know they're illegal in this city."

"It's confetti," Angie said immediately.

"That's right," Vinnie agreed. "Chinese confetti."

"We had some popcorn down here, too," Connie added. "When Lexington wasn't looking, Angie put it in a box of confetti and lit the box."

"Yes!" Angie cried, giving Connie a thumbs up. "It began to pop, and this is the result."

Paavo frowned. "If that's the case, where's the popcorn now?"

"I was hungry," Earl said. "Sorry, boss, but I t'ink I ate da evidence."

Paavo looked from one to the other, shook his head, then said simply, "Let's get this mess cleaned up."

A charred and still smoking green hat popped up from behind a cabinet in one corner and a quaking voice called out, "May I please go home now?"

35

Exhausted, Connie entered her apartment, kicked off her shoes and flopped onto the sofa. Seven days had passed since the fireworks at Wings of an Angel. Amazingly, the insurance claim on her shop had already been approved. For the past week, she'd been picking out paint colors, and had gone on a buying spree for figurines and knick-knacks, plus a line of more upscale home decorations—brass and pewter and pottery pieces, unique tea, coffee and chocolate sets, rustic crockery—the kinds of gift items Angie thought would be appealing.

Using her own style and taste, Connie ended up with unique and not too expensive merchandise shoppers couldn't find in big department or "big box" type stores. The activity was fun, and filled her with new enthusiasm and excitement about her business.

She flipped through her mail and stopped at a letter from Zakarian Jewelers.

After Angie remembered about the pawn ticket they'd found at Veronica's, the two of them went to the pawn shop to retrieve the merchandize. It was Connie's missing antique doll with a porcelain face. At first, both were puzzled as to why Veronica would have taken it and then pawned it... until they realized what the doll had been used for. Angie handed Connie the doll, saying it was hers to do with as she wished, and then left.

Over a million dollars' worth of diamonds lay hidden in the doll's stuffing. Connie quickly understood what Angie was saying to her. She could attempt to smuggle them out of the country and then sell them for a fortune, or fence them locally for a smaller fortune, or turn them in. It was her choice.

Her life.

But Connie had seen firsthand what wrong choices could do to a man, or a woman. She turned in the diamonds, knowing they belonged to the Zakarian Jewelers. She offered to split the reward, if there was one, with Angie.

Angie refused any part of it, only saying she was glad for the choice Connie had made.

Nervously, Connie now opened the envelope from the jewelers. Inside was a check for $40,000 in reward money. Her heart nearly stopped at the sum. Even after taxes, it would do a lot for her store.

Check in hand, Connie brewed a cup of tea, glancing again and again at the tidy sum.

After all the trouble she'd gone through, the thought came to her that it was only right for her to do something special with at least a small part of the money. But what?

This whole mess had started with a blind date, a date who'd stiffed her. Maybe she could create a dream date for herself. One so hot it sizzled.

Carmel, California, was one of her favorite places. What about a date there? Romantic images filled her head of a helicopter ride down the Pacific coast to Carmel, dining at the very best restaurant, dancing at the most fun nightspots, a helicopter ride back to the city, and then breakfast at dawn at the top of the Fairmont Hotel. Yes! She could really get into this.

Her dream bubble burst. Who would she take?

Girlfriends were out for something like that, fun though it would be to go with Angie, or even Helen Melinger, whose latest motorcycle riding companion bore a striking resemblance to one of the inspectors Paavo worked with. What was with that?

Anyway, Helen wasn't much fun, and Angie was too busy trying to convince Paavo to take the Corvette she wanted to give him. So far, he was stubbornly refusing.

For something this cool, Connie needed a male friend.

If she took Stan, she'd have to shoot herself.

Max was a possibility. The other day, she ran into him on the street near Wings of an Angel. The money Veronica embezzled had been recovered from the overseas account—Dennis turned in all the information he had about it in hopes to get a suspended sentence and not jail time for his involvement in Veronica's embezzlement scheme. Max had used the money's return to settle claims from his investors and the insurance company, with some left over for his own losses. He seemed to be well on the way of regaining some of the old fire that had made him one of the city's top financial advisors. He acted as if he wanted to get together with her—just to talk, he said. But she refused. She wasn't ready for talking about all that had happened as yet.

Which brought her to Dennis. He had phoned to apologize for the trouble he'd caused her. She accepted the call, but ended it as quickly as she could without being rude. His career was on the rocks, and he was going to have to find out what he was all about after a lifetime of having had it—in many ways—too easy. He needed to learn about right, wrong, and consequences, and how lucky he was that Max didn't press charges against him for conspiring with Veronica, and that there was no proof he'd profited from Wallace Jones' counterfeit autographed sports memorabilia.

And, of course, there was Keith. After learning all she'd been through, he'd begun calling her regularly. He hadn't been lying when he said he'd been clean for over a year, which was a record for him. The last time he called, they'd talked for over an hour without getting angry or uttering a single swear word. A record for them.

What to do?

She decided to sleep on it, and when she awoke the next morning, she had her answer. When she thought back on the way all this had started, she remembered that it wasn't, in fact, about a blind date. The blind date had been her second choice.

Connie got into her car, glad she'd have another week before her shop would reopen. After a drive across town, she pulled into a parking lot, and went into a city building. The doors had just opened to the public.

Drawing in her breath, she got out of the car, uncertain of what she was about to face. Then, she decided to go for it. This was what she wanted, and she could only pray it worked out. It was, in a sense, a blind date with destiny.

After filling out the necessary forms, Connie waited in line, and when it was her turn, she went up to the customer assistant, her heart pounding at what she was about to do.

"I'd like to adopt a dog," she said. "I live alone, with a goldfish." She forged ahead, her words falling from her lips in a torrent of emotions. "I'd like a female. She doesn't need any fancy pedigree, just a mutt is fine. I don't want one that's big, and not too little, and not a puppy. A dog with a few years on her, some maturity, a little experience in the ways of the world so to speak. One that doesn't want or need much exercise. A walk a few blocks each day, and one who doesn't mind hanging around a shop with a small backyard while her owner works. Just a nice companion."

The woman studied Connie's face, then suggested, "Maybe a dog who's known love, but has had some disappointments or misfortunes in her life, and now hopes to settle down in a quiet but warm and loving home. Does that sound right?"

Connie brightened at the woman's understanding. "Exactly."

"Come this way."

Nervously, Connie followed her to a small room. About ten minutes later, the woman led in a medium-sized dog that resembled a cream-colored dust mop. Big, bright, dark brown eyes peered up at Connie as its stumpy tail wagged.

"Her owner was an elderly woman who died recently. She's been here a month already. Few people seem to want an older dog, especially a mixed breed. She's a healthy five-year-old, which isn't really old at all. She's very well trained, well behaved, quiet, and loving."

Connie knelt down to play with her a bit, and when Connie sat back down, the dog sat in front of her, looking up with a hopeful expression that melted Connie's heart. "She seems perfect. What's her name?"

"Oddly, she was named after a woman of ill repute in the old West called Diamond Lil. Everyone calls her Lily."

Diamond? Connie laughed. Definitely perfect. She ran her gently hand over the dog's head. "Lily, my girl, looks like it's you and me, now."

Lily gazed up adoringly, and happiness filled Connie head-to-toe. This was the perfect ending to a perfect date.

Dear Reader,

*I hope you enjoyed this installment of The Cook and Inspector Mysteries. The next mystery is **The Taverna Affair** in which Angie is on pins and needles over her engagement party at the same time as* *her clueless neighbor, Stan, finds himself swept into a whirlwind romance with a mysterious woman he meets at a Greek taverna.*

As murders happen around the taverna and as the murders shift closer to home, Angie and her rather long-suffering fiancé, Inspector Paavo Smith, need to solve the crimes and to somehow get through their engagement party without a full-blown family meltdown.

Here's the opening of **The Taverna Affair**:

A fat, salty tear trickled down Stanfield Bonnette's narrow cheek. He pulled a Kleenex from its cellophane packet. The tissue tore apart and he ended up with half in his hand, the other half still stuck in the packaging. A metaphor for his life.

Real men don't cry. He'd heard that often enough from his father, and believed it, even as he fought to stop his tears while walking down the steep hills away from his top-of-Russian Hill San Francisco apartment.

Real men especially didn't cry out of self-pity over losing girlfriends they never had who were engaged to men they didn't like. Men who were more macho, more sexy, and definitely more exciting.

They didn't even cry when they had a job they despised, a father who scorned them, and they received no respect from anyone, ever.

Another tear formed in the corner of his eye and he wiped it away, even more disgusted with himself.

Outwardly, he had everything--a well-paying job at a bank, good looks, a nice apartment, and access to his father's money whenever he needed it. He was in his early thirties, single, slim, with silky light brown hair, brown eyes, and—he'd always heard—boyishly handsome looks.

As he crossed Union Street, he faced San Francisco Bay and Alcatraz--old, solitary and squalid, much the way he felt.

At the foot of Russian Hill, where the ground became level and flat, past the old red brick Cannery that had been converted into tourist shops and eateries, he reached Jefferson

Street, the heart of Fisherman's Wharf. To his right were famous restaurants and tourist attractions, but where he stood the buildings were wooden, single-story and windowless, with company names painted over doorways or garages, all a part of the real world of fishing boats, warehouses, and fisheries.

Many of the area's restaurants featured Italian food, yet another reminder of the woman he was mooning over, Angelina Amalfi. Okay, maybe it was true that they'd never dated, and that she'd never indicated that she felt anything for him other than friendship. But as she talked about her upcoming engagement party, he suddenly realized how much she meant to him. He had no doubt her engagement party--being planned by her mother--was going to be the biggest and most lavish ever held in the city of San Francisco.

If his mother were to plan an engagement party for him, it would probably consist of Kentucky Fried Chicken and Hostess Cupcakes. To say his mother wasn't thrilled with him or the way he was living was an understatement. And her disappointment was exceeded only by his father's.

At times like this, he couldn't help but think his parents were right. After all, he'd lost Angie, and now he would never have a chance to convince her that their relationship might become more than friendship.

No, that wasn't exactly true either. He'd tried. More than once. She'd never noticed. What did that tell him?

He sighed woefully. She would have been perfect for him, too. Beautiful, smart, ambitious...rich...and a great cook. He loved food. Loved to eat. Day. Night. Mid-day. Middle of the night.

Angie's kitchen was one of the Seven Wonders of the World. He could knock on the door to her apartment, right across the hall from his, she'd invite him in and he'd head for her refrigerator. It was like a magic box, filled with the most delectable leftovers the world has ever known.

And if she married the inspector and moved away, this wonderful, scrumptious, mouth-watering phase of his life would be over.

Tears threatened again.

Not that he cared about her only for her culinary skills. She understood him. She never nagged or pressured him, but just accepted him for what he was. Or wasn't. In fact, he had a longer relationship with her than he'd had with any other woman.

With a heavy sigh he wondered what scrumptious feast Angie's mother would serve at the engagement party. At least he had that to look forward to.

For some unknown reason, still thinking about Angie, Stan turned down one of the small roadways off Jefferson Street that led back to the rough wharves where fishing boats were docked. It was an area where tourists never ventured and homeless people sought shelter--smelly and dingy with gulls swooping overhead, and saltwater, oil spills and worse at his feet.

A small building, separate from the others, caught his eye. A sign in Greek-style lettering proclaimed The Greek Taverna. One story with a flat roof, the once-white paint was now gray and peeling. The windows had scrolled bars over them in a pretty design, but bars nonetheless. In the window, a cardboard sign read "Fresh Fish! Greek Specialties Served Here."

Stan stepped closer to the Greek Taverna and sniffed. A blend of lemon, cinnamon and clove wafted over him. All his thoughts about Angie's kitchen had made him hungry. Perhaps a little nourishment would help allay his sorrows.

To find out what happens next, continue with **The Taverna Affair.**

ABOUT THE AUTHOR

Joanne Pence was born and raised in northern California and now lives in Idaho. She has been an award-winning, *USA Today* best-selling author of mysteries for many years, but she has also written historical fiction, contemporary romance, romantic suspense, a fantasy, and supernatural suspense. All of her books are now available as ebooks and in print, and most are also offered in special large print editions. Joanne hopes you'll enjoy her books, which present a variety of times, places, and reading experiences, from mysterious to thrilling, emotional to lightly humorous, as well as powerful tales of times long past.

Visit her at www.joannepence.com and be sure to sign up for Joanne's mailing list to hear about new books.